D0191786

Sexy
Beast

Sexy Beast

KATE DOUGLAS
NOELLE MACK
VIVI ANNA

APHRODISIA

APHRODISIA BOOKS
www.kensingtonbooks.com

APHRODISIA BOOKS are published by

Kensington Publishing Corp.
850 Third Avenue
New York, NY 10022

All Kensington titles, imprints and distributed lines are available at special quantity discounts for bulk purchases for sales promotion, premiums, fund-raising, educational or institutional use.

Special book excerpts or customized printings can also be created to fit specific needs. For details, write or phone the office of the Kensington Special Sales Manager: Kensington Publishing Corp., 850 Third Avenue, New York, NY, 10022. Attn. Special Sales Department. Phone: 1-800-221-2647.

ISBN: 0-7582-1485-5

First Printing: March 2006

10 9 8 7 6 5 4 3 2 1

Printed in the United States of America

CONTENTS

Chanku Rising

Kate Douglas

1

One moment, she was a tall, elegantly dressed African American woman with long, darkly waving hair and eyes of brilliant amber. In less than a heartbeat, her dress lay on the redwood deck in a tumbled shimmer of blue satin. The woman had become the wolf, amber eyes glinting angrily in the last dying rays of the sun, canines glimmering like ivory blades. With a single low growl and a flick of her tail, she leapt over the deck railing and raced through the damp meadow.

Anton Cheval threw back his head and laughed. Keisha hated to lose an argument, any argument.

"You gonna let her get away with this?"

Anton turned to the couple sitting behind him, snuggled close together on the big porch swing.

Grinning broadly, Stefan Aragat lifted his wine glass. "She *is* your mate. You better chase her down. We'd help, but Xandi and I plan to enjoy the sunset before we run."

Anton glared at Stefan for a brief moment, then shook his head in resignation. Stefan was right. If he didn't chase after Keisha and work this out now, he'd never hear the end of it.

Anton's abrupt shift from human to wolf left his clothing in a messy pile on the deck. So unlike him, he thought, not to remember to undress first and fold everything neatly. He glanced once more at the dark pants and black cashmere sweater laying in an untidy heap, then cleared the deck railing and the garden beyond in a single bound.

Maybe laughter hadn't been his best response.

Only Keisha could leave him so flustered.

Or so turned on.

Anton's powerful forelegs stretched out and he gathered speed with each thrust of his haunches, but his mind was not entirely the wolf. No, he was reacting like a very protective male, no matter the species, and he knew it irritated the hell out of his alpha mate.

It didn't matter. He was not, under any circumstances, going to allow her to return to San Francisco by herself. It went against all he stood for, all that the Chanku were. Their strength lay in the pack, not in the individual.

The memorial garden Keisha had designed for Golden Gate Park was moving forward according to schedule. She'd made enough trips, accompanied by either Anton or Stefan, to ensure everything would be perfect for the dedication. There was no reason she needed to go back early.

Not with that damned tabloid reporter, Carl Burns, once more on her trail.

Anton snarled and almost missed the leap across a small, partially frozen stream. The mere thought of the persistent reporter raised his hackles, made his heart race faster, his blood run hotter.

Burns was the one man who could expose them, the one person who not only suspected the existence of Chanku, but had actually witnessed Keisha's shift from woman to wolf.

Anton knew his ability to mesmerize was extraordinary, but even he had his limits. He'd hoped the mind-job he'd done on the tabloid reporter would erase the smut-peddler's memories of Keisha for a longer time than they had, but the bastard had suddenly reappeared in their lives on Keisha's last trip to the city.

Why hadn't Keisha let Anton file harassment charges? Carl Burns was a menace, a threat not only to Anton's mate but to the pack as a whole.

No matter. Anton's meetings in Boston would be over in less than a week and they could make the trip west together. He had a lot of money riding on this latest investment. Stefan was learning the business, but he wasn't up to handling an entire board of directors for a multi-national company all by himself.

Following the frosty trail with his wolven mind, working through the problems concerning Keisha with his human side, Anton loped across the familiar ground. He still wasn't certain what he could say to make her wait, but somehow he would convince her of the danger.

He had to.

Danger!

Keisha's warning hit him like a solid object. Another scent assaulted his sensitive nostrils. Anton ducked low, twisted and slipped off the trail.

Male. Not Chanku. Human male. More than one, very close. Anton raised his nose and sniffed the air. He scented excitement, fear and the sour sweat of unwashed human.

Keisha's scent was strongest, to the right.

Pain. Anger. Fear.

Her emotions washed over him, impossible to understand, beyond speech, beyond coherent thought. Anton veered off the main trail and, keeping his body low to the ground, raced down a narrow, bramble-filled ditch. Tufts of dark hair clung to some of the thorns. He scented blood and his hackles rose. Either she was so pissed she was ignoring the thorns, or something— someone—had hurt her.

All thoughts of meetings, investments, humanity, evaporated. Pure wolven rage filled Anton's heart, seared his thoughts. His lips curled back in a dark snarl, exposing sharp canines.

Anton!

Keisha's mental cry, clear now, ringing true as a bell in his mind, sent ice running through his veins.

Anton! Take care! Poachers. Armed with crossbows.

He skidded to a halt, one foot raised, his sensitive nose finding Keisha's scent, smelling blood along with her unique, feminine fragrance, pinpointing her location. At the same time, he reached out with his thoughts to touch Stefan and Xandi.

The connection was instantaneous, their response immediate. Satisfied, Anton raced toward his mate. *I'm coming. Are you hurt?*

Just grazed. Stay low. Can you reach Stefan? I can't find him.

I've already contacted him. He's on his way. He'll bring the four-wheeler and he's armed. Xandi's called the sheriff. Where are the poachers?

Near the pond. They've built a blind at the far end, above the beaver dam.

Anton passed the information on to Stefan. Scanned the thick underbrush along the near edge of the pond. Keisha's scent and the odor of fresh blood were strong, her fear and anger a palpable thing. *Where are you?*

Near the birch stand. Low, in the bramble patch.

He found her there, curled into a tight ball, her blood dripping steadily into the remnants of one last patch of crusty snow. She'd packed the shallow wound in her shoulder with ice, at least as well as she could in wolven form. Tiny crystals tinged with blood clung to the stiff whiskers along her muzzle.

Anton inspected the wound, licked the matted fur around it, grabbed a mouthful of ice and pushed it tightly against the seeping gash. Thank goodness, it didn't appear life threatening.

He licked Keisha's muzzle, wiping away the bloody snow with a careful swipe of his tongue. *I should kill them. They need to die.* Anton's thought ended on a snarl of pure rage.

No, you should have them arrested. They're idiots. Let the law deal with them.

Keisha's calm statement helped slow his racing heart. Still, he growled, unwilling to concede too easily. *I will, but I don't have to like it. I'd rather kill them.*

Keisha raised her head and glowered at him through eyes shimmering with pain. Sighing, Anton nuzzled her once more and waited impatiently for Stefan to arrive with clothing for both of them . . . hopefully before Xandi brought the sheriff.

This made the third set of poachers on their land this season—all of them hunting wolves.

Naked, Keisha sat on the toilet seat lid, hunched over in pain and seething with anger while Anton cleaned the shallow gash across her left shoulder. Her body trembled, a delayed reaction to the shooting.

Stefan and Xandi would be back later. They'd followed the sheriff into town to give more of a statement after one of his deputies had taken Keisha and Anton's. Now, alone here with Anton, Keisha felt the full impact of the night's attack.

"Are you sure you don't want to see the doctor?" Anton's fingers caught her gently under the chin and lifted, forcing her to face him. "It's not all that deep, but it could leave a scar."

"Then it leaves a scar. I'll be fine. Damn them. I hope they rot in jail." Her voice shook, but it was rage, not pain that had her hanging on the edge of tears. "Somebody put them up to this. They were too stupid to come here on their own. I just know it."

Anton placed a gentle kiss on her lips. "I agree. I just wish we knew who it was. I doubt those men know enough to shed any light on the situation. Unfortunately, I imagine an attorney will have them out of jail in a few hours."

"Well, I'll be long gone. I'm planning to leave for San Francisco the day after tomorrow. I've already got my flight arranged." Keisha tilted her head, daring him, waiting for his argument. Anton's eyes narrowed but he kept his mouth shut. Instead, he carefully bandaged Keisha's wound and drew her slowly into his arms.

She went willingly, inhaling the musky scent that was all Anton's, reveling in the strength of his embrace, the deep sense of love and safety that surrounded him. It would be so easy to lose herself in Anton's arms, to forget the memorial, the dedication, the fact that someone hunted her as if she were nothing more than a wild beast.

So easy to forget the danger when Anton held her tight.

"I was terrified when I heard your warning of danger, when I sensed your fear." Anton's voice cracked on the words and a deep shudder passed through his body. Keisha clung to him, suddenly awash with guilt. She'd been thinking only of herself, of her desire to see the job through. What if it had been Anton wounded today? What if she'd followed his blood on the trail? Found him curled up in a ball of pain, hurting and frightened?

Could she have controlled her rage as well as Anton did? Would she have even tried? It hit her like an epiphany, the explosive awareness of how wild her nature had become since embracing her Chanku heritage. Keisha accepted a new reality—if Anton had been the one injured, the two shooters wouldn't have survived long enough to go to jail. She'd killed men before. As much as she abhorred violence, she could do it again if her mate were threatened.

It took her a moment to tamp down the rush of bloodlust that almost swamped her. Finally, she swallowed back a growl and nuzzled close to Anton's chest. "I wasn't afraid, not once I knew you were close." She wrapped her arms around his neck and rose up on her toes to kiss him. "I'm never afraid when you're with me."

Anton groaned, the sound a sensual rumble against her breasts. Keisha whimpered, a tiny, needy sound deep in her throat. She inhaled his scent, drawing strength from his warmth and innate power. She rocked her hips close to his, rubbed her mons over the smooth fabric of his pants.

Anton groaned, then kissed her hard, his tongue plundering, his teeth scraping her lips, along her jaw, nipping at her with a wild frenzy. His lips demanded. His hands raced across her back, over her breasts, swept down to her buttocks where he grabbed her with bruising strength and pressed her body closer to his.

Caught in his feverish desire, Keisha cried out against his mouth. She felt the heat of his erection through his black chinos, the hard edge of his belt buckle abrading her belly. The flap of fabric over his bulging zipper pressed against her swollen clit. His tongue found its way once more between her lips and he caught her up in a swift and carnal rhythm, plunging into her mouth, lifting her body hard against his.

She wrapped her legs around his waist and pressed her pussy close against his straining cock, but it wasn't enough, not nearly enough to soothe the fire raging hot and wild inside.

Keisha writhed in Anton's powerful grasp, all the anger and pain, the fear and frustration of the past few hours coalescing into heat and passion, need of an almost feral intensity, driving her heart, inflating her lungs, making her gasp as if she'd run miles. Keisha lowered her legs, planted her feet firmly on the tile floor and let go of Anton's neck, then grabbed at the hem of his sweater. She raked her fingernails over his ribs as she tugged the garment past his head.

The moment he shed the sweater, Anton dragged her against him for a deep, tongue-twisting, mind-searing kiss. Gasping for air, he backed away and stared deeply into her eyes, his nostrils flaring, his dark pupils narrow slits, dark shards of obsidian surrounded in amber.

Keisha reached for his thoughts and found them blocked, surrounded by something dark and impenetrable. Whatever he felt for her, whatever he thought of her, remained hidden behind those watchful eyes.

Fingers trembling, Keisha raised her right hand and touched Anton's cheek. He turned and kissed her palm, groaning once again. She felt the press of his lips all the way to her womb. The tight clenching of her vaginal walls, the rush of welcoming fluids, the ache deep within her gut wrung a cry from her lips and she thrust her breasts against his bare chest, rubbing her sensitive nipples in the thick mat of his dark hair.

Anton nipped her palm, took a deep breath, then grabbed Keisha by the hips and spun her around, pressing her belly against the cool tile surrounding the bathroom sink. Shoving the first aid kit aside, she spread her palms wide and braced herself on the counter. With his left hand in the small of her back holding her down, Anton found her wet and waiting pussy with the fingers of his right.

He thrust two fingers, then three inside, slipping easily into her drenched pussy, stroking her inner walls, trailing his thumb lightly across her anus, then pressing harder, finding entrance there as well.

She felt the tight muscle relax, then close once more around the base of his thumb as he once again found a seductive rhythm. In, out, penetrating both passages, slow and deep, his thumb pressing against his fingers through the thin wall of sensitive flesh inside her body.

Gasping for air, Keisha spread her legs even wider, flattening her belly hard against the tile. Once more she tried to reach Anton's thoughts.

Still she found them closed to her.

Her climax was rushing forward, but she heard the sound of his zipper, the rustle of cloth and Anton's body was there, the broad head of his cock pressing hard against her wet and waiting pussy, her swollen and sensitive lips parting, giving Anton passage.

His body, but not his thoughts. His skill as a lover, but not his love. Suddenly Keisha understood as awareness flooded her mind, left her soul wanting, her heart hurting.

This was not an act of love at all, at least not love as Keisha expected it. No. This was something darker, something ancient and ritualistic.

This was something she must fight or accept, the way of Chanku.

The way of the alpha male subduing his bitch.

Pressing Keisha flush against the smooth tile until her breasts were flattened and her cheek rested on the hard surface, Anton thrust hard and fast, establishing his dominance, his power and physical strength over his mate.

Keisha thought to struggle, then accepted. He might be physically stronger, yet she was the winner, the one who cried out in mindless pleasure when Anton pumped his seed into her, the one who begged for more, then milked him with powerful muscles until his legs quivered and he leaned across her back to keep from falling to the floor.

The one who opened her mind at the point of climax and found his waiting—conscience-stricken, apologetic and remorseful beyond description.

Each harsh breath forced his chest against her back and her tight vaginal muscles continued their steady contraction and release around his shrinking cock.

Anton sensed no anger from her, no fear, no emotion beyond love and her underlying compassion.

He couldn't believe what he'd just done! This was no better than rape, this harsh and forced lovemaking . . . no, he couldn't begin to call it lovemaking. Keisha would never forgive him.

She shouldn't forgive him.

How would he go on living if she didn't?

He raised his head, spread his palms out on the cool tile to separate himself from Keisha's warm body.

"No. Please. Not yet." She turned and smiled at him. "Damn. You feel too good inside me. Don't go yet."

"But . . . ?" Anton frowned. "You're not . . . ?"

"Not what? Pissed?" She grinned, a lopsided smile that tore at his heart. "A little. On the other hand, if I'd wanted to stop you, all I needed to do was tell you to stop, right?"

He thought about that a minute. He would have quit in a heartbeat, no matter how angry, if he'd thought she wanted him to. "Okay, that's true, but . . ."

Keisha reached up and brushed her knuckles across his chin. "I didn't ask you to stop, Anton. I love you. We were both a bit overdosed on adrenaline. Do you love me?"

You know I do. I love you more than life itself.

Then why did you block your thoughts?

Anton sighed, then slowly withdrew from her body. He grabbed a yellow washcloth, held it under running water a moment, then wrung it out and handed it to Keisha. She turned around, leaned against the counter where they'd just had the most amazing sexual encounter, and unselfconsciously began to clean the semen and fluids from between her legs.

Anton watched her for a moment, mesmerized by the sweep of the damp yellow cloth against her dark skin and realized he wanted her again. He would always want her. He sighed, took the washcloth after she rinsed it in the sink and held it. "I didn't want you to see an anger I couldn't fully comprehend, didn't want you to think less of me, to realize I can't always control the beast inside."

Keisha grinned, grabbed the washcloth hanging limply in his hand and began to wash his no longer limp cock. "You control the beast admirably, my love. Just don't try to control me."

She raised her head and gazed at him for a long moment. Anton watched her perfect breasts rise and fall with each breath she took, then looked up, into her eyes. "If you do," she said, and her voice was tight with emotion, "you'll lose me forever."

2

"I don't like it one bit. What's a few more days?" Anton practically growled at her. If he'd been in wolf form, Keisha knew his hackles would be up. Obviously, their explosive lovemaking right after the shooting hadn't had the impact on Anton she'd hoped for.

Standing face to face with her lover in their large bedroom, Keisha held her ground and glared at Anton. Her shoulder hurt and she had one hell of a headache, but she was not giving in on this. "It's the difference between doing my job right and not. You of all people should understand that."

Anton sighed and pulled her gently into his arms. "I do, sweetheart. I really do. I don't have to like it, though."

She went willingly, her anger evaporating as quickly as his. "You said your meetings in Boston will be over by Friday. You can join me this weekend. It'll give me time to get my work done without a lot of, um, distractions, okay?"

"But I love distracting you. I'll worry. It's dangerous for you. Stefan suspects Burns might be behind the poachers."

"Then it's probably safer in San Francisco than here." She

leaned back in his embrace and smirked. "I've never been shot at in San Francisco. Kidnapped, assaulted, but never shot."

Anton shook his head, obviously unhappy. She rarely made reference to her deadly attack and wished she could take back the words said half in jest. Now wasn't the time to remind Anton of what she'd barely survived just a few short months ago.

Keisha rubbed her bandaged shoulder, then closed the gap between them and brushed her lips over Anton's. "The dedication's scheduled for the first Sunday in June. With travel, that gives me less than a week . . . not a lot of time for me to make sure everything is ready. This is important to me, Anton. I have to go. I promise I'll be careful."

"I know." He leaned close, his lips softly brushing hers.

She tilted her hips forward, pressing her pubic bone against his growing erection, at the same time sending out a silent call to Xandi and Stefan.

This would be the last night for all of them to spend together for more than a week. If nothing else, she knew sex with her packmates was a sure cure for the headache that lingered.

Anton smiled against her mouth. He'd obviously caught her signal to the others. She knew nothing pleased him more than when she initiated a night of pleasure for the four of them.

Unless of course, it was just the two of them, perfectly in sync.

Last night, after her attack, after the sheriff and his deputies had hauled off their captives and Keisha's injured shoulder had been properly cleaned and bandaged, after she and Anton had made love, they'd all shared the same bed. There'd been no sex among them then, merely loving, supportive bodies holding her close, helping her heal.

Tonight, Keisha wanted more.

Anton's hands were roughly kneading her taut buttocks when Stefan slipped into the room and wrapped his arms around both Keisha and Anton. "Xandi's on a grocery run. She'll join us later."

Keisha turned to Stefan and kissed him. "Hmmmm. Poor girl doesn't know what she's missing." Stefan's tongue found the seam between her full lips. Practically purring with the sensual promise in his kiss, she welcomed him inside. Her mouth moved with his as Anton's lips found the sensitive spot below her ear. Stefan's hands worked the buttons on her blouse, Anton's released the snap and zipper on her jeans.

As if they'd rehearsed each move, the men stripped her clothes from her body, following each item of clothing with wet, open-mouthed kisses and sharp little nips of their teeth.

At the same time, Anton and Stefan shed their own clothing, helping one another until all of them were nude. Sandwiched between two hot, male bodies, Keisha gave herself up to pleasure.

Not so long ago, the very fact that two men touched her, tasted her, loved her, would have sent her over the edge into mindless panic, dredging forth horrible memories of the night she was brutally raped by three men. Now, she reveled in not only the sensual touch, but her own healing. There was nothing she feared from these men she loved and trusted.

Nothing she wasn't willing, even eager to try.

Stefan swung her up into his arms and carried her to the bed. Anton took her from Stefan and settled her on the cool sheets, on her back with her legs spread wide, bent at the knees. Both men knelt beside her. Keisha closed her eyes and, moving her injured shoulder carefully, reached over her head to grab the headboard railing. She knew her silent acquiescence would set them free to take her however they wished.

She wanted whatever they offered. It wasn't often Keisha got both men all to herself.

Mouths, hot and greedy, found her breasts, suckled her nipples hard and deep, tongued the sensitive peaks, nipped at the turgid flesh.

She cried out, aware of each man, how different, how similar their touch, their scent. Fingers stroked her hips, her thighs, teasing close to her center, then moving away. Finally, after what seemed an eternity, both men's fingers came together in the nest of curls between her legs.

The suction on her breasts grew stronger, the long fingers trailing between her legs crept deeper. Moaning, Keisha arched her back, begging silently for penetration. One hand circled her left buttock and she recognized Stefan's touch. The other slipped between her swollen labia as Anton teased the creamy opening to her pussy.

Together, both hands moved between her legs, two fingers slipped into her wet heat, twisting and turning deep inside her. Then only one remained, stroking very slowly, in and out. She felt the rough pad of Anton's thumb against her clitoris, the damp tip of Stefan's forefinger pressing gently against her anus.

Anton slipped two more fingers inside her just as Stefan breached her ass and pressed deep. His finger slipped easily in and out, easing the taut ring of muscle. She felt him insert a second finger, then a third. Still, there was no pain, nothing other than a sense of pressure, of building excitement.

She knew the men could feel each other through the thin wall of flesh, wondered if they would carry this further, something they'd never done without Xandi present.

Anton's thumb made wet circles around her clit, his fingers penetrated her dripping pussy, and his mouth suckled her nipple so hard he narrowly skirted the barrier between pleasure and pain. Stefan tightened his lips around her just as hard, then let her sensitive nipple slip loose, tugging it gently with his teeth before releasing her.

His fingers, however, continued their relentless, rhythmic penetration, stretching her sphincter muscle, preparing her. Keisha arched her back, lifting her buttocks off the bed. Her stomach muscles rippled with the steady thrusts from both her lovers, with the hot suction from Anton's mouth.

Caught up in Anton's touch, she was barely aware of Stefan, thought she heard the sound of foil tearing, was only truly certain he'd donned a condom when she felt him settle between her knees. Once more his fingers sought her, slick now with some sort of lubricant, something warm and soothing. He shifted and she felt the solid pressure of his erect cock against her ass as he sought entry where his fingers had been mere moments ago.

She knew Stefan wanted this. No so long ago, he had prepared her so that she might take Anton without fear or pain. Because of his love, she could enjoy the act that had terrified her since her attack. After a moment of gentle teasing, Stefan's cock speared her deep, filling her ass, a smooth, painless entry that left him supported tightly between her legs with his balls pressed against her buttocks.

Her fingers tightened on the headboard. She moaned, then practically whimpered as Stefan carefully adjusted her legs, settling her even closer, filling her deeper.

Keisha let the sensations flow over and through her. She actually felt Stefan's cock expand even more, now he was inside her. Felt each ridge, even the thick vein throbbing with blood against her sensitive tissues. His balls were warm, the soft fur covering them tickled her ass.

Filled with Stefan, she jumped when Anton twisted his fingers deep inside her, turned them to touch the back wall of her vagina. He was stroking Stefan! Anton's fingers, buried in her pussy, traced the contours of Stefan's huge cock through the fleshy barrier.

Anton opened his thoughts to her, allowed Keisha to share the sensations with him, the hot, wet sheath a nerve-laden boundary between Anton's supple fingers and Stefan's pulsing cock.

Stefan groaned, leaned over and bit down on her nipple then suckled it against the roof of his mouth. He thrust harder, then slowly withdrew, as if loath to give up either Keisha's heat or

Anton's touch. At the same time, Anton pulled his fingers slowly out of Keisha and released her nipple with a wet sounding *pop*.

Stefan licked the very tip of Keisha's breast, then released it. He lifted her hips and sat back on his heels, at the same time pulling her away from the headboard so they were centered in the middle of the bed. His big hands grasped her buttocks while her legs dangled over his forearms, his cock filled her ass, slowly entering and then withdrawing. She felt Anton shift over her body and smiled when his cock brushed her lips.

A not so gentle hint, my love? She drew the hot crown between her lips and sucked hard, tonguing the sensitive tip before drawing him deep into her mouth.

I'll make it worth your while.

His thought had barely entered her mind when Anton's tongue circled her clitoris. His silky hair tickled her belly and thighs and she wondered how it felt for Stefan, wondered at the sensation of his cock buried deep in her channel with Anton's mouth locked on her pussy. Did Stefan feel Anton's hair brushing his groin? Did the silken strands drift across Stefan's hard thighs with the same soft sweep as Keisha felt?

The image of the two men she loved, each loving her in his own way, took Keisha higher, sent her blood running hotter with each lick and thrust. Stefan continued his slow, deep penetrations, but it was Anton, his tongue and teeth, his warm lips and hot breath, taking her faster, farther into oblivion.

Her breasts ached, her nipples felt cold without the warm mouths sucking and biting them, but the rest of her body was hot, so hot she imagined steam rising from her flesh.

Keisha grabbed Anton's firm buttocks, holding his hips in place while she sucked and licked his cock, seeking and finding the same rhythm the men had with her.

Lord, how she loved the smells and tastes of her lover! Stefan was dear and his technique beyond reproach, but Anton stole her soul, owned her heart, invaded every cell of her body. It scared her, sometimes, to realize how much she loved him, how very much she needed him.

How easy it had become to lose herself in his love.

Keisha twirled her tongue around the crowned tip of his beautiful cock, licked the tiny eye and tasted the first drops of his seed. Some day, hopefully not too far away, Anton would take her as the wolf, make love to her in the deep, dark woods, and with his seed plant a new life, a child within her womb.

The image consumed her, the thought of binding herself irrevocably to this man, the knowledge that a child would link them for all time, would be the constant reminder of their love.

Love. Dear God, the emotion was more frightening than she'd ever imagined. It made her vulnerable, made her afraid.

Made her whole.

Complete.

Reality replaced thought. Keisha's orgasm slammed into her without prelude, hot and fast, a raging storm overwhelming her senses. Fueled by love, by need, by emotions so intense she feared to understand them, her climax took control of conscious thought, of the blood in her veins, the beat of her heart, the air rushing into her straining lungs.

Stefan thrust hard, his body tightened, and he took her even higher. Gasping for air, Keisha released Anton's hard cock and screamed, back arching, hips tilting forward, thrusting her pussy against Anton's mouth, tightening her muscles around Stefan's cock.

Anton continued lapping and sucking her streaming pussy, even as Stefan collapsed over both of them. Grasping Anton's thighs firmly, drawing a great shuddering breath, Keisha silenced her moans with his cock, filling her mouth once more with him, drawing him deep and running her fingers over his testicles, milking Anton's seed as he joined their climax. She felt

Stefan move deep once more, pause, finally withdraw. Vaguely sensed him easing her legs down to the bed and moving away from her quivering, clenching body.

Heard his murmured words of love, both to her and to Anton.

Still she tongued and suckled Anton, swallowing each drop he shared with her, licking him, then merely holding his flaccid cock within her mouth until he rolled to one side, away from her. She lay there, gasping for air. His mouth remained fixed to her spasming, clenching pussy, his body shuddering against hers in the aftermath of passion.

She lifted her hand, touched his shoulder, caressed the firm skin, absorbed his heat. Her eyes drifted closed and her breathing slowed.

Anton rested his tongue against her clit, sensed the final spasms of her climax, tasted the flavors unique to Keisha. She was so beautiful, so welcoming of their lifestyle, their Chanku heritage. Anton knew he would never get enough of her taste, her scent, her body . . . her wonderful, independent mind.

Damned if she wasn't going to drive him nuts! He ran his hands along her relaxed and pliable body, spread her legs wide, shifted position and knelt between her knees, taking the place Stefan had just vacated. Now, though, Anton pressed the head of his recovering cock against her waiting vagina and entered in a single, smooth thrust.

She arched and cried out, coming apart before he'd fully penetrated her. He felt her muscles tightening, rippling along the length of his cock, felt the fresh release of lubricating moisture and thrust even deeper. His cock found the hard mouth of her womb and pressed close before he slowly withdrew.

What would it be like, to know his child grew there? The image of Keisha, round and full with their baby brought tears to his eyes. She would be a wonderful mother, strong, protective, fierce. One day she would carry his child, the truest evidence of her love, of his love for her.

Now, though, she arched her hips and took all of him, took his heat and strength, his very essence deep inside. He tried to lose himself fully in her welcoming warmth, but fear still fluttered silently in the back of his mind.

The coming separation scared the crap out of him. Frightened him beyond measure, but he would help her pack and take her to the airport without further argument.

What was that old saying . . . if you love something, set it free?

Stupid saying.

Anton didn't want to let go of Keisha, not for a moment. He'd do it because she asked, because he loved her . . . because to hold her too tightly would be to lose her.

With that thought in mind, his soul filled with the fear, the love, the frightening vulnerability of having given his heart to this woman, Anton took her once more over the edge.

Crying out, thrusting hard and deep, he followed her into oblivion.

3

Keisha shoved the last of her clothes into the carry-on bag and slowly zipped it shut. She stared at the bag for a moment, going over all the reasons she had to go to San Francisco. As much as she needed to make this trip, it wasn't easy to leave the people she loved.

There was a soft tap at her door. Keisha turned around just as Xandi cracked the door open and stepped into the room.

"You okay? Should you be carrying that much weight? You've barely had two days to heal." Xandi touched Keisha's shoulder near the bandage. "How's it feel?"

"Hurts, but it's shallow. The arrow just grazed me. It didn't penetrate, so there's no permanent damage. I have to admit, besides shifting, one of the nicest things about being Chanku is that we seem to heal really fast."

"You scared Anton half to death." Xandi turned and closed the door behind her. "Stefan and me, too. I'm sure Anton's told you he and Stefan are worried the poachers may somehow be connected to Carl Burns. We've had so many of them this year.

They're all focused on wolves, not deer or elk, and not one of them seems like a real hunter. They're just thugs."

"We can't continue to live our lives in fear, Xandi." Keisha plopped down on the bed. "I've lived that way far too long. Being Chanku is giving me a strength I never knew before. I will not be a victim again. Anton has to understand that."

"He does. He's also very much in love with you, so he worries." Xandi sat down on the bed next to Keisha and grasped both her hands. "Do you have any family in San Francisco? Someone you can stay with? You've never mentioned parents, siblings or . . ."

Keisha shook her head. "No. I had a wonderful family, but not anymore." She blinked back a sudden rush of unexpected tears. It was all so long ago . . .

"My mother was killed by a hit and run driver when I was just a kid. Her sister, my Auntie Camille, was shot and killed in a mugging a few years later. She had a daughter, my cousin Tianna, but Tia and her dad just sort of disappeared out of my life after Camille's death. I have no idea where Tia or Uncle Ulrich are now. Then my father died of a heart attack a couple of years ago. That was tough. I was an only child, so . . ."

Keisha swallowed back a lump in her throat, then flashed a quick smile at Xandi. "Now there's just me."

Xandi squeezed her hands tightly. "Never just you, sweetie. Not anymore. We—Anton, Stefan and me—we're your family. I didn't know that about your mom or your aunt, that both of them died so violently. How awful!" She reached up and brushed Keisha's hair back from her face. "Let me come with you. That way you won't be alone and Anton won't worry so much. It'll give me a chance to get back to the city and shop and do girl stuff. Would you mind?"

Caught off guard, Keisha turned and looked deeply into Xandi's gray eyes. "You'd do that for me? Leave Stefan here so you can babysit me in San Francisco?"

Xandi's laughter was free and totally uninhibited. "Babysit? You? The alpha bitch? You've got to be kidding! You want the honest truth? I want to go to a play, eat out in really expensive restaurants and go back to your place for some totally kinky sex. We haven't gotten together, just the two of us, for weeks. The guys keep barging in."

Keisha snorted. "So true. I never realized how much it turned a guy on to see two women having fun. It's like shooting them with a sex gun. Kapow! One look and they're both naked and panting."

"So true. Deal?"

Keisha smiled at Xandi. "Even though I know Anton put you up to it, yes, it's a deal. I'd love to have you come with me." She grabbed Xandi's hand in hers. "Don't tell Anton, but I was scared to death when the poacher shot me. It hurt so much, at first I didn't realize if I was badly injured or not. When I left the house, I was mad at Anton and didn't pay attention to my surroundings. I'm lucky they didn't kill me. I actually stumbled over their hiding place before I even saw it."

Xandi laughed. "Well," she drawled, "I think Anton's figured all that out, but you know I'd never betray a confidence. I'll pack some things and be ready as fast as I can. Shouldn't be too hard for me to get a ticket once we arrive at the airport, flying midweek like this." She stood up and headed for the door, then turned and struck a pose against the frame. "Oh, I need to thank you. Whatever you and the guys did yesterday afternoon certainly put Stefan in the mood! I'm almost glad I got home too late to join you." She brushed her hand over her heart. "Talk about hot! Whew . . . he wore me out last night!"

Laughing, she turned and headed down the hallway. Keisha just shook her head and grinned. Suddenly, this trip was beginning to look a lot more interesting. She'd be doing the work she loved, seasoned with a girls' night out . . . or two.

She'd have four days with Xandi before Anton showed up . . . four days to play with her best girlfriend ever.

The skies over San Francisco were a clear blue when their plane landed at San Francisco International Airport. Xandi chattered on about the sailboats on the bay and the heavy traffic along Nineteenth Avenue, but Keisha barely heard her friend's voice. There was a lump in Keisha's throat as their cab pulled up in front of her townhouse late in the afternoon.

She stared at the freshly painted exterior for a moment, then stepped out of the cab and grabbed her bags. Xandi paid the cabbie and the two women climbed the stairs to the front door. Keisha took a deep breath before she stuck her key in the lock and opened the door.

Keisha peered into the dim interior and inhaled a lungful of musty air before finally stepping inside the foyer. She heard a soft *thump* when Xandi set the bags down on the wooden floor behind her. The hollow sound emphasized the lonely sense of abandonment. There was an uncomfortable chill in the air and a thin layer of dust covered the once beloved, still beautiful antique furnishings Keisha had spent so much time collecting.

She'd found peace here before the assault, but it hadn't truly felt like sanctuary to her since, even less so, now that Carl Burns knew where she lived. No, that peace was strongest in the deep forests of Montana when she ran with her packmates.

Feeling a gentle sense of loss over her once treasured home, Keisha reached for the thermostat and turned the heat up a notch. She sensed Xandi's concern and her shoulders slumped.

"You okay?"

"Yeah." Keisha turned and leaned back against the wall. "It just feels really weird, coming back here. It's not home anymore." She swept her fingers slowly across the textured wallpaper. "I decorated every inch of this place, made it into exactly the space I wanted. Now I realize it's not what I want at all."

Xandi nodded as if she understood completely. "Maybe it's time to sell. Move on. It was a positive step for me when I resigned my job, gave up the apartment . . . gave myself to Stefan without any ties holding me anywhere else."

Keisha stared at her friend for a long moment. Xandi had never seemed happier, more content than she was now that she'd permanently moved with Stefan to Anton's Montana home.

Keisha wanted that same feeling—the solid foundation of Anton's love—but what of her hard-won independence? Her need to control the direction of her own future? Would Xandi understand?

Would she have any answers?

"Xandi, do you ever feel as if Alexandria Olanet has become lost in Stefan Aragat? Do you worry about losing *you* in *him*? Losing your identity, your sense of self?" She held her hand up, giggled and shook her head. "Now I sound like my shrink!"

"No you don't. You sound like a very serious-minded woman who is still a bit unsure of this whole life-changing set of events." Xandi drew Keisha into a brief but loving hug. "I finally decided, just like Popeye, *I yam what I yam*. I'm not merely human. I am Chanku. I've had to reevaluate my feelings about a lot of things. Being mated to a hard-headed shapeshifter is only one of many adjustments." She laughed. "Try not to worry. You will always be Keisha Rialto, even though you are Anton Cheval's mate. It works. Trust me."

Trust. That's really what it's all about, isn't it?

Xandi nodded, smiling. *Exactly. C'mon. Let's unpack and go eat. I'm starving.*

They went out just after dusk and found a popular restaurant and bar combo in the Castro district. It was near a small restaurant just like this one where Keisha had been kidnapped so many months ago. Would she ever totally get beyond the seemingly random act of violence that had changed her life in so many ways—changes both good and bad?

A tremor ran along Keisha's spine, a reaction to the memory of her horrifying assault—the bloodied bodies of the three men who'd attacked her, their torn remains spread about the apartment after her first unconscious shift to wolven form. Then, shortly afterwards, Xandi had appeared on her front step and changed into a wolf before her disbelieving eyes.

Keisha had awakened to Anton Cheval's beautiful amber eyes staring into hers, awakened to the face of the one man she knew she would love forever.

No, life would never, ever be the same.

Shivering, Keisha grabbed Xandi's hand at the crowded entrance and held on tight.

A massive bouncer blocked their way. His muscular arms were folded across his broad chest and he looked the women slowly up and down, as if assessing their attributes. His gaze lingered a bit too long on Xandi's full breasts and there was a curl to his lip as he took in the women's tightly linked hands.

Xandi returned his insolent gaze. "Hello, big boy. Seen enough, or do I need to strip for permission to enter?"

Blinking in surprise, the man jerked his head in a quick nod for them to go inside. Keisha still held tightly to her hand but Xandi burst into giggles once they got past him.

Keisha jabbed her in the ribs. "You're not supposed to taunt the help."

Xandi laughed. "Have you ever been tempted to just say to hell with it and shift, right in front of everyone? I bet that big jerk would have peed his pants."

Still grinning, Keisha glanced over her shoulder as Xandi found them seats at a table near the back. The bouncer watched them.

A waitress brought menus. Xandi studied hers, but Keisha

couldn't concentrate. She felt the hair on the back of her neck standing on end. A shiver ran over her arms. She shuddered.

Xandi looked up, obviously sensing Keisha's discomfort. *Is something wrong?*

"I don't ..." Keisha turned slowly and looked across the crowded restaurant toward the entrance. The bouncer was leaning over, obviously in deep discussion with a small, dark-haired man. Suddenly he looked directly at Keisha and Xandi and pointed. The man looked up, hesitating as if giving his eyes a chance to adjust to the dark.

Keisha felt her heart skip a beat.

"C'mon. Act like we're going to the restroom." Keisha grabbed her purse in one hand and Xandi's wrist in the other and dragged her to her feet. "Get your bag."

Walking quickly, fighting the urge to run, she found the narrow hallway to the restroom and from there a door that led through the kitchen. Ignoring the cook's orders to go back the other way and Xandi's questioning looks, Keisha dragged her friend through the small kitchen and out a door that led to a dark alley.

What's going on?

Carl Burns. I'm positive that was him talking to the bouncer, and the big oaf pointed directly at us. "Hurry." Keisha hiked up her calf-length skirt and took off at a run down the alley. She heard Xandi's footsteps just behind her.

Keisha heard her thoughts as if Xandi had spoken aloud.

We'd move a lot faster if we shifted.

Without slowing her pace, Keisha shook her head. *That's the last thing we want to do with a tabloid reporter on our tails. I think his camera is surgically implanted.*

Within minutes, the two of them rounded a corner across from Keisha's home. Breathing hard, they ducked behind some shrubbery. Keisha studied the street in front of her house. "Looks clear. Let's make a run for the porch and get inside. I do not want to talk to that man!"

They raced across the street and up the stairs. Gasping for breath Keisha fumbled with her keys.

Hurry, hurry, hurry. Xandi's frantic mantra echoed in Keisha's mind.

Keisha jammed the key in the lock and twisted, then ripped the door open. Stumbling over the threshold, Xandi slammed the door behind them. Keisha twisted the deadbolt and both women leaned back against the door, gasping for breath.

Xandi turned to Keisha and burst into nervous giggles. "You sure know how to show a girl a good time."

Keisha slumped against the door and sighed. "That wasn't exactly what I had in mind. Why does he keep following me? At least he's so familiar to me now, I can usually sense when he's near." She shoved herself upright. "C'mon. I've got some stuff in the freezer we can heat up for dinner. Hanging out in town has suddenly lost its appeal."

"You need to call Anton and let him know what's going on." Xandi sipped her glass of wine and tried to look relaxed. She couldn't pull it off. Her actions felt jerky and her veins practically sizzled. She'd been running on adrenaline ever since they'd fled the restaurant and the slimy reporter. If she didn't find an outlet soon for all her pent up energy, she knew she'd explode.

"I know. I'll wait and call him in the morning, before his meeting." Elbows resting on her knees, the wineglass clasped in both hands, Keisha turned her head to look at Xandi. She sighed and her shoulders slumped. "At this point, I think we can charge Burns with harassment. Anton wanted to call the newspaper and complain the last time he followed me, but I wouldn't let him. My mistake, I guess. Anton worries so much about me. He'd want to fly out here immediately, and he can't do that. Let the man at least get a good night's sleep. There's nothing he can do tonight, anyway."

She set her wineglass down and rubbed her hands up and down her arms, as if warding off a chill.

"Agreed." Xandi gave Keisha a sideways glance, then spoke in a soft, seductive drawl. "You look as wound up as I feel. Obviously, with Burns following you we can't shift and run, but there're other ways to burn off excess energy. Might take our minds off of things."

Keisha answered with a broad smile. She took a final sip of her wine, then both women set their glasses down and headed for the bedroom. At the last moment, Keisha leaned over and whispered softly into Xandi's ear, "I'm the alpha bitch, sweetie. Remember?"

"Like hell you are." Laughing, Xandi swatted Keisha on the butt and chased her through the door.

They kissed, briefly. Xandi could kiss Stefan for hours and never grow tired of the feel of his lips on hers, but for some reason, when she was with Keisha, Xandi wanted more direct, more physical contact than mere kisses. She slipped her sweater over her head as Keisha removed hers. Their bras landed on the floor and Xandi moved into Keisha's embrace.

There was something immensely erotic about rubbing their taut nipples together, standing breast to breast, hips thrust forward, their hands grasping one another's buttocks and kneading firm flesh through fabric.

Equally erotic was the difference in their color. Xandi's fair skin against Keisha's darker tones never failed to excite her. Keisha's nipples were the color of dark berries; Xandi's were lighter, the areolas larger and more defined. Standing together, rubbing lightly against one another emphasized their differences as much as their similarities.

Keisha was the first to pull away and slip out of her skirt and underpants. Xandi didn't waste a minute. Naked, trembling with need as much as the adrenaline rush still coursing through her body, she pulled Keisha back into her arms, this time bending down to take one of Keisha's firm nipples in her mouth.

Xandi rolled the taut flesh between her lips, drew it in and pressed the nipple tightly against the roof of her mouth with her tongue. She sucked hard, drawing a soft moan from Keisha and a hard thrust of the other woman's hips against her own.

Xandi arched her back, releasing Keisha's nipple with a satisfying *pop*. She felt the scratchy brush of Keisha's pubic hair tickle her recently shaved mons and moaned. Breath rasping in her throat, Xandi caught Keisha's rhythm and tilted her hips even closer, rubbing her sensitive pubes back and forth across Keisha's coarse thatch of hair.

Keisha palmed both of Xandi's breasts, then quickly slipped her hands lower to grab Xandi's buttocks once again. With her hips rotating slowly against Keisha's, Xandi scattered wet, open-mouthed kisses across her friend's throat and along the line of her jaw before covering Keisha's mouth and breathing in her soft, moaning breaths.

Xandi held Keisha close with one hand tightly clenching her firm buttock in a bruising grasp. She kissed her deeply, nipping at lips and tongue, then slipped her fingers between their bodies and found the crisp nest of curls covering Keisha's pussy.

So much heat, so slick and ready. Xandi felt the first trickles of moisture along her own inner thigh. She knew Keisha hovered on the brink of orgasm, just as Xandi did. She let her fingers creep slowly through the tangle of wet hair, then probed slowly, carefully at the swollen, weeping mouth of Keisha's pussy. Keisha moaned when Xandi gently circled her protruding clit with the tip of one finger.

Then Xandi pressed the sensitive bit of flesh between her fingers. Keisha's legs buckled and she cried out, but she didn't come. Xandi forced her fingers deep inside, deeper still, where firm muscles danced, clenching, releasing, clenching once again. Together, the women tumbled onto the wide bed. At the last moment, Xandi shifted, twisting her body so that she landed on top, her lips now firmly compressed once more about Keisha's nipple.

Xandi quickly rediscovered Keisha's pussy with her free hand. Her fingers slipped easily into the slick, hot channel, first one, then two, finally four fingers buried deeply, with her thumb resting firmly against Keisha's clitoris.

She felt Keisha's hands frantically rubbing, touching, grasping, sliding across her breast, then slipping down between her legs to skim lightly over her sensitive clit.

Xandi wanted to laugh but didn't dare release Keisha's nipple. Their sex play had become an unspoken battle of alpha bitches, with each of them trying to bring the other to orgasm first.

Keisha's fingers clenched tightly around Xandi's buttocks, pulling her cheeks apart, finding the sensitive sphincter muscle, probing none too gently until she gained entrance with her middle finger.

She pressed hard, sliding her finger in and out, then adding a second and going deep.

Moaning, panting with rising excitement, Xandi released her tight suction on Keisha's nipple. She shoved her fingers deeper inside Keisha, now using her palm to rub back and forth across her friend's clit, finding her rhythm, thrusting in counterpoint to each of Keisha's deep strokes.

Keisha twisted, leaned forward and caught Xandi's nipple between her tongue and teeth and sucked hard. At the same time, she speared Xandi with two fingers deep inside her anus and pressed down on her clit with the pad of her thumb.

Xandi threw her head back and howled. Wave after wave of pulsing heat, shimmering sensation and pleasure verging on pain swept through her. She tried to bring Keisha with her but her hands wouldn't obey. Gasping, giggling, her mouth opening and closing like a fish on dry land, she collapsed beside her friend.

"Okay. Alpha bitch. You win that round. Just let me get my breath . . ."

"And then?" Keisha leered at her.

"And then you . . ." Xandi took a couple of deep breaths and rolled over on top of Keisha, slipped her hand down between her friend's legs and found her hot, wet center. Suckling her nipple tightly between her lips, she tongued the sensitive tip while her fingers tangled in the nest of curls between Keisha's legs. She slipped between the pouting lips, dipped into Keisha's moist heat and stroked slowly, deeply, in and out.

She felt the slight rise and fall of Keisha's hips as she tried to hold back and slowly lost the battle. Heard her soft moan, felt the fluttering muscles deep inside as they tightened imperceptibly around her fingers.

"Then it's your turn."

Xandi found Keisha's clit, ran her thumb over the hard little bud, faster, harder, her fingers thrusting deeper. She sucked hard on the nipple still caught between her lips, tightened her lips about the tip and pressed them together hard.

Keisha arched her back and screamed, her hips pumping against Xandi's thrusting fingers, her hands clutching at the rumpled blankets beneath her.

Xandi brought her down slowly, stroking Keisha's quivering flesh, finally just rubbing her slick, engorged labia with the palm of her hand. Keisha's body shuddered, she sighed and lay still.

"Damn. I think I'll sleep well tonight." She giggled. "Wow . . . we haven't done that for ages."

Xandi lay down next to her. "I know. I'm still not sure if it's better sex or just different, but I like it."

"It's all sensation and sharing. Touching someone and knowing exactly what parts to touch, where to taste, how hard to apply pressure."

"Sensation without the emotional intensity." Xandi laughed. "Sometimes when Stefan and I make love and I realize just how *much* I love him, it scares me." She turned and touched Keisha's shoulder, running her fingers over the bandage. "I love you, too, but it's not so intense, not as frightening."

"I know." Keisha looked soberly at Xandi. "I've felt exactly the same way." She leaned closer and they kissed. "G'night, hon. Sweet dreams."

4

Xandi found Keisha at the kitchen table in the morning. She stared blankly out the window, but turned when Xandi entered the room. Her lips were trembling, and her hand holding the half-empty coffee cup shook.

"I heard the phone ring. What's wrong?"

Keisha sighed. "I just talked to Anton. I called him first thing, told him about Carl Burns. He contacted Burns's publisher to complain. Anton just now called me back to say the paper fired Burns more than a month ago. It looks as if he's not working on a story. He's stalking me."

"Have you called the police?" Xandi poured herself a cup of coffee and sat across from Keisha. "Is Anton coming out?"

"Anton's stuck in meetings until Friday . . . he may even have one Saturday morning. I told him not to come."

Xandi snorted. "You mean he listened?"

"I don't think he's got a choice. This deal involves millions of dollars. It's a huge investment for him. I've got a call in to the detective who worked my assault case. I'm hoping he can tell me how to keep Burns away from us."

"In the meantime?" Xandi took a sip of her coffee.

"In the meantime, I need to check on my project, make sure we're still on schedule. The next couple days are going to be really busy." She smiled sadly at Xandi. Her amber eyes filled with tears. "Why won't he stop following me? Why won't he leave me alone? It doesn't make any sense."

"When was the first time you were aware of him?"

Keisha frowned. "Not until the article came out in the paper, the story about my assault."

"How did he get there so soon? He was at the crime scene really fast. I saw the pictures. There were still bodies in the room."

"I don't know. I was so out of it. I never saw Burns, at least that night. At first I thought the photos were from the police files, but I learned later they weren't."

"Did the police let him in?" Xandi recalled the lurid black and white photo, the torn and mutilated bodies of three men, the superimposed photo of a rabid, snarling wolf covering the picture. "Could he have been there before the police arrived?"

Keisha slowly raised her head. "I don't know. I can't imagine the police letting him take pictures. It was a crime scene, but he had to have been there right after it happened to get those shots. How could he have known?"

Xandi reached behind Keisha and grabbed the phone. "Call the detective. Now."

Early Friday morning, Keisha surveyed the stark stone monument, its sharp edges softened by the gently swaying grasses she'd carefully selected for the design. She'd picked them out of hundreds of other similar plants in the months before her attack, long before she knew Anton, Stefan or Xandi, or anything about the Chanku.

Now Keisha leaned over and plucked a single golden stem and slipped it between her lips. She straightened up, chewing thoughtfully, to study the finished project.

She found it absolutely fascinating, realizing her body had known the nutrients she needed to discover her Chanku heritage. Somehow, instinct had led her to choose exactly the right combination of plants for the memorial, had driven her to chew on the woody stems and suck on the slender grasses until her body had responded, until the tiny gland near her brain stem had finally developed enough to let her shift from human to wolf.

Thank God it happened in time, or she would have been the one who died in that bloody apartment so many months ago.

The sun chose that moment to break through the morning fog and cast shadows exactly as she'd planned, reflecting a jagged silhouette reminiscent of the Himalayas. Keisha nibbled on the stem of grass and studied the dark line of stone.

She stared blindly at the monument, but she hardly thought of it, nor did she consider the impact it would have on the people who came to view it for the first time. No, her mind was filled with thoughts of her mother, of her Auntie Camille and her missing cousin and uncle. Of her father, a proud and hard-working gardener who'd taught Keisha to love plants and all growing things.

Had he been the one who carried the Chanku genes? Most likely not. Anton believed it was recessive in men, but dominant in women. Had her mother shifted? Her Auntie Camille? Or had they gone through their brief lives without knowing their own potential?

What of her cousin? Tia would be a grown woman now, at least in her mid twenties. Did she carry the Chanku genetics within her DNA? If so, as Keisha had been for most of her life, was Tia unaware of her heritage?

Keisha started when Xandi slipped an arm around her waist. "It's a fitting tribute, sweetie. Absolutely gorgeous. I can see why your design won the competition."

Xandi's praise should have filled her with pride. Instead,

Keisha was aware of a terrible emptiness. If only her mother could be here . . . or her father. She put the impossible out of her mind, remembering instead her brief and unproductive conversation with the detective. She'd finally reached him after two days of calls, only to learn there wasn't anything they could do to stop Carl Burns from following her. Not until the reporter broke the law.

She sighed. One more thing she'd just as soon not think about. Shoving thoughts of Burns and the San Francisco Police Department aside, Keisha returned Xandi's hug. "At least the project's done, under budget and on time. I just wish I could feel more excited about it."

"You will. Once everyone shows up for the dedication. Stefan and Anton haven't seen the finished project. They're going to be amazed at how gorgeous it turned out. Now let's clean up around here so it's perfect for Sunday. Your rake, m'dear?"

Sighing, Keisha took the rake from Xandi and began clearing away the accumulation of branches and leaves left by the workmen. She missed Anton. She missed Stefan.

She missed the sense of peace she'd lost the moment Carl Burns came after her again.

Unbidden, thoughts of her mother and her Auntie Camille crept back into Keisha's mind once again. Why now, of all times, would she find herself mourning both her mother and her aunt?

Mourning the dead and wondering about her cousin . . . where was Tia? Why was the sense of the missing women in her life so strong, here in the midst of Golden Gate Park?

Hours later, standing in the neatly cleared garden, Keisha still couldn't find answers to her questions or the sense of achievement she'd hoped to feel.

She'd won a national landscape design contest, created something lasting and beautiful, yet all she wanted was to get as far away from San Francisco and Carl Burns as possible.

"Xandi, I think we should go home." She slanted a look at her friend. "Back to Montana. Let's skip the dedication and just leave. I have a really bad feeling about . . ."

Xandi planted her rake in front of her and shook her head. "No. You've worked hard. You deserve recognition for this. Besides, I'm staying alert. I've been watching. I don't think Burns is nearby. One of us would sense him."

Keisha shook her head. "What if we don't? They can't arrest him because he hasn't done anything. There's no record of his stalking me, but I certainly don't want to give him an opportunity to hurt either of us just so the police will take notice. How do I make him leave me alone? I'm not even certain why he's following me." Keisha wrapped her arms around herself and shivered. She'd been feeling so strong, so in control. Feeling like her old self, for the first time since her attack.

Not now. Now the old fears were seeping into her bones, the insecurities, the lack of confidence . . . it was all coming back.

"If he's been fired from his paper, he probably wants film to prove you exist, that you shift." Xandi's eyes continuously swept the park as she spoke. "He wants his job back and figures you're the key. We just won't give him the opportunity."

Keisha sighed, staring blankly at the memorial garden she'd worked so hard to create. "Do you miss it as much as I do? Shifting? Last night I practically lost it. I stood at the window in the middle of the night, tired from working out here all day, yet wanting so badly to shift and run . . . but I didn't dare."

Xandi leaned close and gave her a tight hug. "Two more days. You can make it. Anton and Stefan will be here tomorrow, the dedication is Sunday morning, and our flight leaves Sunday night."

Keisha nodded, then turned to Xandi and grinned. "Okay. Two more days. I can do this. You realize, of course, I'm gonna be real tense."

Laughing, Xandi grabbed Keisha's hand. Together, they walked back to the car. Keisha paused by the driver's side and brushed one hand across the back of her neck. She turned her head slowly and scanned the lush park behind her. There was no one visible, but a subtle sense of contact, of being watched, lingered.

Xandi?

Xandi paused in the act of opening the door on the passenger's side. *Yeah?*

Don't turn around. Just smile like we're talking about the project. In fact, look back in the direction of the memorial and see what you feel.

Okay . . . why?

Do you sense anything? Anyone?

Xandi laughed and looked back in the direction of the memorial. After a brief moment, she turned back. Keisha noticed a small frown between Xandi's eyes when she looked at Keisha over the roof of the small rental car.

I'm not sure. For a moment there, I thought I sensed a wolf. That doesn't compute. The guys won't be here until tomorrow at the earliest.

I know. I felt the same thing. Keisha sighed, then laughed, but even in her own ears, the sound lacked humor. "It's probably just wishful thinking. Let's get home. I'm beat."

Anton tossed his briefcase on the wide bed, thoughts of Keisha filling his mind, teasing his body. More than three thousand miles away with that blasted tabloid reporter on her tail and not a damned thing he could do about it. Thank goodness Xandi was with her.

One more meeting early in the morning and they'd head west. He ached for her, needed her sweet body as much as he needed to breathe, needed to feel her beneath him, crying his name, wrapping her gorgeous legs around his hips.

Needed . . .

To run. To feel the wind against his muzzle, the cool grass beneath his feet, the sensory input that kept his Chanku soul alive. The need to shift was almost overpowering, but it wasn't worth the risk. Not here, not in the heart of the city.

Which brought him back to a toss-up between what he could have and what he needed. He'd have to find another way to burn off the energy.

A good fuck? Anton glanced at the door separating his room from Stefan's and wondered if his packmate was as exhausted as he was, as wound up from their day.

He tossed his coat on a chair and tugged at his necktie, then stretched and grimaced at the crackling in his joints. Damn. As tired as he felt, he was still high. He'd never worked with a partner before, much less one who read his mind. It had been an amazing experience, communicating telepathically while pulling off a huge business deal.

Before long, Stefan would be as adept at handling their investments as he was, though he couldn't imagine anything more effective than the two of them working together.

Which brought him full circle to how the hell he was going to burn off all his excess energy. Anton glanced back at the connecting door and grinned. The available options had an immediate effect on his libido. Remembering Stefan, his amazing mouth and aggressive tongue, had Anton's cock surging against his zipper. He loosened his belt, appreciating the fullness, the heat of his erection.

Imagining what Keisha and Xandi might be doing together even now sent a fresh surge of heat to his cock. He cupped himself through his slacks, recalling other business trips, other lonely hotel rooms. Evenings had been the worst. Occasionally, there'd been a woman to share a meal and more, but even feminine companionship hadn't eased the aching loneliness, the soul-deep yearning he'd felt for a true mate.

His thoughts turned once more to Stefan.

With Keisha on the other side of the country, a packmate would do in a pinch. Stefan had already proved that. He wasn't Keisha, but he wasn't bad. Anton's grin broadened. No, Stefan wasn't bad at all.

The door between their rooms swung open. Stefan stood there, barefoot and shirtless, a big smile on his face. "I keep hoping to sense Xandi. Instead all I pick up is your sad but horny refrain."

Anton laughed. "Damn right I'm horny. The women are too far away. I can't reach Keisha, either."

Stefan sauntered into the room, all alpha male swagger and sex appeal, a man fully aware of his effect. "So . . . you think I'm not bad, eh? That's all I get? A 'not bad'?"

"It's a start, don't you think?"

"Barely. You can do better."

"I intend to." Anton began unbuttoning his shirt, taking each button in slow motion. He sensed Stefan's growing excitement . . . as well as an unusual sense of hesitation.

"I . . . uhm." Stefan cleared his throat.

Anton bit back a smile. Ah, that explained it. Stefan still had trouble initiating sex with another man, no matter how often the two of them had made love. Not a problem Anton shared.

Stefan cracked his knuckles and cleared his throat once more, before the words tumbled out of him. "I ordered in tonight. A couple of rare steaks, some potatoes . . . the basics. You looked tired and I know I really don't want to go out. Hope that's okay."

Maybe things were changing. Anton ducked his head to hide his smile. "Sounds good. Have you heard anything at all from the girls? I checked my phone—no messages."

"No, but it's early in California." Stefan glanced at his wristwatch. "Just a little after three for them. They'll call later. This was Keisha's last day to work on the project before the dedication, so I imagine they've been busy."

"I've been worried about her . . . about both of them. I wish they weren't so far away."

"They'll be fine. She and Xandi can take care of themselves for one more night. I have to admit, though, I'll feel a lot better when we're all together again."

"Me, too." Anton threw his shirt in his laundry bag. He straightened up slowly when he felt Stefan's hand brush lightly over his bare shoulder. "Isn't dinner on the way?"

"Not for an hour. I suggested they deliver it around seven. That gives us a little time to unwind. Why don't you sit and let me rub some of the knots out of your back? It'll help take your mind off Keisha."

Anton laughed. "You must really want something if you're offering a massage."

"Oh, I do." Stefan laughed but didn't say anything more enlightening. He did, however, slowly remove his slacks and briefs.

Anton turned away. The need to fall on his knees in front of that perfect body, to grab Stefan's cock and roll his tongue around its blood-filled head, to suck him deep into his mouth . . . damn. It would probably shock the hell out of Stefan. Generally he was the one kneeling in front of Anton.

He bit back a grin. This was Stefan's show. He decided to let the younger man call the shots, at least this once. Anton took a shaky breath and willed his cock under control. His legs felt like rubber.

Sighing, he practically fell onto the desk chair. He turned it backwards, straddled the seat and leaned his forehead on his crossed wrists. Stefan stood close behind, straddling his back, his big hands working magic on Anton's sore muscles.

Stefan's solid cock brushed against Anton's spine. The feel of that hard length burning across his bare back sent a shiver through Anton, a charge that grounded itself deep in his gut.

His own cock pressed against his zipper. His balls drew up

tight and hard between his legs. He shifted on the wood seat, managed to lean closer to Stefan. He opened his mind to Stefan's thoughts and found them blocked.

Wondering, not knowing what his packmate was thinking, turned Anton on even more. That and the hard length of cock riding back and forth across his backbone.

"I could do a better job if you took off your clothes and stretched out on the bed."

"I'll bet you could." Laughing, Anton stood up and reached for his zipper, but Stefan beat him to it. It was the first time another man had ever unzipped Anton's pants for him. Anton grabbed the desk behind him as Stefan's fingers slowly peeled the fly back and released the snap. Then, moving even slower, touching only the tab, Stefan dragged the zipper open, one metal tooth at a time.

Anton gritted his teeth. This teasing, confident male was a new side of Stefan, one Anton hadn't experienced. He put his hands at the waistband, intending to slide his pants down, but Stefan shook his head.

"I'll do it."

He slipped his hands inside the waistband and slowly lowered both Anton's slacks and briefs. The elastic of Anton's briefs caught against the root of his erection. Stefan shoved the loose slacks to the floor, but left the briefs in place.

The band pressed against Anton's cock, holding it down between his legs unnaturally close against his body. The elastic cut lightly into his ass. Stefan led Anton to the bed and gestured to him to wait while he threw a heavy towel over the bedspread.

Anton lay down, still partially clad in the white briefs.

The sensation, though not uncomfortable, drew Anton's attention to both his cock and his ass, as Stefan straddled his hips and began to rub his back. Stefan's huge cock rode against his cotton briefs, prevented from sliding up and down the crease between Anton's buttocks by the thin layer of soft cotton.

Anton's frustration grew. Generally, he penetrated Stefan—took him in the ass while either Xandi or Keisha sucked hard on Stefan's cock—but this was totally different.

Just the two of them, Stefan on top and Anton squirming beneath him, trying to find relief from the growing pressure in his cock, the hard ache in his balls.

Stefan continued to massage his shoulders and back, but the touch of his hands was secondary. Anton shuddered under the weight of his packmate straddling his hips, the tantalizing sweep of Stefan's cock over his ass, the rough abrasion of coarse hair on Stefan's legs sliding across his thighs.

After long minutes of rubbing and teasing, Stefan rose up on his knees and slipped Anton's briefs down over his legs, then tugged them past his feet.

He spread Anton's legs apart and lay on top of him. Anton shifted, better to wedge Stefan's long cock tightly between his cheeks, then he grabbed the top edge of the mattress, wishing for his bed at home with the stout iron railings.

He waited, breath caught in his throat, heart practically stuttering in his chest, for Stefan to fuck him. Instead, he felt fingers reaching under his belly, finding his cock, stroking it in long, slow, teasing sweeps.

Groaning, twisting beneath Stefan's weight and heat, Anton thrust his hips down, pressed himself into Stefan's grasp, practically wept when Stefan slipped his hands away.

"It's been a while, hasn't it? I figured it was your turn for the bottom." Stefan chuckled, then slipped away from Anton. "Don't move."

Anton lay there, remembering. The first time they fucked was the first time either of them had ever had a sexual encounter with another man. Stefan had returned to Anton, caught halfway in his switch between man and wolf, angry, needy, so frustrated he literally bristled in his half wolf, half human pelt.

Unaware of his Chanku heritage, Stefan was convinced Anton had cast a spell on him. He had no idea the shift had occurred within himself, that he alone was responsible for his bestial appearance.

For five long years, Anton had waited for Stefan to come to his senses, to realize he needed Anton. It had taken Alexandria's love and compassion to convince Stefan it was time.

Stefan had been afraid and belligerent at the same time, and he'd burned with a sensuality that was almost intimidating. Anton's breath caught as the full memory blasted through his mind. He'd shifted, half afraid of his prodigy. He'd become the wolf and wrestled Stefan to the ground, had speared him with his wolven cock without care, had taken him in what would have been an act of rape if only Stefan hadn't wanted it so badly.

Not merely taken him—he'd screwed Stefan in front of Alexandria. Fucked him hard and long, shifting from wolf to human, filling Stefan's firm ass with his sperm and bringing the young magician to an incredible climax.

Then he'd walked away and let Stefan and his future mate sort it all out themselves, something they'd done admirably.

Later, the tables had reversed. With youth and anger, passion and lust on his side, Stefan eventually bested his mentor, but there'd been no losers, only winners . . . packmates, and just as important, friends.

A new beginning.

The bed dipped. Still lying on his stomach, Anton spread his legs wider, giving Stefan access. He felt the gentle touch of Stefan's fingers, rubbing some sort of lubricant between his legs, around his sensitive ass. Anton groaned when Stefan slipped one finger inside his tight sphincter muscle, then shuddered when

Stefan slowly guided him up on his knees and rubbed his balls and cock.

Stefan's hands stroked and teased, fingers circled Anton's balls, then traced the sensitive length of his cock, slipped back between his legs to lightly squeeze and massage his balls once more.

Trembling now, Anton buried his head on his crossed arms and braced himself. His breath rushed in and out in short puffs. Stefan's hands were everywhere, rubbing his cock, circling the hard crown, massaging the pulsing vein back to his balls.

He felt the solid head of Stefan's cock pressing tightly against his ass. Grunting, forcing himself to relax, he sighed as the huge crown pressed hard, harder, then slipped past the tight sphincter. Anton shuddered again as Stefan filled him in one long, slow, burning thrust.

Both of Stefan's hands wrapped around Anton's cock. Covered in lube, they slipped to the very end as Stefan withdrew, then slid back against his belly as Stefan thrust forward.

Anton felt Stefan's balls pressing against his for the briefest of moments, then once more Stefan was sliding out, moving his hands in the opposite direction.

In, out, faster, harder, Stefan's fingers tightened around Anton's cock with each thrust . . . pressure increased in balls and gut, breath rasping, muscles clenching, Anton's mind open and screaming on the edge of orgasm.

Suddenly Stefan was there, deep in Anton's thoughts, sharing the sensations of heat and pressure, of cock stuffed deep in his lover's hot bowels, of the slick slide of fingers over straining cock, a link that went full circle, growing, building, layering sensation upon sensation, peaking as one, coming as one, both of them crying out, hanging there in a sensual high for what seemed like forever.

Yet lasted only seconds. Mere seconds before Anton's cock was shooting his seed all over Stefan's hands, mere seconds before Stefan's cock was spasming, pumping his ejaculate into Anton's welcoming body.

Minds open, hearts open, both of them linked as tightly as two people can be. Open to each other.

Open to love, to emotions so deep and powerful there were no words to explain.

Together they heard Keisha's mental scream.

5

"Quit that!" Laughing, Keisha slapped Xandi's hands away from her crotch and climbed out of the car. "It's impossible to drive when some little bitch has her hands between your legs. Now cut it out!"

"Like you want me to stop? Admit it. You love it." Grinning like the very devil, Xandi followed her up the stairs to the front door.

"You're a traffic hazard, woman. I probably left a wet spot on that fine leather upholstery. Explain *that* to the car rental agency!" Keisha opened the door and stepped inside.

"Oh, damn." Xandi paused at the threshold. "I left the bag of groceries in the trunk. Let me have the keys."

Keisha tossed her the keys as she leaned down to unlace her boots. Xandi closed the door and ran back down the steps.

Keisha hoped she'd hurry. She was hot and wet, her pussy so ready for more of Xandi's talented fingers, it wasn't even funny.

Xandi, make sure you lock the doors. You got me so hot and bothered I can't remember if I did or not.

Hell, she'd barely been able to remember where her townhouse was, as turned on as she'd been while they drove along the crowded streets with Xandi's fingers beneath her skirt, slowly stroking her very receptive clit.

Xandi? Did you hear me?

Xandi?

Dread curled, dark and potent in her gut. Keisha raced back to the front door and yanked it open.

Groceries lay scattered on the sidewalk in front of the steps. The rental car was gone.

So was Xandi.

"Ms. Rialto, you don't know for certain it was Carl Burns who took your friend."

"Who else would it be? The man's been following me for weeks. You've got to find her!"

"We've got people working on it. If you hear anything, call me." The burly detective handed his card to Keisha. "My cell phone's the best way to get hold of me."

The detective had been gone less than a minute when the phone rang. Keisha burst into tears when she heard Anton's voice. She needed him with an almost paralyzing desperation. Needed both of them—Anton's steady strength, Stefan's quick humor and compassion.

After a short conversation, Keisha slowly set the phone back on the table. Anton and Stefan were already at the airport. Somehow, they'd heard her, somehow, in spite of the distance, they'd known something terrible had happened.

Her packmates were due to arrive in San Francisco shortly after midnight. They'd cancelled their morning meetings, left their luggage to be shipped later by the hotel.

They'd dropped everything to protect their women.

There wasn't a thing she could do now but wait. Once more Keisha sent out a quick mental search for Xandi. *Nothing.*

Wrapping a faded afghan around her shoulders, she curled

up on the end of the long couch. A heavy layer of summer fog
settled over the city, muting the sounds outside, sending the afternoon into an early dusk. Keisha opened her mind, searching
blindly for Xandi.

It was frightening, after so many months of sharing thoughts,
to have no one answer when she called, but she kept her mind
open, the plea to Xandi running in a steady litany, time mean-
ingless, the silence oppressive.

She glanced at the clock over the fireplace. Almost seven.
She'd been huddled here for almost three hours. The men would
be in the air by now, completely out of touch. Sighing, she settled deeper into the soft couch, closed her eyes. Once more she
silently called out.

Xandi? Why can't you talk to me? What has he done to you?

Keisha? What . . . ?

Stunned, blinking in surprise, Keisha leapt to her feet. Finally!
Contact!

*Where are you? You can't be too far or we couldn't connect!
What happened?*

*I'm not sure. Someone hit me on the head. I've got a hell of a
headache. I think I'm just now waking up. How long have I
been gone?*

About three hours. But where . . . ?

*Three hours! Shit . . . okay. Think. Smells like fish . . . near
the ocean? I'm almost sure I'm naked, handcuffed, tied and
blindfolded. Other than a headache from where someone conked
me, I'm okay. I don't sense anyone else around. If I shift, the bind-
ings might come off and . . .*

*Don't shift! If it's Burns, he's watching you. I know he is.
Anton and Stefan are on their way. They should be here a little
after midnight . . . it's just after seven. Keep your mind open to
me. I'm coming to find you.*

There was no time to consider, no time to worry if this was
the right course of action or not. The fog was growing thicker,

the night darker. She called the detective's cell phone. Left a message that she'd heard from Xandi, though she obviously couldn't tell him how. Tucked her own cell phone into a small nylon fanny pack.

Keisha took a deep breath. Damn, if only Anton were here! He'd know if she were doing the right thing. It was risky, but her senses were sharper as a wolf, her legs faster, endurance and strength multiplied. The fog would help hide her, but the risk of discovery was great.

Xandi's life depended on Keisha. She had no other choice. Keisha could do things as a wolf she could never accomplish in human form.

She stripped her clothes from her body. Naked, pack slung about her neck, Keisha slipped out the back door, checked to make sure no one was watching, and shifted.

Within seconds, a wolf leapt the back fence, raised her head to sniff the smells of the city and, with the small black pack hanging loosely around her neck, raced in the direction of the mental touch she'd felt just moments ago.

Xandi blinked against the darkness, praying her blindfold would slip, wishing she could see something, anything that would lead Keisha to her. She'd lost track of the time but still she worried about her packmate. Every moment Keisha searched as Chanku put the entire pack at risk of discovery.

Xandi rubbed her face against her shoulder but couldn't reach the blindfold, tugged at what felt like handcuffs holding her wrists but only succeeded in making her wrists bleed. If she could be certain she was alone, Xandi knew she'd risk shifting. It would be so easy to free herself.

No luck. I can't move the blindfold. Keisha? What if you link, the way we used to do during sex? Then you'll see what I see . . . if I ever see anything! We'd know if anyone was watching me and you might get some idea of how to get me out.

You're too far away for a complete link. I'm nearing the Presidio, paralleling Lincoln, heading toward the Golden Gate... I just cut through the park. Your mental signal is growing stronger. Keep feeding me anything you sense.

Xandi opened her mind, absorbed the sounds and scents around her. She drew on her Chanku heritage without shifting, delving deeper into her basic wolven instincts.

Fear hovered just beyond. She refused to acknowledge its presence.

The scents grew stronger, the sound of water lapping nearby, the roar of cars overhead.

Overhead?

Keisha? Is there any place under a bridge or overpass where he might have me? I smell fish and hear water, but I also hear lots of cars going overhead.

Fort Point!

What?

Fort Point. It's just at the foot of the bridge, an old military base. I'm not that far away and your signal is stronger in that direction. Hang on.

Xandi sensed his presence even before she heard the door squeal on its hinges. Her body tensed. *He's here. In the room.*

So am I. Not physically, not yet. But I'm getting closer.

Xandi felt Keisha's thoughts enter her mind, the strength of the link now almost a physical presence. She almost sagged with relief, but instead, she forced herself to sit straighter in the hard-backed chair and take a deep, calming breath.

"Who are you? Why are you keeping me here? I want my clothes, dammit!"

She sensed movement, felt the brush of fingertips along her cheek and immediately recoiled. Her heart pounded beneath her ribs.

"Who are you?" It was all she could do not to scream. Heart

racing faster, breath rasping in her throat, Xandi reached deep to find a calm she didn't feel.

It's Burns. I can feel him. But what the hell is he trying to prove? Keisha's soft mental voice tinged with her usual steel helped quiet Xandi's pounding heart.

She felt the man's presence, stronger, closer. Her Chanku senses heightened with the rush of adrenaline and she smelled him, the acrid odor of unwashed body, old cigarette smoke and stale breath. Her stomach roiled and churned and she clamped her teeth tightly together to keep from gagging.

His lips brushed against her ear, dry and disgusting, and he whispered softly, "Why haven't you shifted? I know you're one of them. Shift. That's all you have to do. Turn into a wolf for me and I'll let you go."

"You're crazy." Xandi practically spat the words, then had to swallow quickly to keep from vomiting. His smell suffocated her, his breath found its way into her nostrils and she drew back and swallowed again.

Quiet laughter echoed in the room. "Ah, no crazier than your friend. That little black girl's hiding a secret that's going to make me rich. No, I'm no crazier than your friend . . . or her mother. The bitch!"

Did you hear him? Keisha, could your mother shift? Xandi turned and faced the direction of the man's voice. "What's her mother got to do with this? I don't know what you're talking about."

"Oh, yes you do. You know what your friend is like. She's a tease, just like her mother. A monster. A wolf in human form. I think you are, too."

I don't know if my mother could shift or not. I told you, she died when I was little, but I had to get my Chanku genes from one of my parents. She's the most likely. Keep him talking. Get him to take the blindfold off if you can. The more I can see, the better my chance to get you out of there.

Xandi raised her head and looked in the direction of Burns's voice. "I don't know anything about her mother. Keisha does not turn into a wolf. Are you nuts?" She shook her head and laughed. "Well, I guess that's a given. Take this blindfold off of me. There's no point in hiding. I know who you are, Mr. Burns."

Her head jerked back with the force of his backhanded slap. "Ah!" Xandi tasted blood, but at least he ripped the blindfold away.

"You're playing a dangerous game, bitch." Burns stared down at her, his sallow face illuminated by the glow from a small flashlight clutched in his hand. "How come your friend hasn't come to save you? I know you communicate. Is it telepathy? Do you read minds? Are you aliens? What the fuck are you?"

Xandi ignored his questions. She took in all she could of her dark surroundings, hoping Keisha would grasp the images.

Burns set the flashlight down on a small table and walked around Xandi, trailing one finger along her collarbone, over her shoulder, across her back. Her nipples puckered in the cold air and she prayed he wouldn't touch them. She couldn't stand the thought of this disgusting creature putting his hands on her.

The narrow beam of light sent a crazed pattern against the wall, over his fleshy hand. Xandi shuddered, aware even as she struggled to hold still that Keisha fought the same battle within her mind.

Xandi stiffened her spine as Burns slipped his fingers along her shoulder, then rudely flicked one nipple with his fingernail. He chuckled and did it once more. Xandi turned her head away, unable to watch her own violation.

Frantic, she reached for Keisha. *Where the hell are the police?*

I left a message and I have my cell phone with me. Maybe the detective isn't taking my calls.

Not the time for humor, m'dear. Xandi turned to follow Burns as he circled her, his hands now trailing over her arm. She had to keep him talking, keep his mind occupied. It was her only chance. "Why did you kidnap me? If you're so convinced my friend is a wolf, why would you want me?"

"You really want to know? Might as well tell you, since your friend is taking longer than I expected."

He squatted down in front of Xandi. His eyes were surprisingly clear, not the crazed look of a madman. Mere inches from her crotch, he stared directly into her eyes. Xandi found his calm demeanor unsettling.

"Her mother was a wolf. Yeah, you look at me like I'm nuts, but I saw her shift. We went to high school together. I worked on the school paper. It was late, the school was almost empty, and I imagine she thought she was alone. I was in the journalism room, putting the paper to bed, when I saw her in the quad outside. Just standing there, sort of staring at the woods beyond the campus. I watched her . . . I used to watch her a lot. She was gorgeous, so sexy. But she was black, you know?"

He stood up, paced back and forth, agitated. "I couldn't date her. My old man would've had a fit. Nah, I didn't want to date her, but damn, did I ever want to fuck her."

He looked off in the distance, as if remembering, then licked his lips. Xandi felt a shiver run down her spine.

"She sort of shimmered, this cute little black girl. Damn, she was such a hot babe. She just . . . shimmered. Then there was a pile of clothes on the ground and a huge wolf standing over them. She turned and saw me. I'll never forget that. I almost peed my pants. She snarled. Man, did that bitch have a mouthful of teeth! I slammed the window closed and locked the doors. When I looked back, she was gone, but I know she saw me."

Keisha? Did you hear him?

Yeah. I've got a bad feeling about this.

"I watched her after that. Followed her for a long time without her knowing it. She got married. What a mistake. The guy was a gardener, a real loser, but eventually she had a baby. I kept waiting and watching, but I never saw her shift again . . . not until years later."

Did Keisha know any of this? Xandi watched Burns as he rocked back on his heels. Though he looked directly at Xandi, she sensed he was somewhere else. Somewhere in the past. Keisha's presence was a roiling tension in her mind.

"One night in Golden Gate Park I spotted a wolf." Burns laughed. The sound scraped across Xandi's already raw nerves. "Like wolves were a regular occurrence in the park? I don't think so. I followed it. It loped along without a care in the world, but right at the edge of the park, right there near Fulton and Thirty-fourth, the wolf disappeared into the bushes. It looked back, like it was checking to make sure no one was watching, but I saw it. I went back and got my car. Figured I'd look farther down the road. Suddenly, a slim, black woman dressed all in dark clothes stepped out into the crosswalk. I hit her. Didn't see her in time and I ran right over her."

Xandi felt Keisha's gasp in her mind. She struggled not to react to her friend's pain. Burns shook his head, rubbed his hand across his eyes. "Of course, I recognized her immediately. I was driving an old, beat up car already covered with dings, so one more didn't make a difference. No one ever found out who killed her. I parked a block away and went back. I was already a reporter, so I had my camera. I waited in the bushes."

He looked at Xandi as if everything he said made sense, as if his actions had been perfectly acceptable. She held still, kept her face passive in spite of the growing nausea, the sense of evil filling the dark room.

Burns shrugged his shoulders. "I thought she might turn back into the wolf when she died, but she didn't. She just lay there in the center divider, her body all twisted and broken, caught up in the landscaping. She might have looked like a woman, but I knew better. I knew she was just an animal. Made me think of road kill. That's all she was. Road kill. A dead wolf on the side of the road."

Burns turned around and walked away, disappearing into the shadows. His voice echoed out of the darkness. "Of course, that wasn't the end of it. I knew she had a kid. Figured, like mother, like daughter, right? But I never could catch the little brat shifting. All those years . . . the pictures and story could have made my career."

Oh my God.

Keisha's agonized cry echoed in Xandi's head. *Keisha, it's okay. He's nuts. Totally nuts. Where are the police?*

I don't know. He killed her. He killed my mother!

Honey, hang in there. We'll get him. Just hang in there.

You're the one tied up. I need to get you out of there, need to . . .

No! Just wait. Please. Just wait. Frantic, Xandi tried to follow Burns' movements in the shadows while she silently begged Keisha to stay out of sight.

"I finally figured it out. Decided that she could turn into a wolf, just like her mama, but she didn't know it." Burns wandered back into the narrow beam of light. "I waited for years, waited and watched. I was real patient."

He squatted down in front of Xandi once more and rested one fat hand on her knee. She backed away, as far as the chair would allow, but she couldn't escape the clammy feel of his palm against her bare skin, the twitch of his fingertips emphasizing each word he spoke.

"I got to thinking, maybe she was like the Hulk, ya know? Remember that show, where the guy had to feel really strong emotion to change? I figured, why not? It wouldn't hurt to try. I hired two losers. Not sure where the third guy came from. They were only supposed to scare the crap out of her, not rape her. Scare her good enough that she'd shift. I figured there might be sort of a 'fight or flight' reaction, ya know? Like the Hulk? I was there. I watched it all. It was pretty ugly, got totally out of hand, but it worked. I took some pictures when the little bitch shifted but then she killed them. God, she just tore those poor bastards to pieces. It was awful. What's worse, I panicked."

He stood up, brushed his hand across his face. "I am not proud of myself for that, believe me. God. I was so damned stupid. Would you believe I actually burned the film? I was so afraid someone would connect me with the murders . . . with her rape. That film could have made me a fortune and I panicked."

Burns whirled around, his eyes wide. "Where the fuck are you? I know you're here somewhere. Show yourself, damn it. Shift!"

No! Keisha, no!

Xandi sensed Keisha's outrage, her unleashed anger, and knew there'd be no stopping her. Xandi jerked at the handcuffs binding her wrists, tugged at the cords holding her to the chair, but it wasn't enough. She heard a loud crunch against the door. The sound of scratching and panting. Another loud cracking noise.

"I knew it!" Burns grabbed a camera off the floor and slipped the strap over his neck, then yanked a knife out of his pocket and slashed the rope holding Xandi to the chair. With her hands still cuffed behind her back, it was all she could do to rise without stumbling. Burns looped another rope around her neck and dragged her to a door at the opposite end of the room.

The door behind them creaked, wood splintered. The hinges groaned.

Keisha? Don't let him see you!

Sensing only blind, animalistic rage, Xandi tripped over her own feet. She tried to drag Burns to the floor with her, but he caught his balance then twisted her around, holding tightly to her cuffed wrists and tugging on the rope cutting into her throat.

Even if she wanted to shift now, Xandi couldn't risk it. He literally had her leashed.

Burns grabbed a bulky camera bag in his free hand and slung it over his shoulder, then shoved the door open. With a final curse, he pushed Xandi out into the darkness. She tumbled to the rough gravel surface, scraping her knees and falling hard on her shoulder as Burns slammed the door behind him.

She felt the rope cut into her neck as he yanked her upright, then shoved his forearm against the middle of her back. Pushing and pulling, Burns forced her across the parking lot to the stolen rental car. Rocks and broken glass cut into her bare feet.

The twisted strands of rope sawed at her throat. Gasping, choking, she struggled for each breath. The noose around her throat tightened and black spots danced before her eyes. She had no choice but to follow Burns when he yanked on the rope and dragged her across the rough gravel.

A loud crash echoed from the far side of the building. Burns shoved Xandi into the front passenger seat. She landed on her side, one leg caught beneath her, but the noose around her neck loosened when Burns released his end of the rope. Gasping for breath, twisting around, she raised her head in time to see a large wolf leap over the retaining wall at the back of the building.

Burns snapped one quick shot with his camera before throwing his equipment in the back seat and speeding away.

6

Panting, paws torn and bleeding, muzzle covered in bloody froth and saliva, Keisha watched the car fishtail out of the parking lot. Her tail hung low, her body quivered with barely suppressed rage and sorrow.

Everything awful, every terrible thing that had happened in her life . . . all of it caused by this man. Her mother's death. Her own rape and assault. All of it because Carl Burns wanted proof.

Well, he had his proof now, only he didn't know it.

He had Xandi, an innocent bystander, a victim to one man's sick desire for fame and fortune.

Xandi?

No answer. Keisha glanced at the sky and wondered if Anton and Stefan's plane was on the ground yet. She reached for them but there was nothing. She'd never needed her mate more, never felt this vulnerable, this bereft. She raised her head and howled, a long, keening cry of pain and sadness.

The mournful wail echoed eerily across San Francisco Bay, fading slowly away until the only sounds were the passage of cars overhead and the gentle lap of water against the rocky shore.

Keisha's breathing returned to normal. Though her body still trembled, her heart rate slowed and her mind cleared. It had to be well after midnight. Anton and Stefan would be here soon.

Xandi? Where is he taking you? Where are you?

A car horn honked overhead. Far off, a siren sounded, and a mockingbird called from a nearby tree. Keisha waited, but there was no familiar mental reply from Xandi.

Keisha's cell phone rang. She stared at it a moment, then nuzzled at the small pack laying on the ground in front of her and caught it in her teeth. She trotted into the shadows and shifted.

Naked and shivering in the foggy night, she answered her phone.

Unwilling to wait for a rental car, Anton hailed the first cab he saw at the airport. He stuffed a hundred dollar bill into the cabbie's hand. "Four more of those if you can get us into the city in under twenty minutes."

The cab was moving before either Stefan or Anton had their doors closed or seatbelts buckled. Immediately, Anton felt Keisha's mental touch. He sighed his relief, but the feeling was short lived. Their minds linked and he sensed her fear, her disgust with herself, her overwhelming anger.

While her thoughts poured into him, the cab raced down the freeway. Keisha broke the link to return to her search for Alexandria. Anton tapped the cab driver on the shoulder. "Make that the Golden Gate Bridge. Fast." Anton reached out for Stefan but kept his gaze on the road ahead.

Stefan, have you been able to reach Alexandria?

No, Anton. Keisha?

Yes. Just now. She's waiting for us just below the Golden

Gate Bridge, near a place called Fort Point. The detective called
her a few minutes ago. Said he'd gone back over evidence from
her assault. Found Carl Burns's prints. They'd been taken from
a closet door in the apartment. The crime lab hadn't matched
them before now. Didn't think they were pertinent.

Shit. How's Keisha?

A wreck. Worried about Alexandria. Afraid people will find
out about us.

That's the least of our worries. Stefan swung his head around
to glare at Anton.

Anton turned and held Stefan's gaze for a brief moment. "I
know." He touched Stefan's arm. Felt the tension coiling within
his packmate, his lover. "We'll get to her in time. Hang in there."

Suddenly Stefan jerked. "Xandi!" Anton linked immediately, felt the familiar mental touch of Stefan's mate. He pulled
Keisha into the link.

You're all here! Alexandria's relief was obvious. I'm not sure
what he's up to. We're parked near the north end of the bridge.
I think he's setting up some camera gear, but I'm not sure. He's
outside, hidden in the shrubbery. He's got me cuffed to the steering wheel.

Are you okay? Stefan's calm mental voice shouldn't have
surprised Anton. Stefan would never let his own fears affect his
mate.

I'm fine. Just madder than hell. This man is evil, Stefan.
More evil than any of us imagined. Keisha, are you okay?

I'm so sorry, Xandi. I tried to get to him, but . . .

Anton interrupted. Don't worry. We're in a cab, sweetheart.
We'll pick you up and cross over to Xandi's side of the bridge.
Keisha, are you coming as woman or wolf?

Her relieved laughter bubbled through all of their minds.
Hairy wolf or naked woman. Take your pick.

If I had my choice, you know what I'd choose. Stefan's silly
comment seemed to melt away fear. Even Alexandria laughed.

Keisha's mental voice sounded clear and calm. *I don't want to shock the cabbie. He's probably seen a naked woman before . . . the wolf would scare him to death. Are you wearing a coat? I can put that on.*

At Anton's request, the cabbie pulled over to the side of the road near the tollbooth at the south end of the bridge. Stefan opened the rear door. Keisha raced out of the shadows and crawled into the backseat of the cab, slithering right over Stefan's lap like a naked seal.

Anton quickly slipped his coat over her shoulders and Keisha wriggled her arms into the sleeves. Anton leaned forward and handed the cab driver four one hundred dollar bills. "Drop us off at the far end of the bridge, and thanks."

Shoving the bills into his back pocket, the cabby pulled back onto the road. Anton thought the man spent much too long looking in his rearview mirror. He wrapped his arms protectively around his mate.

Poor guy is gonna wonder about this odd group forever! Keisha snuggled close to Anton.

He didn't answer. He couldn't. She felt too damned good curled up in his lap, so warm and alive. So safe. Anton glanced over the top of her head and smiled grimly at Stefan. "We'll get Alexandria back."

Stefan merely nodded. Obviously he was still linked with his mate.

Wrapped in Stefan's loving thoughts, Xandi felt her racing heart calm and her panic subside as she sensed her packmates growing closer. She still wasn't certain what Burns was planning. He'd left her in the car, hands cuffed to the steering wheel, rope tied tightly around her neck. The car was just outside the regular parking lot, close up against the side of a hill.

Car lights flashed nearby on the freeway.

Xandi pressed on the horn. She wanted to raise her muzzle

and howl, but the loud beep was almost as satisfying. Stefan's laughter echoed in her mind and his thoughts immediately touched hers. *Where the hell is the jerk?*

Xandi took a deep, steadying breath. *I don't know, but I imagine I'm bait and he's nearby with a camera.*

All he's gonna get is a shot of a really pissed off adult human male hauling your sweet ass out of his car. The police should be right behind us. Hang on, sweetheart!

Whatever you do, don't shift. I mean it, Stefan! He's already got a shot of Keisha in wolf form. We have to get his camera.

Suddenly Stefan was beside her, tall and strong and so beautiful he took her breath. He kissed her hard and gently removed the noose from around her neck. Then he threw his jacket over her body. *Shift, pull your hands free of the cuffs, then shift back.*

It was all so simple. Xandi's paws slipped out of the cuffs beneath the coat, and she immediately regained her human form. She was free, enveloped in Stefan's arms, and he was pulling her out of the car, wrapping his coat around her naked, shivering body, taking her to safety.

Stefan glanced down at her bare feet and lifted Xandi close against his chest. She wrapped her arms around his neck, pressed her body close to his and finally breathed a sigh of relief. Nothing could harm her while Stefan held her close.

Where are Anton and Keisha?

Taking care of the camera.

A scream nearby filled the night. Snarls and yelps. Something heavy raced ahead of them through the thick brush. Moments later, Xandi spotted a man running along the pedestrian access to the bridge.

A howl, long and low, then another.

"Sounds like they're on it."

"What are they doing to him?"

"Making sure he doesn't take any more pictures or plan any

more assaults. Keisha told us about her mother and about her assault."

Flashing lights suddenly appeared near the southern end of the bridge. Xandi and Stefan watched from behind an outcropping at the opposite end. Xandi held her breath, praying the police wouldn't shoot at Anton and Keisha.

What could have been two large dogs chased a man along the narrow walkway, then quickly stopped when he crawled up on top of the railing to escape them. One animal leapt for his camera bag, barely missing the strap.

The lights from the police cars drew nearer. Sirens echoed eerily across the water.

The man balanced for a moment on the edge of the railing, his body outlined by the harsh bridge lighting, arms flailing, the camera bag swinging from one hand. Suddenly the heavy bag seemed to pull him off center and he tumbled, almost in slow motion, falling end over end from the center of the span.

The animals watched briefly then turned and raced back along the walkway. They disappeared into a small construction area just beneath the bridge abutment, hidden from the oncoming policemen.

Moments later, Anton ran across the road with Keisha's hand tightly clasped in his. He wore his slacks and a white dress shirt. Keisha had on his suit coat, but her legs and feet were bare and bleeding.

Xandi was caught in a full-body hug, laughing and crying at the same time with her packmates when the police finally pulled into the parking area.

7

There was a lavender glow in the sky, but the sun hadn't yet breached the horizon by the time the police interrogation ended. Keisha could hardly believe the four of them were finally free to go. She was so tired, standing upright was a struggle.

At least the hospital scrubs they'd gotten at the emergency room were about as comfortable as clothes could be. She and Xandi had spent almost an hour having their cuts and bruises treated while Stefan and Anton paced impatiently outside the small cubicle.

Now Keisha held tightly to Anton's arm as they walked slowly and stiffly down the flight of stone steps from police headquarters. Her feet were bandaged and sore from running barefoot in human form, but Xandi's injuries were worse. The tears on her wrists from the handcuffs would probably leave deep scars, and she wore a sling on her right arm to protect her badly bruised shoulder.

It had been a long, long night and sleep sounded heavenly. Keisha yawned and leaned against Anton's solid frame as Stefan closed the door behind them. It shut with a satisfying click and the four of them headed down the stairs.

A large, well-dressed man stepped out of the shadows. "Keisha? Keisha Rialto?"

Keisha's head snapped up and she blinked in surprise. "Wha . . . ?" She squinted and leaned closer. It couldn't be! "Uncle Ulrich? It is you, isn't it? What are you doing here?" She felt Anton's grasp tighten about her waist. Stefan and Xandi paused on the step above, alert and watchful.

"Please." The man nodded to Anton, glanced up at Stefan and Xandi, then returned his attention to Keisha. "I know you must be exhausted, but I need to talk to you. It's important or I wouldn't intrude." Almost as an afterthought he added, "I had no idea how much you had in common with your mother and your Aunt Camille, my dear."

Keisha lost herself for a moment in the man's amber-colored eyes, her mind roiling with the memories of her mother and her beautiful young aunt, both dead now for so long. She'd wondered over the years why her uncle had disappeared. Now, seeing Anton's eyes in his, she thought she finally understood.

"Whatever you have to say, Uncle, can be said in front of my mates."

He nodded in understanding. "So I suspected." He stared off into the distance, a tall, proud-looking man with a shock of white hair and those oddly familiar amber eyes. "I heard a wolf howl last night. More than once . . . and more than one."

Keisha swallowed, on the verge of asking a million questions. Suddenly the wolven presence in the park made sense, and she glanced behind her, catching Xandi's eye. Xandi's slight nod and tight smile gave Keisha confidence. Anton's arm looped solidly around her waist steadied her even more.

Her uncle gazed at the four of them for a moment, then nodded, as if agreeing to some inner conversation. "I love the sound of wolves. It reminds me of legends I've always enjoyed." He turned and smiled at Keisha and she suddenly remembered him from long ago, when Auntie Camille had been alive and Tia was a baby and he'd held her in his lap and told her stories.

Stories she'd forgotten until now. Keisha blinked owlishly at him as the memories flooded into her mind. There was a catch in her throat, a lump she had to swallow back before she could answer.

"I remember. You told me about the Chanku, a magical race of wolves who became human, who lived among us. I remember the stories. I really do remember. How could I have forgotten? I loved those stories." She turned to Anton and saw the growing look of wonder in his eyes as he watched the older man.

Xandi and Stefan waited warily on the step above them. The day grew marginally brighter as the sun rose above the low hills on the eastern side of San Francisco Bay, but most of the city still slept, so early on a Sunday morning.

"I'm pleased to know you remember. That was a special time in all our lives, when your mother and my beloved wife both lived and all was right with our world. I want you to know you're not alone, my dear. None of you are alone." Ulrich handed Keisha a plain business card with his name and a couple of phone numbers on it, then turned his attention to Anton. "I should introduce myself. I'm Ulrich Mason, Keisha's uncle. I was married to her Aunt Camille until my wife's untimely death many years ago. When you feel ready, please contact me. We have much to discuss."

He shook Anton's hand, then Stefan and Xandi's as well. Bemused, Keisha stared at him, her heart pounding in her chest with the flood of memories the big man's presence released. He turned back to Keisha and she was suddenly wrapped in a familiar bear hug, transported back to a childhood she'd long forgotten.

"I have so many things I want to ask you." She pressed her cheek against the rough fabric of his coat, embarrassed by the quick rush of her tears.

"There will be time for that later." Ulrich stepped back and brushed her damp hair away from her face. "Rest now. All of you. Know we're here and contact us when you're ready. There are others, though not many. I'm just very glad I was able to find you."

"Mr. Mason?" Anton stepped forward and held his own card out to Keisha's uncle. "We'll be returning to our home in Montana, but I promise we'll get in touch with you. You have no idea how many questions . . ."

Mason laughed. "Ah, but I do, young man. I do . . . probably as many as I have." He turned once more to Keisha. "It's good to see you, to know you're healthy and happy. To know your mother's blood runs so strongly in your veins. She would be very proud of you."

"How did you find me?" Keisha tilted her head, seeing Ulrich Mason as the younger man she remembered. "Why did you disappear in the first place?"

"I was always here, but life was difficult after Camille died. I decided to look for you when I saw the memorial garden in the park. Only another of our line would choose the same plants. Knowing your father's work, knowing your mother's creative talents . . . well, let's just say I had a pretty good idea who designed the memorial. It was time to find you. Take care."

Before Keisha could ask another question, Mason turned and walked away.

Oh my God. Xandi let out a breath with such force Keisha heard her.

"My sentiments exactly." Stefan hugged Keisha. "Well, at

least we know where you got your Chanku genes. It's strange, though . . . knowing there are more of us so close. Unfortunately, I'm exhausted and I know you guys are, too. Let's sort this out later."

Keisha stared after the man walking briskly away from them, then turned to the tall man at her side and the couple waiting patiently behind her. She didn't know whether to laugh or cry. After so many years alone, she actually had an uncle right here in the city, a family link to her mother and her aunt.

More importantly, she had her pack, her mate, the truth of her heritage and the strength and power of the wolf.

It didn't get much better than that.

Stefan finished his shower and crawled into Keisha's big bed to join the other three. They'd talked of splitting up, each couple going to their own room, but the night's call had been too close. They needed to be together.

Stefan wrapped Xandi in his arms and held her tightly, much too aware of how easily he could have lost her. He wondered about the other Chanku in the city, how many there were, what they were like, if they might be a threat to the balance he'd found with these three.

"Interrogations aren't all that bad when you can link."

Anton's wry comment made Stefan smile. He'd worry about Ulrich's pack later. "I think the police bought the idea the man was nuts, that he was fixated on Keisha and his weird idea she was a werewolf."

"I'm just glad they didn't see you and Keisha chasing him across the bridge. That would have been tough to explain, though from where Xandi and I were, you just looked like a couple of big mangy dogs."

"Watch it, buster." Anton leaned over and cuffed Stefan lightly on the shoulder. "We are not dogs. We're wolves. There's a difference."

Stefan barked.

Keisha sighed. "Thank goodness you found the video camera. I can't believe Burns actually filmed me shifting right here on my back porch."

There'd been one small camera hidden inside a hanging plant, another near the greenhouse. Stefan had discovered both and destroyed them. Luckily, they were unable to transmit images, merely store them. Burns hadn't collected the images. Now, he never would.

"He'll never film anyone again." Anton leaned over and kissed Keisha full on the mouth. "No more Burns. No more cameras. No record. Period. Police are happy, the case is closed, and we're going home in the morning."

Xandi groaned. "No, we're not. It's already morning and we've got a dedication to attend. We've got time for about an hour's nap before we leave. I am not missing this, not after all we've been through."

She snuggled closer to Stefan, her round bottom fitting perfectly against the cradle of his hips. His cock wedged comfortably in the crease of her behind.

"Napping is the last thing on my mind, woman. It's been a week, and that's too damned long to go without sex."

"Excuse me? What was that we were doing last night?" Anton lifted himself up on one elbow, looking properly outraged.

Keisha laughed. "Yeah. What *were* you doing last night? How the hell did you hear me? We can't link that far."

Anton lay back down and tucked Keisha close under his chin. "I don't know what happened. Stefan and I reached climax at the same time and that's when we heard you scream. Somehow, the orgasm must have heightened our senses, allowed us to pick up your thoughts. I don't ever want that to happen again."

Stefan snorted. "What, a mutual climax? It's not nearly as

much fun alone." His fingers trailed between Xandi's legs, where he found her wet and ready. It was such a simple, marvelous thing to slide his cock slowly inside her welcoming pussy.

From the look of pleasure on Keisha's face, Anton was doing the same thing to his mate. Both women sighed. Xandi wriggled her butt, giving Stefan better access. He thrust inside, slow and smooth, withdrawing just as slowly. His mind opened, his thoughts spilled out over all of them.

He sensed Xandi's pleasure, her need, at the same time felt Keisha's response to Anton, experienced Keisha's heat and the full, even slide of Anton's huge erection filling her, touching the mouth of her womb, pausing a moment and then slipping back along the rippling muscles.

Xandi and Keisha closed the narrow gap between them. Keisha leaned forward and sucked at Xandi's nipple. Stefan felt the pull between his legs, between Xandi's legs.

The four of them moved as one, their bodies sliding together in a slow and graceful ballet, sensation building on sensation as the link grew stronger. They shared the common coil of pending orgasm, the heat building, the gut tightening, their bodies so perfectly in sync it was difficult to tell where one began and the other ended.

Thrusting harder, faster, finding a perfect rhythm, filling Xandi, filling Keisha, *being* Anton, Keisha and his beloved mate, Stefan tipped over the edge between light and dark, felt his body take flight, his mind and soul in perfect communion with the three he loved.

Gasping, crying out Xandi's name, he came in a rush of heat and life, his seed filling her, his body wrapping around hers and holding her close, holding Keisha and Anton as they arched and cried out together.

Suddenly, a gate seemed to open in Stefan's heart, a blossoming in his soul that was as fierce as it was unexpected. The memories of pain and misery, of his years caught in the darkness, between worlds both human and wolf, were so totally overwhelmed by love and light that the harsh sob raging out of his chest caught him unaware.

He held Xandi in his arms, his tears falling into her thick mass of hair, remembering how alone he'd been, how much the outcast, half wolf, half human, unaware of his true heritage, unaware of the gift that was Chanku.

The gift made whole by these three who loved him, who so completely loved one another.

He opened his thoughts, halting their worry, their loving concern, showing them what was in his heart. Sharing his memories.

Anton's hand reached across the two women, his fingers tightened around Stefan's shoulder.

"I know."

Two simple words of understanding. Male to male, their women between them, basking in the strength of the pack.

Epilogue

Keisha's speech at the end of the dedication was short, simple and filled with her wry sense of humor. It felt even more special, knowing her Uncle Ulrich stood there at the back of the small crowd, his head held high and his smile creasing his handsome face. He nodded to Keisha as she ended her talk, gave her a small salute, then slipped away as people surged forward to congratulate her on the beautiful design she'd created.

Smiling, graciously accepting the accolades she'd worked so hard for, Keisha turned to step down from the podium. San Francisco's handsome young mayor held out his hand to assist her. Anton quickly stepped between them.

"Excuse me, sir. We have a plane to catch."

The mayor nodded, grinned at Anton and stepped aside. It was obvious he was reluctant to let go of Keisha's hand.

Anton wrapped Keisha's fingers around his forearm and quickly guided her around the rows of folding chairs and past the bandstand to where Xandi and Stefan waited near the car.

Keisha burst into laughter once they were away from the

crowd. "Could you have been any ruder to the poor man? He's the mayor, Anton!"

"I didn't bite him."

"Yeah. He didn't pee on the man's pants leg, either." Stefan laughed when Xandi punched him lightly on the shoulder.

"And I thought men were bad. Wolves are worse." Xandi punched Stefan again, as if to emphasize her comment.

"Thank goodness." Keisha stopped next to the car. "And thank you. All of you, for talking me into staying for this. Did you see Uncle Ulrich? He was there, too. I saw him standing in the back of the crowd."

Xandi nodded. "We spoke to him briefly, just before you gave your talk. I like him, Keisha. I tried to hear his thoughts. No go. His mind wasn't open to me, but I didn't sense anything wrong about him, just a need to retain his privacy. Sweetie, he's so proud of you . . . your mom and dad would have been proud of you, too." Xandi pulled Keisha into a quick hug. "Just as we are."

Stefan gave Keisha a quick kiss, then drew Xandi away. The two of them slipped into the backseat of the rental car.

Keisha bit back tears as she gazed across the green expanse of park, at the memorial garden she'd designed and the small groups of people slowly dispersing now that the dedication was over. She turned and looked behind her, at the city that had been her home and realized it no longer held her, in spite of her newfound family.

Ulrich Mason was a link to her past, one she fully intended to follow, but Anton Cheval was her future. Keisha tilted her chin and gazed up at him, caught, as always, by the perfection of his profile, the strength in his jaw and his sensual mouth, his lips tilted now in a half smile as he gazed steadily back at her.

"Sweetheart, we need to go now." He ran his finger along her jaw, then planted a very light kiss on her mouth. "It's time."

Bemused, Keisha nodded and gazed once more across the green expanse of park. He was absolutely right.

It was time to head back to Montana, back to the place where she now belonged.

It was time to run through the cool, dark forest, to hunt with her beloved packmates, to prowl along hidden trails and race the moon.

Time to make love on the mossy forest floor, and maybe, just maybe, time for babies.

She turned and smiled at Anton. Let him see the dreams in her heart, the future she envisioned.

He watched her, his amber eyes glowing, his love for her obvious in the tender curve of his lips, the soft touch of his hand, even the tilt of his head as he leaned over to kiss her softly on the mouth.

A benediction.

A promise.

Keisha felt the truth of his love blossom deep within her heart. When he slowly pulled back from their kiss, she looked up at him, at his beloved face, and she knew.

There was no doubt in her mind. This was the time for Chanku.

Tiger, Tiger

Noelle Mack

For JWR, born in the Year of the Tiger.

1

The crevasse reverberated with the sound of her scream as she went down . . . then Dani's climbing rope caught on a rock somewhere above her.

My lucky rock.

She hadn't seen it on the way down. But then she hadn't seen the hole to hell, either. The sudden snowstorm, fierce and fast, had covered it—the Himalayas were full of freaky surprises.

Hey. Breathe.

Dani forced herself to inhale and exhale, her throat raw from screaming. She swung back and forth like a clapper in a giant bell, looking down into . . . blue-black nothing.

Her moist breath crystallized in the air as her swings shortened little by little. She uncurled the fingers of one freezing hand and reached out, but she was too far away to touch the glistening walls of the crevasse. She looked up, hoping Moe's head would appear in the hole.

He had to have felt the violent tug on the rope that joined them, had to feel the drag of her weight on it now. But there was no answering tug. She clung with both hands again to the taut rope, grateful for the kernmantle core that had absorbed the impact of her fall and added an extra six or seven feet of stretch. The trace eight knot Moe had tied had held. He'd added another at the end just in case that gave way. Just in case she had to hang on.

Justinfuckingcase. If the trace eight failed . . . but it wouldn't. That knot only got tighter when pulled. She knew it was a straight drop onto bone-shattering crags of ice that lay in the darkness below.

Dani turned her attention to the rope. The strong strands were undamaged. She rested her cheek on it, trying to think. Most likely it would hold her until Moe came back and pulled her up.

The storm had kicked up about twenty minutes before she'd stepped into air. Afraid of losing her in the blowing snow, he'd connected them with the longest rope they had, then gone on out of sight. Older than she was but a lot faster on difficult terrain, Moe wanted to set up camp so they could sit it out in relative safety. He'd taken all the heavy gear and fastened it to his pack to spare her. Good old Moe. Her brother's best friend and like a brother to her.

Where was he? She yelled once. Twice. Her cries rang, echoed, then died away. A few thin shards of ice fell past her.

She looked up. Cracks had appeared around the hole. Dani hung on to her lifeline, trembling with fear as she saw her rope begin to shred, pulled tight against razor-sharp ice by the momentum of her body's swing.

The last strands parted as the ice overhead gave way with a sickening crack. Snow poured in, covering her face and goggles, filling her mouth and nose with suffocating powder. Screaming soundlessly, she let go and fell into white oblivion.

* * *

Dani opened her eyes and saw . . . more white. A white that breathed, rising and falling with soft growls. Dazed, she reached out to touch pale fur marked with brushstrokes of soft black. Blue eyes, piercing and predatory, outlined in black, gazed into hers.

Hi, tiger.

Okay, it was a figment of her imagination. Last thing she remembered, she was falling . . . so she must have banged her head.

But the tiger radiated a healthy heat that warmed her. Dani raised a hand to her cold face. Her goggles were gone, and her cheeks were scraped and dry. The tiger's moist breath felt good on her skin.

Dani caught a whiff of something that seemed indisputably . . . male. And pleasantly musky. Almost spicy. *Not aftershave,* she told herself. *This is an animal. A wild, carnivorous, climber-chomping animal.*

She stared deep into the penetrating blue eyes, which regarded her with . . . hunger. Dani hoped it wasn't hungry because it—he—was huge. Male tigers were bigger than females, if she remembered right. Okay. It was huge and it was hungry and it was male. *Hi, tiger,* she thought again. *Come here often? Mind if I leave?*

Trying to get away, she stretched a hand out and touched the brittle edge of whatever she'd landed on, feeling bits of ice break off.

Dani waited for the sound of something hitting bottom, but the abyss swallowed the falling ice as soundlessly as it had swallowed her. The huge tiger stood over her, inhaling her scent and growling again. She cowered, battered and bruised, against the sheer wall behind her. No handholds that she could see. Her rope was gone.

There was no way out and she had no idea how far she'd fallen. It was darker at this depth—much darker. The immense white tiger seemed to glow against the blue ice. His jaws opened and she caught a glimpse of long teeth and the wet pink flesh of the inside of its mouth. Once again the fragrance of its breath hung in the air between them, something like incense and something like sex.

She *had* to be hallucinating. Or dreaming. Unless she was dead. Did dead people dream? Hell, she couldn't be dead, because she hurt all over.

The predatory eyes widened slightly and she felt another blast of hot, sweetly spiced breath. Then the tiger lowered its heavy head . . . and licked her ear. And the side of her neck. The rough rasps were weirdly stimulating. Dani submitted, helpless, but grateful that his instinct was to groom her and not eat her.

Then the tiger took her thick braid, which had fallen out of her hood, in its mouth, almost as if it were playing with her. It tugged, pulling her head up from the ice. The sudden motion hurt and she yelped. The beast let go and her head cracked back.

With one powerful paw, the tiger rolled her onto her belly and grasped the back of her neck in mighty jaws. Dani screamed, cutting her lip on a jag of ice, struggling to escape the killing bite that would sever her cervical vertebrae.

In seconds, a half-remembered TV show on big cats played in her mind with hideous clarity. Lions bit through the necks of their prey. Tigers tore out throats. Or vice versa. Oh, hell. She wasn't going to remember how she died.

Bye, Moe. Bye, life.

She waited, motionless and silent. But the tiger didn't seem to be tearing or biting. Maybe the high collar of her down jacket and the puffy hood were keeping her from feeling its teeth sink in. The jaws tightened and she had the strangest sensation of shrinking to kitten size as the tiger grew larger still. Then it lifted her with gentle ease—she didn't dare struggle—and moved swiftly away on noiseless paws along a ledge.

Dani heard ice crack and saw the shelf she'd been lying on

crumble and fall. The tiger entered a hollow that widened into a cavern and paused, looking down, holding her carefully in its jaws. She went limp, her gloved hands and boot-shod feet dangling under her nose as she took one last look down the bottomless crevasse. Then she blacked out.

Somewhere, somehow, the tiger put her down. Thick white fur striped with black enveloped her and warmed her. A huge, powerfully muscled body held hers in perfect safety and the deep, pulsing thrum of hot blood rushing through big veins steadied her racing heart. Her befuddled brain surrendered to the experience of being embraced by an animal powerful enough to kill and devour her.

Unable to comprehend what was happening, she slept . . . and she woke, unable to move. The tiger still clasped her but no longer curled around her back. Her cheek rested upon luxurious folds of hot fur—its chest. Dani pulled back a little, not wanting to move away from the comforting warmth, and gave the tiger a tentative pat.

She listened with odd pleasure as a soft, rhythmic growl, like a gigantic purr, rolled from within its throat. Then its heavy, whiskery chin settled upon the top of her head. Feeling her stir, the tiger batted at her gently, keeping its long claws sheathed. The rough bottom of its paw rasped against the ripstop nylon of her jacket.

It tried to lick her neck, but the beast settled for an exposed ear it seemed to find tasty. Dani managed to wriggle a few more inches away, still groggy from sleep and the impact of her fall into the crevasse, confused by mingled sensations that her brain could not make sense of.

Fear—that was definitely one. And arousal. Go figure. The tiger could eat her in a few bites, beginning with the ear it was now nipping tenderly, but she was aroused.

The tiger lowered its massive head and its wonderful eyes,

twin circles of intense, otherworldly blue, looked into hers. An erotic charge shot through her, settling right between her legs. *The usual place,* she thought wryly. And for her, the usual reaction to an attractive male. Of her own species.

Probably a good idea to distract the tiger—and herself—in case it was feeding time at the . . . zoo? Not that she had the slightest idea of what time it was or where she was. And what did cats, big or little, like? She'd never had a cat, never wanted a cat.

You have a cat now. A really, really big one. Dani forced herself to concentrate. *Oh, right. Chin scratch. Might work.* She scratched the stiff hair under there with one tentative finger and the tiger closed its eyes, grinning blissfully.

Would this dream never end?

She realized that, according to the few functioning brain cells that had not been anesthetized by the terror of her fall, she didn't want it to. Lulled by the soft growling of the slumbering tiger that held her, Dani allowed herself to float away into an irresistible fantasy of animal desire. Yet it seemed only natural . . .

A swishing sound, interspersed with a familiar fluttering, like laundry on a line, brought her slowly back to semi-consciousness. Dani lay in a room built of stone. She saw a black-and-white striped tail, long and thick, curl around the edge of a wooden doorway carved with demons and dragons and fantastic animals. The tip of the huge tail gave a final swish around the open door and vanished.

The tiger, she thought, stretching sleepily. *The morning after.* Then Dani opened her eyes all the way. There were no tigers in Tibet. She had been saved by Sherpas . . . or fellow climbers . . . or Moe. Where was Moe?

The window afforded a glimpse of prayer flags in constant movement, blowing in the fierce winds that raked the high country of Tibet.

Om mani padme hum. The fluttering string of flags was connected to the gilded spire of a stupa, rising in thirteen levels that represented the thirteen heavens, painted at its base with the all-seeing eyes of the Buddha, divine eyes that looked out to the lost horizon. The flags were faded and shredded, but silently echoed their mantra in endless refrain. *Om . . . the jewel in the lotus . . . hum. Om mani padme hum.*

Okay, she was somewhere now. Somewhere real. Dani struggled to sit up, wincing when her bruised elbow connected with the side of the wooden bed. The thin mattress was comfortable enough, even though it was stuffed with—what? She patted its plain-colored canvas ticking. Straw? Yak hair? Something like that. But the comforter that covered her legs was made of brilliant silk brocade in an unusual pattern, quilted over thick batting.

Nice. But not as nice as having your own personal tiger to keep you warm. There is no tiger, she reminded herself. Dani wiggled her toes, covered in two pairs of wool socks. Forget the polypro, Moe always said. Nothing like real wool for natural warmth. He'd knitted her socks himself, on a long flight to a different country with high mountains and not too many other climbers.

Not domestic by nature and as macho as a man could be, he'd been taught how by a Peruvian woman during the blizzard-bound start of his Andes climb a decade ago. Moe was pretty good at it, even if he didn't care about matching yarn colors. Her left outer sock was gray and yellow, and the right one was solid pink.

He must have taken off her boots. And her down jacket. And her gloves. And most of the rest of her clothes.

Dani looked around and saw it all neatly piled on a chair, with the boots beneath it, along with her light daypack. That must have snagged on something just before she'd fallen down the crevasse.

She was wearing only a long-sleeved undershirt—Moe's deft fingers had undone and removed her front-fastening sports bra. Okay, her brother's friend had gotten a look at her boobs. Big deal.

She still had on her favorite boycut underwear that didn't hike, so to speak, when she climbed. And the long-sleeved undershirt had kept her warm, even though the air inside the room was cold and dry enough to chap her lips.

She put a finger to them to see if the cut had healed. It was gone—completely. Her lips were soft, as if someone had soothed them with balm. Her cheeks were no longer raw, either. Amazing.

Somehow she'd had survived a potentially deadly fall by a miracle that someone was going to explain. Somehow she'd been brought to an abandoned monastery, a very old one, given first aid and then been allowed to sleep. What little she remembered seemed more than ever like a dream.

Especially the part about hugging a gigantic white tiger. Okay, they had done more than hug. *Dream, dream, dream,* she reminded herself. It was a *dream.* Or a hallucination after a head injury. Dani ran her fingers gingerly into her hair and over her scalp, probing for a bump.

Nothing. And why was her hair so smooth and glossy instead of tousled? Someone had undone her braid and combed it out carefully while she was sleeping. There must be women trekkers somewhere around here.

Sure as hell couldn't have been Moe. He didn't care about hair—his, hers, or anybody's. He left his coarse curls uncombed and grew thick gray stubble to warm his chops when he was trekking or climbing.

The thought of her gruff climbing partner made her smile. He'd been doing her brother a favor by taking a relative novice along. He rarely climbed with women anymore, not after losing two girlfriends in a row to younger and studlier guys.

He claimed to be still looking, though. But he'd never made

a move on Dani. Not that she'd ever, in a million years, have sex with any man named Moe. Just not the kind of name you wanted to yell in the bedroom.

She sat up, feeling along her legs for injuries or bruises. Nothing. Hard to believe. Pulling her out of the crevasse must have been a struggle, even for Moe. And he couldn't have carried her down the mountain by himself, as strong as he was. Maybe he'd gotten her out, stashed her in a tent, and led rescuers to the spot.

He had to be around here somewhere. Probably cooking breakfast with a blowtorch, like a real Tibetan—wood was too scarce at this altitude to be used as fuel—and wowing the women who'd helped with her hair.

Yet she heard nothing, no footsteps, no voices, no sound of another human being, just the prayer flags fluttering outside. Meditatively, Dani began to rebraid her hair, separating it into three strands, taking her time to weave them over and under each other, and tucking the last wisps into the very end of the braid.

A long, broad-shouldered shadow fell across the brilliant silk of the comforter and she looked up, startled.

A huge man had come into the room without her hearing him enter. She looked down, feeling inexplicably shy, and noticed what he had on his feet. Traditional Tibetan boots made of felt, with thick, multi-layered soles. That explained his silent arrival.

"Sleep well?"

She looked up. The rest of him was covered in black sweatpants and a white T-shirt. His pale hair was close-cropped but thick, and his eyes were as piercingly blue as the tiger of her dreams. His eyelashes were black, and the effect was tigerish, too. His nose was wide, broken once and not set well, over a lopsided, sensual mouth and a strong chin that gleamed with pale blond stubble.

She mentally added whiskers to his chops and stripes to his ears. Yeah, he was the tiger she'd imagined. Whoever he really was, she'd gotten him confused with the crazy idea that a huge cat had come to her rescue.

The blond guy towered over her, his hands on his hips. The T-shirt fit snugly across his broad chest and the cool air made his small male nipples stand out. Dani felt a tightening in her lower body and forced herself to look only at his face.

"Yes. Thanks for asking. But where's Moe?"

The man only shrugged and folded his arms across his chest. "I don't know."

"Well, maybe he's downstairs with the others." The man gave her an odd look but didn't say anything. Dani knew she was about to talk too fast, the way she did when she was nervous. Moe, on the other hand, could be terse to a fault. Maybe he hadn't told the tiger man who she was. "Um, I'm Dani Fairweather. I was climbing with Moe—Moe Briggs, you know who he is, right?"

He had to. She waited for an answer. There weren't that many high-altitude mountaineers. The dedicated ones lived for the adrenaline high of extreme sport and didn't mind the idea of dying young. The few veterans like Moe and the new dudes generally knew each other.

The tiger man—she couldn't help thinking of him that way, especially since he hadn't mentioned his name—definitely had the physique and stance of a world-class climber. Arrogant. Powerful. Confident. And just about too sexy to live. But he was very, very alive.

The room seemed to be filled with his presence and the intriguing, faintly musky scent that emanated from him was making her dizzy. She rubbed her eyes. "The room is spinning. Whoops—okay. It stopped."

"Uh-huh," the man said. His tone was clipped. "You need

to eat. You've been asleep for hours. Time to get dressed." He went to the chair and turned his back to her as he bent over to rummage through the pile of her clothes.

How thoughtful of him to wear sweatpants. Taking the opportunity to admire his gorgeous, muscular butt and exceptionally long legs, Dani stayed sitting up but kept most of herself under the comforter, not sure she wanted to bounce up and out of bed in her underwear in front of a total stranger. Especially since she wasn't wearing a bra, and with breasts as full as hers, she was sure the tiger man would stare.

Not sure of her next move, she flipped her braid over her shoulder, feeling it fall against her spine with an inaudible thump. Wait a minute—had *he* heard? His ears had most definitely twitched back, kinda like a cat's. Cool trick.

He turned and tossed her climbing pants at her. "The knees are shot but at least they're dry. I'll find you something else that fits. Got a ton of clothes and gear and just about everything else you can think of. Left by folks who, uh—" He stopped himself from finishing the sentence.

"Didn't make it back down the mountain?" Dani said. Her voice was calm. "Could have been me."

"How much do you remember?" he asked softly.

"Not much." She was not, repeat not, going to tell him or Moe or anyone about the tiger.

"Probably just as well. But let's get some food into you. And I'll find you some clothes that aren't ripped. Never mind where they came from."

"Hand-me-downs, huh? I have an older brother but no sisters. I never had to wear hand-me-downs." Dani examined the abraded knees of her climbing pants, grateful that the pads on the inside had provided the advertised protection. "But thanks."

The tiger man grinned. "Thank the trekkers and climbers who leave stuff behind."

Uh-oh. He had a *wicked* grin and devil dimples too. Not to mention a pull-down-your-panties growl in his voice that was making her squirm under the covers.

Since he'd flashed a smile, she could begin flirting. Good a way as any to celebrate being alive. "Is that what you do? Scrounge around for used parkas and stuff?"

His grin vanished. "Sometimes."

Dani hadn't meant to be rude but he seemed to have taken her lame joke the wrong way. Hell. She wanted to see him smile again, and ventured a smile of her own. "What's your name, by the way? You never said."

"Jack."

"Jack what?"

He shrugged, as if he didn't care what she called him. "Jack Flash, if you have to have a last name. Is it that important?"

"No, not really. Jack Flash. Born in a hurricane, huh?"

He grinned at her again and his blue eyes really did flash. Optical illusion, she thought, unnerved. Once you got above thirteen thousand feet—and a lot of Tibet was higher than that—and didn't have cuddly layers of atmosphere to soften perception, it was possible to see all sorts of strange things.

"No, I wasn't. So tell me something about yourself."

"Before we go down and join the others? Okay. My life story in ten words or less . . . here goes." She took a deep breath and his gaze dropped to her braless breasts. Dani realized that her nipples had to be erect. Well, let him check her out. She didn't mind. Hadn't she scoped him thoroughly when he'd bent over to look through her clothes? Butt, balls, and all. Yummy, yummy.

The tiger man gave her a look of pure lust and a wink. "I could wait on the life story. Want to fool around first?"

Holy cow. *That* was fast, even for the turbocharged sex drive of high altitude climbers. Hmm. Wouldn't be the first time she'd indulged in a no-strings-attached romp with one.

Dani looked him up and down, just to make sure she hadn't missed any detail of his fine—make that mega-fine—body.

She decided to take at least five minutes to think about it. The first aid kit in her daypack did have a couple of condoms, if it came to that. "Maybe later."

He smirked, looking disgustingly confident that later was likely to be pretty damn soon. "Okay, put on your pants. Nothing I haven't seen."

It occurred to her that he had helped Moe take them off. "Did you undress me?"

"Yeah."

No wonder he was so bold. He'd already gotten a good, long look at everything she had. Apparently he'd liked what he'd seen. And he still did. His eyes glowed with a sexual hunger that mesmerized her. "Bra too, huh?"

The thought of his touching her naked flesh while she slept didn't bother her. In fact, it excited her way down deep. But she didn't have to let him know that—not right away. Dani realized that Tiger Dude was talking to her and snapped out of it.

"Interesting clasp, by the way. But I figured it out. Engineering degree."

"From?"

His sensual mouth tightened. Clearly, he didn't like being put on the spot. "MIT," he answered reluctantly.

"Oh, cool. When'd you get that?"

"Long ago."

"You don't look much older than me, and I'm twenty-seven."

His face clouded over. "I'm not."

"I thought MIT turned out legions of geeks. You are so not a geek, though."

The confident—no, call it cocky—look came back. "Is that a compliment? Well, okay, I shared. So what's your life story? Before we fool around."

That seemed to be a given, she thought with a flash of pleasure. "Trauma unit, junior nurse. Long shifts, but a fair amount of downtime. I took up climbing to blow off the stress. Bim, bam, boom. Here I am in Tibet."

"That was way more than ten words. Did this Moe guy show you the ropes? Is he your—"

"No. And no. Come here."

His ears twitched and his blue, blue eyes widened. "Huh? Did you just say *come here?* Want to see how fast I can take off my clothes?"

Dani laughed lustily. "Yeah. And then you're going to help me find Moe." She just hoped her climbing partner would stay downstairs. "Lock that door," she added hastily.

"Deal." He yanked the white T-shirt over his head, revealing a muscular belly that was totally firm and totally natural. Not a trace of that gym-rat ab segmentation. You had to hand it to the rock jocks. Climbing gave them incredible bodies.

She admired the light dusting of gold hair on his chest and his armpits, and the way his nipples looked dark against it, even though he was really tan. He rolled the bunched-up T down over his biceps and forearms, throwing it on the floor. Then Jack pulled the massive door shut and slid its bolt into place. He grabbed the waistband of those soft black sweats next. Dani didn't miss the erection that made the front stick out.

A lot.

He paused, running a finger around the inside of the waistband. "I feel like a stripper."

"Go for it." Dani gave him a very encouraging smile. "And do it quick. Before anybody comes knocking on that door." She was giddy, filled with a strange, animal exhilaration that made her want this man in a way she'd never wanted any other. She watched him eagerly.

"Okay. Here goes. Welcome to the Roof of the World, Tibet's exclusive all-male revue. For ladies only. Starring one male. Me."

He inched down the sweats to where his groin muscles began, running his fingers over the taut flesh and pressing his erection back with one huge, cupped hand. "Mmm. I'm already hot just from you looking at me. Like to watch men get off, huh?"

"Yeah. I do."

He caressed himself slowly and sensually, keeping his eyes on her face. "How am I doing so far?"

"Great. Keep it up," she added, feeling bolder by the second.

"You asked for it. Go ahead and stare. Makes me really hard." He began to rub his cock through the soft cloth just as if he was alone, pleasuring himself, with no one watching. Dani couldn't take her eyes off him. "This feels so good it almost hurts."

"Been a while?"

He nodded. "How'd you know?"

"Seems obvious."

Jack took his cupped hand from the bulge in his crotch, touching the tips of his thumbs together and using the rest of his fingers to frame his very healthy package. He would look *totally* hot in a climbing harness, she knew, with two straps around each powerful thigh and more straps around the crotch and under his butt cheeks. That big bulge in front would really show.

He wasn't wearing anything underneath the sweats that she could see. Not briefs. Not a jockstrap. She could see the head of his cock straining against the cloth. And his fingers brought his balls, temptingly large, up and forward.

"Hey. I want to suck you. Right now." She almost reached out a hand to pull down his pants but stopped. Watching him put on a show like this was a lot sexier than doing all the work herself.

He grinned. "You're not shy, are you?"

"No." She watched him hungrily. Jack eased his sweatpants over his erection and the cock to rule all cocks just about jumped out. He took himself in one hand, and pumped slowly, letting each stroke reach the heavy, plumlike head but never covering it.

He was *huge*. Dani almost gasped. More thick than long, especially at the base, which was just fine with her, because it wouldn't hurt when he rammed it in, and she suddenly wanted to be really rammed.

He used his other hand to stroke his balls. His hands were just as sexy as his genitals, with roped veins that pulsed as he pumped his cock. She pulled his sweatpants farther down and slid a hand between his powerful thighs, stroking upward until his balls tensed at her touch.

"Like what you see, Dani?" he murmured.

"Yeah."

"Then I guess you do want to suck me." He stopped playing with himself and kicked off his boots. She yanked his pants down the rest of the way and helped him step out, his hard-on high and proud. "Want a condom on it?" he asked.

"Are you assuming I have one?"

"Um, yeah." He gave her a guilty look, like he'd looked in her daypack while she was sleeping. "I mean, I respect chicks who come prepared."

"Give me a freakin' break," she said indignantly, but the flash of annoyance she felt didn't change the fact that she was up for some hot, fast fun.

Not that she usually asked total strangers to jerk off for her viewing pleasure, but these were unusual circumstances. And the strange feeling of freedom that surged through her had to be the result of her near death experience. Not to mention dreaming about sex with a tiger.

Just looking at his slow masturbation was *incredibly* erotic. Dani threw the comforter back and got on her knees on the bed, kissing his taut belly and ignoring his cock, which throbbed insistently, for a few seconds. She was glad she was tall and long-limbed, able to reach around and easily caress his ass. No matter how much guys talked tough about how not gay they were, they all loved to have their butts petted.

The light sensation made him suck in his hard belly and his buttocks tightened under her touch. She traced the hollows on their sides and brought her hands around his narrow hips, trailing her fingertips along his groin and down into the golden blond pubic hair.

Jack moaned under his breath. A pearly drop of cum, and then another, appeared and merged on the tip of his cock. Dani swiped it off with her fingertip and used it as a lube to stroke his taut scrotum, watching him keep right on pumping and fondling himself.

"Careful," he growled softly. "That gets me hot."

She stopped to admire his stuff and sat back on her thighs. "Come on my tits. We can skip the latex." She yanked her long-sleeved undershirt high on her chest and cupped her big, bare breasts, offering them up.

He really growled. And he let go of his cock and balls.

"You saw them already," she said nonchalantly. "When you took off my bra."

"Not like this." With the sure touch of a man who was good with his hands in every way—she knew from experience that only climbers had that combination of strength and sensitivity in their hands—Jack rolled her nipples in his fingers, rolled and tugged and rolled until she cried out with pleasure. "Yeah. Oh, yeah. Like to get your nipples teased, huh?"

She murmured yes, gazing up at him with half-closed eyes.

"Oh, yeah. Give me that look . . . and keep those tight little shorts pulled up into your wet cunt. You are so hot. So fucking hot."

He pushed her back on the bed, and Dani stretched out her legs, getting between his as they rolled so that she was on top. Where she liked to be.

The light fur on his body was deliciously tickly, and the power of the big leg between hers was a total thrill. She straddled his quad and pressed her pussy on it, enjoying the friction of her soft cotton underwear between her labia and the hot, rocklike flesh of the top of his thigh.

She was the proud possessor of a healthy, curvy, athletic body, but in every way that counted, Jack was bigger and stronger. Much, much bigger and stronger.

He put his hands on her ass cheeks and let her rock on his hard thigh. She pulled her undershirt all the way off, threw it on the floor and put her mouth on his, making him open his surprisingly soft lips with her tongue.

He bit her lower lip gently, then kissed her hard, getting even more excited, judging by the way his huge cock was throbbing against her soft belly. He broke off the kiss and nuzzled her neck, moving over the sensitive flesh with his teeth and giving her love nips that made her want to scream with excitement. But she didn't. Someone might hear even though the door was locked, but . . . he bit her again.

"Ahh! More of that!" she whispered.

Jack sucked her earlobe and nipped that, too. She turned her head from side to side, her long hair coming out of the braid, but wanting him to kiss and nip her everywhere. Dani had never quite realized how incredible that could feel. The difference was finesse. Jack knew exactly what he was doing.

She got on all fours above him, panting, her hair now completely out of the braid and spilling in dark waves over her back. Her knees were at the sides of his hips. Jack looked at her through half-closed eyes and grabbed her hips, making her move up and sit right on his throbbing cock.

"Slide on it. Rub. Make yourself come." His hands moved up to hold her breasts and he raised himself up, using his strong belly muscles to stay up as he gave one hot pink nipple a long, luxurious, sexy sucking and then did the same to the other.

Dani felt the ridge of his hot cock press between her swollen labia. It was almost as if she wasn't wearing underwear at all . . . but, hell, she was, and the juicy friction and tightness excited her. She'd masturbated on her own with soft underwear before—it would feel even better with a guy this hot watching her do it.

Jack lay back and grasped her more tightly, letting her get the most from his erection, moving his hips sensually up and down. Giving her an *excellent* ride. She wasn't going to stop to put a condom on him. Not when it felt this good.

She stuck her fingers into her underwear to part her labia and tug on her clit. Then she positioned her hips so that the hard bud was against his cock, pressing down with little pulses.

"Ohhh . . . oh! *Oh!*" Dani's pussy tightened deep inside as she came hard and suddenly, not expecting it. She clutched the strong arms that held her, threw her head back to moan, then clawed his chest, leaving a few thin scratches.

Dani collapsed on top of him. He stroked her back, making a noise in her ear that was somewhere between a purr and a growl. "Your turn," she whispered. "Do you want me to get that condom?"

"No." He lifted her whole body with ease and put her at his side. "I want to see you when I come."

She rolled over on her back, cupping her tits again, knowing what was coming when he straddled her torso. His cock was still juicy from her pussy ride but he added a dash of spit to keep the lube going. Pumping himself so hard that his knuckles showed white, his body shimmered with sexual tension until his hand stopped and he sprayed hot white jets over her breasts and nipples, gasping while he watched her writhe between his thighs.

It was more a growl than a gasp—a feral growl that made the back of her neck tingle. Jack let go of his dripping, still hugely erect cock and nuzzled her neck, kissing her wildly but staying above her on all fours, his butt up and his balls tight. He bit her earlobe one last time, just for the hell of it, then stretched out beside her, drawing in deep, utterly satisfied breaths. "Ohh, Dani . . . that was *good.*"

"The understatement of the year," she murmured. "That was exceptional. In every way." Connecting with him sexually had made her forget everything for a few blissfully intense seconds—her fall into the crevasse, the tiger in her dream, her own name. But not his.

Jack drew her against his side with one arm and rested his chin on her head. They dozed off, soothed by each other's warmth, but Dani didn't realize she had until she felt him stir.

He nipped her ear and murmured sleepily, "Guess we better go find what's-his-name. Moe Briggs. Your friend."

Dani giggled. "You say *friend* like it's a bad thing."

He shrugged. "I didn't mean to."

"You don't know him. Good old Moe. He's like my brother."

"Yeah, right," Jack rolled away from her and sat up.

She stretched a hand up and stroked his amazingly muscular arm. "Come to think of it, you don't know me either."

He smirked. "I got the basic facts."

"You don't! Not really." Dani pushed herself up to rest on one elbow and patted Jack's flushed face. "So how can you be jealous of Moe? Don't be ridiculous. You and I, uh, we just met."

"And we just had sex," he corrected her. "So I'm jealous. I'm talking pure male instinct, Dani. You're a highly desirable female, in full heat."

She kissed his cheek and laughed. "Let's go downstairs. I'm starving."

"Better get dressed." Jack got up quickly and scrambled into his black sweats and white T, slipping on the thick-soled felt boots as he watched her wriggle out of her boycut underwear. "Love those hot pants. Can I keep them under my pillow?"

"Hey, they're called boy shorts, not hot pants. That term vanished from the English language, like, thirty years ago. Right before I was born."

"Yeah? Okay, so I'm older than you. We established that."

"Uh-huh. Your babysitter probably wore them back in the day. She was unforgettable, right? You perv. Men never grow up. Here you go." She crumpled her underwear into a soggy ball and threw it at him. "Have your pervy fun."

"Thanks." He caught them with ease and tucked them into his sweatpants pocket.

"How the hell am I going to explain you to Moe?" Dani wiped off her breasts with a towel that was on the chair and chose a few items from the pile for an acceptable-looking outfit, pulling on the torn-up climbing pants last.

"You won't have to," Jack said casually.

She fastened the snaps with little pops, giving up on a misaligned one that wouldn't cooperate. "What do you mean?"

"He won't be able to see me, Dani."

"Yeah, right. I don't think he went snowblind. The storm wasn't that bad."

Jack shook his head. "You can see me, but he won't be able to. Because I'm dead. Technically speaking."

"What? Whoa, nelly. *What* did you just say?"

"You can see me because you're between two worlds right now."

"What worlds? What are you talking about? Are you crazy?" She folded her arms across her still-braless breasts and looked at him like he was. Had she just had sex with a raging lunatic? Thank God Moe was somewhere downstairs to hit this guy with a brick. She had half a mind to call him in here right now.

"Dani, that fall almost killed you. But not quite."

She backed away, letting her arms drop to her sides while she looked for a weapon. The room was nearly empty of furniture, except for the bed she'd slept in and the chair beside it.

The walls were bare, except for a small mirror. And this was a nice, peaceful, Buddhist monastery. Not the best place to find something to bash someone's head in. And Jack—oh, right, Jack Flash, like that was his real name—how could she have *been* so stupid—Jack was between her and the door.

"Stay away from me!"

He looked at her steadily. "Okay. But I'm telling the truth."

"No, you're not. I can't believe I just had hot, totally hot sex with a—a dead guy."

"The body's real," he said carefully. "And I'm real. In a way."

"Prove it." Dani realized she had backed herself into a corner, literally and figuratively. She edged out of it and toward the locked door.

"I just did." He grinned. "And you seemed to be enjoying yourself."

"This is crazy!" She threw up her hands. "Where's Moe? I want to see Moe, I want to get out of here—wait a minute. Are we alone?"

"Yup. Just you and me."

"You led me to believe that there were other people here—oh, never mind." Actually, he hadn't. She had simply assumed that. But since Jack had just announced that he was dead—technically dead, whatever that meant—oh, hell. Dani decided to humor him just long enough to escape. "I have to find Moe. If he didn't rescue me, who did?"

"I did."

"Well, hey. I mean, thanks. But Moe's still up on the mountain and after that snowstorm yesterday afternoon—"

The tiger man shrugged. "A squall line moved through. We got a dusting. Nothing to worry about."

"Excuse me? He probably noticed I'm not at the other end of the rope by now—"

Jack held up a hand. "Wait a minute. You were alone when I found you. And injured. I didn't see him. I think he just left you there."

"No! He never would have done that—unless something happened to him." Dani paused, trying to make sense of a series of events she barely remembered.

"Is he an experienced climber?" Jack asked, in a tone that implied Moe probably wasn't.

"Yes," she said, nettled. "Very experienced. In your league, in fact."

Jack grinned. "And how would you know that?"

Okay, she could add *snotty* to *arrogant, powerful,* and *confident.* And *dead.* But she wouldn't go so far as to say any of that out loud. Not until she found out more about where she was and how Jack had gotten her here on his own if there wasn't anyone else around.

Jack Flash, alive or dead, couldn't just throw a full-grown woman over his mighty shoulder and walk down a mountain. Not from the height she and Moe had been at when she'd gone down the cosmic rabbit hole.

Jack just looked at her. Dani avoided his gaze, not wanting to look into those mesmerizing eyes, not wanting to think about what she'd just done with him . . . but something he'd said came back to her.

You're between two worlds right now. What did he mean? As if she had spoken aloud, he answered in a soft growl.

"Look in the mirror, Dani."

She took the few steps and peered into its silvered glass. She saw herself—saw *through* herself to the rock walls behind her.

2

Dani whirled around to face him. "How come I can't see through you?"

"I don't know," Jack sighed. "It may be that I'm somehow realer to you than you are to me."

"Makes perfect sense." She glared at him, crossing her arms over her chest. She felt substantial enough, even if her body was semi-transparent, which was truly strange. "Gee willy whiskers, why didn't I think of that?"

He shook his head. "Dani, I've been here a long time and I—I haven't gotten any older. But I know I'm not visible to the living, unless they have certain powers of perception. Most people just don't see me as a man or as a tiger—"

"Aha. I was wondering when we were going to get around to the tiger part. So that was you in the crevasse. I thought you were going to bite my head off but you really did rescue me. Thanks for that. I think."

"The monks who used to live here were versed in ancient magic. They rescued me but they couldn't save me. So they put me into the body of a tiger—their protective deity—to, um, store my soul until I could reincarnate."

Dani nodded. "Right. Sure."

"Spare me the sarcasm," Jack said resignedly. "I'll shapeshift right now and prove it to you."

"You do that." Her eyes widened and she gasped involuntarily as his outline shimmered, and his corporeal form vanished. Where Jack had been sat an enormous white tiger with soft, charcoal-black stripes. It regarded her with Jack's eyes, pinning her to the spot where she stood with its mesmerizing gaze.

It—he—seemed to be smiling. No dimples, though. But the blue eyes were exactly the same. Dani didn't know whether to pat him on the head or run for her life.

"Do you—are you—carnivorous?" she asked at last. "Should I be afraid of you?"

The tiger's outline shimmered, the tiger dissolved, and there was Jack again, shaking his head. "Whew. I don't usually do the transfer that fast. The answer is no. I don't feel hunger in either form and I'm not going to eat you."

"What do you feel?"

"Emotion, unfortunately. And desire. The monks couldn't quell that in me."

"Guess not. But how did you get here? You skipped that part."

Jack shrugged. "They found me on Chomolungma—that's Mount Everest to you—and brought me here. My team had to leave me." She raised an eyebrow in an unspoken question. "Yeah, I was already dead," he said. "I got trapped in the Khumbu icefall. Notoriously unstable area."

Dani looked at him curiously. "So I've heard. You just don't seem dead. Not the way you fuck."

"Thanks." His smile was almost bashful, but proud. Even

dead, men still acted like . . . guys. The afterlife was turning out to be a lot like life. "But why are you alone? Where are the monks now?"

"Long gone. The Chinese army closed most of the monasteries and outright destroyed some. Took them a while to get this far into the hinterlands but they did, decades ago. Some of the monks fled to India, some to Nepal. And the abbot who changed me into a tiger—a master magician, by the way—died after a few months in exile."

"Did he tell you to stay here?"

Jack nodded. "I have to gain merit so I can reincarnate eventually. So I help others. I rescue a lot of climbers, who usually don't want to talk about it."

Dani came closer to him, her fear lessening. "Because people would think they were crazy. Of course, mountain climbers are kinda crazy. Or they have a death wish."

"Do you?" Jack asked quietly.

"No. But I do take chances. My mom"—she stopped and looked at him—"my mom died of cancer before she ever got free of my nightmare of a father. I really loved her. The last thing she told me was not to wait to do what I wanted to do."

Jack smiled sadly. "And you didn't."

"No. My brother thinks I'm crazy, but I get around that by not talking to him more once a year. Anyway, I guess he was right. Now I'm dead."

"Not yet."

"I wonder if I'll be able to see my mom."

"Not here."

Dani gave him an exasperated look. "No more cryptic answers, okay?"

"You asked."

"I didn't—" She shook her head to clear it, suddenly aware that she had forgotten all about her climbing partner. Sex with a tiger, finding out you were half-dead . . . she was losing her mind. "Oh my God—what about Moe?" she screamed. "I'm standing here talking to you—but he could be hurt or— We gotta get him down!"

"I'm sure he's all right," Jack said.

"Oh, yeah? You did know that he wasn't here!" Dani pummeled Jack's iron torso with both fists and all the strength she possessed but it didn't seem to bother him. He drew in a deep breath, stepped some distance away from her and she saw with amazement that he was shimmering. His outline dissolved, and there was the tiger again.

I wanted you all to myself for a little while. I'm sorry. Moe really is all right. Padding toward her on silent paws, the tiger rested its massive head on her shoulder and gave her ear a lick. This time it wore, by a magic she couldn't begin to comprehend, a tribal saddle of embossed leather, hung with bells and small pouches, padded with colorful felt. *Hop on. And hang on,* the tiger added.

She hesitated, then grabbed her daypack, which held the first aid kit and the water canteen, she could feel the outline of both—and clambered on.

Ever ride a horse?

"Yeah."

Well, this is different. Because I can fly.

"Holy cow!"

The tiger padded over to the window, nosed it open and rested its paws on the deep stone sill. Dani grasped the saddle horn and soared on its back into the infinite sky of Tibet.

She clung to the saddle, keeping her head down along the beast's powerful neck. At least it was warm. Her ears were ringing from the cold, rushing air—or maybe it was the little bells that decorated the saddle.

It's not the bells.

"I didn't say anything," she gasped.

But I heard you. The bells are supposed to chase away evil spirits. Your ears are ringing because we're going higher.

"Not to mention that it's freezing up here," she hissed into his black-and-white ear, which twitched.

That tickles.

"Keep your mind on what you're doing, tiger." Her hand slipped off the smooth leather of the saddle and she clutched his side, marveling at the strength of the muscles that moved under his fur as he flew on.

The foothills behind the monastery grew higher, rising into nameless smaller peaks cut by deep gorges. The terrain was treacherous and she wondered how in hell the tiger had brought her out.

That's where you went down. Look over my left ear.

Dani sighted the crevasse. The snow and ice that had concealed it were mostly melted now. It yawned open, a blue-black, devouring mouth no longer hidden.

A faint, intermittent track in what was left of the snow led from the crevasse to a boulder field a half mile away, as if someone had been dragging gear back and forth. The track ended at a small meadow.

"There he is! Moe!" she screamed. "Oh, hell, he is hurt!" She let go to point at a small tent directly beneath them and the man struggling to take out the pegs that held it to the ground. His right arm was in a makeshift sling. "Looks like his arm's broken. Moe, wait! We're coming!"

He can't see or hear you, if you're on my back.

"Damn it!" She almost fell off, but a desperate grab at the thick fur of the tiger's shoulders righted her. But the daypack slipped off her shoulder and hurtled earthwards. "Moe, watch out!" she screamed. Dani watched it turn end over end, weighted by the water canteen. No—it couldn't—oh, no—the pack hit him right in the head. Moe toppled over like a felled tree.

Nice work.

Even telepathically, she could hear the sarcasm. "Do something! Land!" She thumped on the saddle, making the tiny bells chime.

The tiger circled, came in lower, and alighted on noiseless paws near the tent. Dani jumped down and ran to Moe, checking his pulse first thing—it was strong and regular—and looking for blood in his nose and ears. Nothing. Thank God. The falling daypack must have given him a glancing blow, just enough to knock him out, but she saw no signs of a skull fracture.

Still, serious head injuries were easy to miss, and they were, what, five thousand miles from the nearest MRI machine? Moe lifted his head and moaned, but his eyes didn't open.

That answered her next question. His neck wasn't broken. Moe kept his head up, only semi-conscious, and Dani seized the opportunity to run her fingers over the back of his skull. No blood. A slight bump that would probably get bigger but again, no sign of a fracture.

She cradled his head in her hands and rested it on the dry, coarse grass that had cushioned his fall.

Thank God he's all right.

Dani looked over at the tiger, which was shimmering in the bright sunlight, preparing to morph back into Jack. He reappeared, big and blond as ever, and strode over to them. He held one of the small pouches that had been attached to the saddle and took out a small flask, uncapping it, and letting a few drops of liquid fall between Moe's open lips.

"What the hell are you doing? He's not fully conscious! I don't want him to vomit."

Jack capped the bottle. "He won't. This is an anti-spasmodic and muscle relaxant. I don't want him to wake up just yet. We have a long way to go."

"What is that stuff?"

"Nothing they give you in a hospital," Jack said simply. "Effective, though. I get it from a shaman. Local guy. He's good, mixes his own herbs. There are healing plants up here that Western medicine oughta know about. He gave me the salve for your cut lip and the scrapes on your face."

Reflexively, she touched the soft skin, remembering how she'd wondered about that.

"His wife combed your hair while you slept," Jack added.

"So some people can see you."

"Well, yeah. Tibetans can sometimes. And the shaman and his wife have unusually strong powers of perception."

"Explain that later." Dani returned her attention to Moe, who lay peacefully on the grass, breathing deeply, his chapped lips curved in a slight smile. "What are we going to do with Moe?"

"Bring him to a place where he can get that arm set. Then we go back to the monastery by an underground shortcut. I don't want to risk flying with an injured guy on my back."

She nodded. "A hospital, right?"

"Kinda."

"I'm not sure I want to risk having a roots-and-herbs guy treat a head injury and a broken bone."

"We're not going to the shaman."

"Then who?"

Jack favored her with a slight smile. "Friend of mine. You'll like her. Now make sure you have his passport and trip documentation so we can get out him out of the country if we have to. We'll have to leave the rest of this gear. It's too heavy and he won't need it."

"Whatever you say, Jack Flash."

He smiled down at her. "That's not my real last name."

"I didn't think it was. How are we going to lift him? If you're going to turn into a tiger and I'm—" She stopped, not wanting to say *almost dead.*

"Levitation," Jack answered. His raised his hands slowly and Moe's body rose several feel in the air to about tiger height. Dani watched her climbing partner roll over in midair and tuck a hand under his grizzled cheek, as if he were sleeping in a comfortable bed.

"Cool. Very cool," she said, impressed. If only she could turn her heavier patients that easily. She reminded herself that his skills wouldn't work in the real world and looked around the campsite. All of Moe's gear—mountaineering rope, climbing rack and harness—was in a neat pile next to his pack.

Dani unzipped the side pocket, finding his documents in a Ziploc baggie. Good ole Moe and his goddamn little plastic bags. Sometimes obsessiveness was a good thing.

"Got it?" Jack asked.

She waved the bagged passport at him and then tucked it into her daypack. "Okay. We're going to have to improvise a med evac. You're the helicopter pilot—"*and the helicopter,* she thought with a wondering shake of her head "—and I'm the trauma nurse. We're a team. Got that?"

Jack nodded. "Tell me what you want me to do."

The tiger padded through gorges and along the edges of crevasses that seemed deeper than the one Dani'd fallen into. She walked alongside, patting the sleeping Moe now and then. His broken arm didn't seem to bother him. She checked the ropes to make sure he was securely and comfortably bound to the saddle. That was magic, too—whatever was needed seemed to appear from its pouches.

Kinda like my mom's purse.

"Oh—did your mother have a purse like that?" she asked the tiger, still surprised by his ability to read her thoughts.

Yeah. She was great. So was my dad. My parents passed away a while ago. They thought I died on the mountain.

"Well, you did."

Technically.

Dani sighed, not wanting to argue the point when her own existence seemed so tenuous.

The monks said I could visit them in heaven when I gained more merit.

"Isn't rescuing climbers enough?"

No. You have to do a lot of things. Go around certain temples a thousand times. Study the sutras. Chant. Make offerings. It's all written in the sacred texts.

"In Tibetan."

I read it. Taught myself. The monks left behind a lot of books when they fled the county, and there's not much else to do when you're dead.

"Besides have sex with females in heat."

The tiger growled but it sounded like a laugh. *Hey, climber girl, you were the only one that ever happened with. Sex with you was fantastic. Did I say thanks?*

"Please don't," she giggled. "That's kinda like leaving money on the dresser afterwards."

Oh. Sorry. Didn't mean to offend. You know, I wasn't sure if you would be able to see me at first.

"You looked totally hot. How could I resist? I was just glad to be alive and—there you were." The memory of his impromptu strip and the revelation of his magnificent body made her feel warm all over. And wet between the legs. She heard his wicked, friendly laugh inside her head.

Do I get to jump you again?

"Just as soon as Moe is taken care of. I wonder how he broke his arm."

The tiger nodded its massive head. *He'll tell you when he comes to. He's going to be okay, Dani.*

Another five minutes of padding over the rocky terrain passed pleasantly enough, while she took in the sweeping views of the vast Tibetan plateau, dotted with yaks and the nomads who herded them. The tiger finally paused at the mouth of a cavern. *Ready to go down?*

"I guess." She looked into the darkness, not wanting to leave the brilliant sunlight, then checked Moe again. He was slumped over the tiger's back, snoring like a hubby in an armchair.

Don't be afraid. This cave is sacred to a subterranean goddess who protects these mountains.

"Okay. If you say so. Moe doesn't seem to be in pain."

He'll be fine. We're going to drop him off at the altar of the Taras.

"And what are Taras?"

The embodiment of feminine compassion. Healers. Kind of like Buddha's little helpers. They come in different colors. There's a green one, and a white one, and—wait a sec. I have an itch. Would you mind? He twitched his ear.

Dani scratched him behind it. "Not at all. I can't keep track of all these goddesses but never mind. Better now?" She scratched a little harder when she heard him purr.

Ooh. You got it. The tiger arched its neck and shook its head. *Thanks. Are you ready to have some fun?*

She tugged on the tiger's ear. "When I'm sure that Moe's in good hands, yeah, okay. Didn't you say I wasn't dead yet?"

The temples at the bottom are amazing. You're going to love the erotic carvings. Beautiful naked goddesses and stuff like that.

"Do I get to pick? I want handsome gods."

Coming up.

They were well within the earth when Dani dismounted in front of a cavern that was also a temple. A green-skinned Tara, her face glowing with tenderness, offered a melodious greeting that Dani didn't understand. Dani was rapt with wonder, noticing the third eye in the goddess's forehead, and the eyes in each of her palms. She wondered about them, but didn't feel it would be polite, as a mortal, to ask a goddess a lot of questions

The tiger read Dani's thoughts and answered silently. *Those extra eyes mean the green Tara can see all the suffering in the world. She's merciful. And very popular.*

"Oh, my." Dani nodded respectfully and added an awkward little bow. The green Tara laughed politely, a sound that was even more melodious than her greeting, and motioned them into an inner sanctum filled with flowers.

"No sun," said Dani softly. "How do they grow?"

The tiger gestured with one paw to a giant crystal that caught the light from a crack in the world above, and focused it upon the Tara's garden.

"This reminds me of an atrium in one of those huge new hotels," she whispered. "You know, with the weird plants."

Shhh.

The tiger and the Tara conversed in an incomprehensible language, and Dani watched in awe as the goddess summoned help from the demi-goddesses who waited nearby. Swiftly and silently, her handmaidens untied Moe, giggling at the way he snored and carrying him effortlessly to a bed padded with brilliant silk that looked familiar.

In fact, its pattern and color were identical to the silk-covered comforter at the monastery. "Just like mine," she said to the tiger.

He nodded. *The design has healing properties.*

Still out cold, Moe curled up on the bed, instinctively protecting his broken arm. The demi-goddesses clustered around and began to remove his clothes, but Dani took advantage of an opening in the circle to bend down and give her climbing partner a kiss.

Moe's gonna be just fine. Let's go.

Dani looked up. There was definitely, very definitely, a grin on the face of the tiger.

She rode on his back through the measureless depths of the Himalayan caverns. "You know your way around down here."

That's how I found you when you fell, Dani. I heard your scream and I came running.

"Thank you again. For real this time."

It's all right. I know you were scared shitless when I started to explain who I was—and what'd happened to you.

"Yeah, I was."

In fact, she was a little scared right now. They were going through dark tunnels, some illuminated with pulsing light that emanated from rocks carved with demons and strange creatures that creeped her out, down here inside the earth. They seemed a little too ferocious, and the pulsing light made it look as if they were breathing. Dani shuddered.

The tiger moved swiftly on, bringing her at last into a temple. Hung with thangkas, the beautiful banners that adorned Tibetan holy places, the vast room was alive with color, lit by numerous lamps that hung from chains, swinging gently and emanating a delicate fragrance, as if someone had just walked through and set them swinging

But they were alone. Dani wasn't exactly sure she wanted to be here, even with a gigantic tiger for protection. "Morph," she told him, getting down off the saddle and landing without a sound on the soft cavern floor.

Say please.

"Please. Be a nice tiger and morph into Jack." She was almost getting used to the shimmering, but this time when he did it, she heard very faint feminine laughter. Jack stood next to her. "There you are. Who was that?"

"The laughing? That was the dakinis." He pointed to the wall. "Beautiful naked goddesses, as promised."

Dani heard the faint laughter again.

"Um, do they know you? Have you been here before?"

He nodded, giving her a wink. "They take good care of me."

"So much for relinquishing desire. I can see why the monks gave up on you. So where are the handsome gods?"

"Someplace else. I lied."

She punched him in the arm.

"I had to do something to get you down here. C'mon, look at these." He took her arm and led her to the sculptures that adorned the temple walls. Sensual, full-breasted bodies intertwined with flowers seemed to reach out long-fingered hands. Dani blinked. Had one graceful stone girl just caressed Jack's face?

"They represent awareness. You have to be naked to be fully aware, reach enlightenment and all that."

"Right. They look really, really aware. Of you."

Jack let his hand rest on a rounded stone breast, and a warm, peachy hue slowly suffused the gray. The entire sculpture suddenly seemed to come alive—and its leg moved as if it was about to step off the wall. "Get back," he said softly. "Not now."

"Okay, that didn't happen," Dani said. "Stone doesn't do that. These women—these statues—aren't alive."

"Sometimes they are. The dakinis are celestial consorts with mystical powers. I mean, if heaven doesn't offer something better than earth, why would anyone want to behave well enough to get there?"

As Dani watched, her mouth open in wonder, the stone goddesses began to dance upon the wall, never leaving it but as Jack said, very much alive.

"This beats hell, doesn't it?" he added. "Some dakinis are ferocious, though. But not these."

"Um, yeah. This is amazing."

The dakinis caressed each other's buttocks and bellies with lascivious abandon, tugging at their nipples and presenting the erect tips to Jack as they held their flowing hair over their heads and thrust out their bare breasts. He put his mouth upon the nipple of the nearest girl and suckled hungrily.

Dumbfounded, Dani saw him slip his strong fingers into the statue's soft labia, pushing aside the strands of delicate gold-and-turquoise jewelry that girdled her hips. As the dancers turned from stone to flesh one by one, he seemed to have forgotten all about Dani, lost in erotic rapture, drawn closer and closer to the wall by the beautifully rounded arms that clasped him around in the neck.

"Wait . . ." Her one softly spoken word broke the spell. The dancers turned to stone again—but in different positions than before. Totally freaking amazing.

Jack turned to her, his blue eyes glittering. "They almost got me. Sorry. That was rude. I didn't mean to ditch you at the party."

"Uh, they were pretty aggressive. But they did seem to know what you like."

Shamelessly, he reached inside his pants and adjusted his erection. "Excuse me. Down, boy."

"No-oo," she said slowly. "I got hot watching you. Stay up."

"You're as bossy as the dakinis," he grinned.

"Well, why not? I want you."

"Same here. And you're real, Dani. You're about the realest thing that ever happened to me." He took her in his arms and bent her back in a melting kiss, teasing her tongue with the tip of his.

"Ohh . . . let's do it. Is there . . . is there a bed?" she asked breathlessly. He had her sweater pushed up over her bare breasts and was suckling her, his mouth too full of nipple to answer. Dani looked over his shoulder and caught a jealous glare from a stone dakini. "He's mine," she whispered, stroking his hair.

Jack let go of her nipple and stood up straight. "Who're you talking to?"

"The limestone bitch," she laughed. "That one." Dani pointed and her sweater fell back down.

The statue turned around in its niche and mooned both of them, displaying her bare stone ass. Jack slipped a finger under the twisted silk cord between the dakini's buttocks—*like a*

Tibetan thong, Dani thought—and let it snap. His touch made the goddess turn into flesh again and in response, she stuck her butt out and wiggled it. Like she wanted more, Dani thought. Jack gave the dakini a slap and Dani heard his hand crack hard.

"Ow!" he howled.

The mischievous goddess had turned herself to stone just when his hand connected. She stood facing the wall, her hip cocked at an angle that clearly said *here comes trouble.* Her sisters seemed to be smiling.

"All right. Be that way. You can stand in the corner for all eternity. You may be divine, but I want a human." He swept Dani off her feet and up into his arms. "This human."

The goddesses treated him to full-lipped pouts and froze into place. He stepped back into the temple proper and pushed through a beaded curtain. Dani caught a few strands and let them trail through her fingers. Beads? Not quite. Rubies and diamonds was more like it.

Jack brought her to a bed with an ornately carved frame, heaped high with silk cushions and covered in material that looked sensually soft. "Welcome to my lair, beautiful." He set her down and stretched out beside her. "We have all the time in the world. You're going to get laid like you've never been laid before."

"Really?" said Dani, still feeling a little jealous of her stone rivals for his attention. "This is your lair? Seems more like theirs."

"Nah." He waved a hand at the bed's frame, and she saw the tigers carved into it. "It's mine. Had this custom made by a Tibetan guy who does restoration work on temples. He made me that rack for my climbing gear too." Jack pointed, and Dani saw a complete array of ropes, cams, belaying devices, hex nuts, carabiners, quickdraws, a chalk bag, and a couple of harnesses.

She remembered with a flush of pleasure imagining how hot

he would look in a harness strapped around his thighs and crotch. "You still climb, huh? Isn't flying easier?"

Jack shook his head. "Sometimes two feet and two hands are better than four paws. Depends on the rescue. And sometimes I climb just for fun. Just because I'm dead doesn't mean I can't stay in shape."

"Right." She picked up a climbing magazine from a stack by the bed. "So, do you subscribe to these or what?"

"Nope. More stuff that people leave behind."

Dani leafed through it, stopping at an article on climbing gear that caught her eye. "*The Advantage of Massive Nuts,*" she read aloud. "Yes indeedy. I know what they're talking about."

Jack just laughed, an easy sound that warmed her all over. "Hey, I gotta read something."

She pulled two more from the stack. "*Hustler,* huh? And *Playboy's Girls of the Big 10.*" She let the centerfold unfold and studied the airbrushed cheerleader with a yawn, then tossed the magazine on the floor and picked up two more. "*Penthouse.* I get the idea. No *Ladies Home Journal.*"

"Of course not. Come here. You can't lie next to me and read."

"What else are we going to do?"

"I can think of something," Jack said wickedly.

"Bet you read aloud to the dakinis."

"How'd you know?"

She gestured to them. "The way their eyes lit up when I started in on that pile."

"Poor things. They really can't get down. They like the Letters column in *Penthouse.* I don't know how much of it they understand, but they like it."

"Let's read it to them now," Dani giggled.

"Careful. They get excited easily. That's how I found out how easy it is to have hot sex standing up."

Dani propped herself up on her elbows and looked around. "I don't want to hear it."

"Jealous?" Jack grinned.

"No. I just wouldn't want to bang my head against a wall. I do enough of that when I'm not having sex."

He laughed. "Me too. But real women—well, that just wasn't going to happen to a guy like me. I used to watch climbers and trekkers go at it sometimes. Not very many made it to the monastery. It's pretty isolated."

"Mmm. So you like to watch. Guess there are a few perks to being invisible."

He drew her closer, rubbing his erection against her thigh. "Some of the guys were so crude—I just wanted to push them off the girls and show them how."

"Aren't you nice," Dani murmured. "I bet the girls wouldn't have minded. But c'mon, you're talking about mountain climbers. Strong. Healthy. Obsessed with their athletic prowess and constantly needing to prove themselves."

He laughed into her neck. "Yeah. Like me."

"I was just going to say that. So you get off looking at a hot couple banging away?"

"Yeah. Who wouldn't? A beautiful girl in ecstasy, getting everything she wants from a really built guy? Hell, yeah. I could stand anywhere, get as close as I wanted, see everything—"

"Tell me."

"You like to watch too, huh? Mmmm." He nipped her ear and whispered into it. "I remember this dark-haired girl, looked a lot like you. Tall, with great tits. She lay back on that bed with nothing on and spread her legs for her guy, masturbating to get him hot. He sat in a chair and just stared. Me too."

"Lucky you."

He shook his head. "An exercise in total frustration. I envied him. She was talking to him in this soft, purring voice, all about how big his cock was and how much she wanted it."

Dani cupped him in one hand. "I understand how she felt."

Jack vibrated an amorous moan into her neck. "Mmm-hm. His cock got a little longer every time she spoke to him—that thing was big."

"Bigger than yours?"

Jack thought for a moment. "No."

Dani had to laugh.

"Honestly, it wasn't."

"Okay, tiger. Whatever you say. So what happened next?"

"She straddled his open lap and let him bury his face in her tits and suck her nipples. He would come up for air and talk about her beautiful hot pussy and how wet it was getting rubbing on his thighs, and how he wanted to worship it for her."

"Good. Pussy worship is always good."

"You're gonna get some. Just you wait." He slid his hand down the front of her climbing pants and right into her. "Juicy." He finger-fucked her with sensual expertise and they kissed for a while, then he pulled his hand out, wiping it on her belly on the way up.

He evidently wanted to take his time. She didn't mind. The exotic unreality of the setting, even the delicate fragrance that lingered in the air, conspired to make her head spin. In Tibet, you could be dead . . . but not. Stone . . . but flesh. Putting one booted, blistered foot in front of the other on an arduous trek . . . then flying through the cold air on a hot tiger.

And was Jack ever hot. She stroked his cock through his pants, letting him push her sweater up again to play with her breasts. He did wonders with nipples. As he had before, his expert touch—and the way he rolled and tugged them, then licked just the tips at the same time—went straight to her pussy.

"I want you inside me this time," she said softly.

"First I'm going to eat you. One last kiss, though." He came up over her and kissed her mouth, long and lovingly, arousing her with his probing tongue.

"Finish the story," she whispered when the kiss was over.

"Huh? Oh, yeah. They kissed for a really long time, sitting like that. It's a tantric position. Then she lay back down again and masturbated really hard, telling him to watch carefully and learn a few things about the proper way to worship a pussy."

Dani poked him in the side. "And did you learn anything?"

"Who, me? I don't have anything to learn."

"All men have something to learn."

"Okay, teach me."

"Finish the story."

"How come you never say please? I may have to put you over my knee and teach you some manners."

"Go right ahead. I like to get spanked."

"Really?" His eyes widened. "You don't seem like the type. You're so independent. Strong-minded."

"So? I still like to get spanked. I like the way it feels and I don't always want to be in charge."

"Cool. You have a beautiful ass. I'd love to."

"First finish the story," Dani said, laughing. "Oops—please."

"Okay. Her eyes were closed by the time he got up, looking down at her hot cunt like heaven on earth was right between her legs. She spread her pussy lips wide and put all four fingers in."

"Mmm. I can see it."

"Her boyfriend got down on his knees and began to lick her clit, once he got her by the wrist and got her hand out. He slid his cock in and rammed her but good. She was totally digging it. Hottest fuck she'd ever had, et cetera. The end. No moral to that story except have a good time while you can have it."

Dani nodded her agreement. "Yup."

He rolled her around and kissed her some more, getting her back in the mood. "Time to get naked. Did you bring a condom?"

"In my daypack. Do we need one?"

"I'm not sure, but what the hell." With a do-my-duty groan, he got up, rummaged around in her pack, found it and set it by the bed. She lay on her back and lifted her pants-clad legs up. Towering over her, Jack stood up to pull them off, stopping when he had them up around her ankles to give her bare ass some preliminary and very stimulating slaps.

"Yow!" She slid her hands over her glowing cheeks, enjoying the tingling.

He let her down on the bed. "Too hard?"

"No . . . just right. Something tells me you've done that before."

Jack grinned and shucked his clothes before he yanked off her pants and then her sweater. He turned her on her belly with one swift move. "That's right. Some women really like it and it turns me on if they do."

"All right. Works for me." Dani felt a slow, sensual heat building deep within her just talking about it. His voice was rougher, more intimate and more male. She rested her face on her crossed arms, hitching up a little so her ass was higher, and crossed her ankles. She was definitely craving some bare-bottom discipline.

He stroked the back of her legs and her behind with his fingertips. "Hot bitch," he said softly. "If you want a spanking, you're gonna get a good one. You ready?"

"Yeah . . . oh, yeah." She felt him take one ankle and then the other, opening her legs really wide. She sensed his eyes taking in every detail of her—her spread-open pussy and her tight asshole, everything—and pressed her blushing face against the soft material that covered the bed. "Tie my ankles," she whispered.

"Too much trouble. Just hold still—and stay wide open without being tied. Just because I said so. That's even sexier." Jack stroked her bare bottom again, then traced his fingertips over the sensitive flesh just under her buttocks.

He stopped for a minute, making her wait for it, then touched her pussy lips, parting them gently with both his hands. She knew he was looking his fill. Dani moaned softly, instantly and deeply aroused, wanting to wriggle with anticipation but forcing herself to hold still. "Good girl. You're not allowed to move, but I like it when you moan. And say please. I want you to ask for it."

"Please," she whispered.

"I can't hear you."

"Please spank me."

"Hard?"

"Yes—oh! Unnh!"

His hand came down on her buttocks, big enough to get both at once, and strong to make it sting. Dani breathed slowly, relishing the awesome sensation that reverberated through her lower body. Her ass cheeks trembled and he stroked them again, intensifying her pleasure.

"Hold still," he said quietly. Jack clasped her ankles again and pulled her legs a few more inches farther apart. She could feel her slick pussy lips part.

She said nothing, knowing that he understood exactly what she wanted. He let go of her ankles and kissed her tingling bottom all over, then got up over her on all fours, caressing her back as he bent his head down to whisper in her ear. "Looking at you, Dani . . . just waiting for it—wow. Totally turns me on."

The heat of his breath, closer than any touch, only made her want him more. She sensed him raising his hand and felt a deep desire throb inside her, then a rush of air as he brought his hand down swiftly, cracking it across her behind harder this time. "Unnh!" The padded silk muffled her cry. Dani, her hair tangled and hiding her face, raised her buttocks, craving what he was giving her.

"Nice. Ass up. Legs open. I can see everything, Dani. And I know you want more."

"Yes," she whispered. "Yes, please."

"Stay still." His expert hands administered the sensual pun-ishment she'd requested for several more minutes, hard enough to send her into a frenzy of arousal that had her pressing her frustrated pussy into the silken bed, but not so hard that he would leave a mark. Then he stopped, stroking her tingling flesh with infinite tenderness. "That's enough. Roll over. Use that soft silk to cool off your spanked ass, Dani."

Like a satisfied animal—well, not completely satisfied—she rolled over on her back and let her legs fall open, rubbing her buttocks against the comforter with little side to side motions while he watched, his wonderful eyes on fire with pure lust.

He stilled her by placing his warm hand on her belly. Then he stroked her, again just with his fingertips, parting her labia and thrusting two fingers inside. Then three. Dani moaned. It felt so good.

"I want you," she whimpered. "Now . . . please. All of you."

"Not yet." Jack buried his face in her cunt, thrusting his tongue deeply inside again and again but keeping away from her aching clit.

Her fingers crept down to it, craving orgasmic release, but he pushed them away. She began to undulate upon the silk be-neath her spanked ass again, needing the soothing coolness of it more than before, especially if he was going to tongue-fuck her like this.

But the motion only heightened her sexual tension. But she couldn't come without clit action and Jack just would not go near it. He kept up the tongue thrusts, getting one finger wet with her flowing pussy juice. Dani knew where that was going.

She felt his fingertip tease the tight puckers of her asshole, then withdraw. He raised his head and wiped his dripping mouth on her thigh. "Want my finger in your ass?"

"Yes," she breathed. "Easy, though." She reached down to grab her buttocks and spread them apart, open to his intent scrutiny. Then she felt Jack's slick finger enter her asshole with a gentle thrust.

She moaned raggedly, giving herself up to the submissive sensation of anal penetration. He moved his soft mouth up to her clit at last, sucking it into his mouth when he pulled his finger out of her ass. He grabbed her buttocks in his big hands and pulled her hips to him, sucking clit like a master. Dani felt the first wave of an intense orgasm hit her hard. Her body shook and she screamed his name, coming in his mouth. She was still coming when he pulled away and let her fall back down on the bed.

He took all of two seconds to roll on the condom he'd set aside, and in another second, he rammed his huge cock between her legs, savoring the thrilled pulsing of the pussy he'd treated so well. His thrusts made her ass pound against the silk bed, which rocked with the power of his thrusts.

She reached around and grabbed Jack's tensed buttocks, pulling him into her hard as she felt him explode in orgasm, imagining rushing jets of his cum filling the condom. He cried out, almost as if he was in pain, not stopping until he drew in a gasping, shuddering breath and collapsed on top of her, utterly spent.

"Oh, wow . . . you . . . we . . . are so hot together." She stroked his back, his hair, kissing him wildly on his chest and shoulders and biceps. "How long has it been since you . . . never mind. I shouldn't ask."

"Years, Dani," he whispered. "Too many fucking years . . . but I'm glad I got someone real. Worth waiting for." He rose on his elbows and let her breathe. Their sweaty bodies came unstuck with a pop. "Wow is right. That was fantastic."

Still caressing him, Dani heard faint murmurs of feminine approval coming from the dakini wall. "I think the goddesses agree."

3

"Now what?" Dani tucked her sweater back into her pants and looked around the temple of the dakinis.

She and Jack had managed to wash up with water from a spring that had been channeled into a carved stone fountain. They got dressed, though all they wanted to do was sleep. But she didn't want to sleep in a tiger's lair. Even if he was her tiger. Being this far underground made her restless.

They sat on the bed, just looking at each other. He sighed. "I guess I have to get you and Moe back to reality somehow."

"Maybe the Tara isn't finished with him. Hey, how much of this is he going to remember? Flying tigers, green Buddha girls, flowers that bloom in the dark . . ."

Jack shook his head. "Not much. We'll bring him back to where he was. However, he was definitely looking for you when you dropped that canteen on his head."

"Hey, it wasn't on purpose," Dani said indignantly.

"Calm down. All I mean is if he doesn't find you soon, he's not going to be happy."

"He'll probably organize a big search-and-rescue effort, get every climber he knows to volunteer—Moe never gives up. You don't know him."

"No, I don't," Jack said tightly. "Even though he's older than me, I'm before his time. It's just too fucking weird to think about."

"Does it matter that much?" she asked softly.

"Since you . . . happened, yeah, it does matter."

"Talk to me."

He got up and paced around his lair. "Couldn't I just growl? The best part about being a tiger is that you don't have to think too much. You go on instinct more than anything."

"Whatever works."

Jack shook his head. "It doesn't. Not if you have a human memory to get in the way. Not if you have to hang around waiting to be reincarnated. You don't know what it's like."

"I get that you aren't very happy. But not every man gets to fly or play with goddesses or morph into an amazing animal."

"It's not that—never mind."

"What do you want out of life, Jack?"

"This isn't life!" he howled. "Hell, I just want to be real." He slammed his open hand against the carved bed frame, making it rattle. "Fuck. Now I sound like Pinocchio."

Dani beckoned him back to the bed. "I'm not going to ask if a hug would help. You'd probably bite my head off."

"No, I won't."

She opened her arms and he flung himself into them, knocking her breathless. "Hug my blues away, angel. Hug me back to life." Dani wrapped herself around him. "Good. That's good. Don't stop."

"Lem um bree—" Dani couldn't speak until he let her go. "Let me breathe!" she burst out, when he rolled off, laughing. "Are you alive yet?"

Jack pinched his arm. "Nope."

"But you can feel sexual sensation and you seem to be the picture of manly health, so how come—"

He held up his hand. "Stop. You're looking at a semi-successful magic trick. Some things work and some things don't. The old abbott who stored my soul in a tiger—well, he got to really die and be reincarnated. I can't ask him how he did it because I don't know where he is."

"Probably working in Vegas," Dani murmured. "But I still don't understand how the Jack body stays in such great shape if you're dead."

Jack flexed his biceps and extended his arms like he was about to take off. "Hey, I have to be both man and beast. And do you think flying through the air with you on my back is easy?"

"Are you saying that I'm fat?" she asked indignantly.

He rolled her over and slapped her clothed behind. "No, you're perfect. Don't lose an ounce."

Dani backcrawled on the bed and threw her leg over Jack, forcing him close to her. For a moment, they lay side by side, just smiling at each other. She touched his face, trailing a fingertip over the pale gold stubble on his jaw. "You need a shave, tiger."

"Nah. I'm a wild beast. Don't have to if I don't want to." He grinned down at her, resting his head on his hand.

Dani sighed. "I could get used to this. Being with you, I mean."

"But you just got here," Jack said. "We hardly know each other."

"I feel like I've known you for a long, long time. Why is that?"

An awkward silence fell. "I don't know," he said softly. "Anyway, I'm not sure you can go back—not right away. So maybe . . ." He didn't finish his sentence, just pulled her against his chest, and she nestled there, listening to the beat of his heart.

"Then I'll stay with you," she whispered. "For now." Dani knew he was smiling.

"Okay. Wow. Guess my karma's improving."

"Explain."

"Karma . . . hmm. Basically it means that what goes around, comes around. The abbott told me that my situation was a chance to atone for my misdeeds in a previous life."

"What about this one, Jack? Who were you before?"

He nuzzled the top of her head. "Born and raised in Southern California. MIT grad—I told you that. Aerospace engineer. Triathlete. Classic car collector. Money to burn and more girlfriends than I knew what to do with. I got into mountain climbing just to find some peace and quiet."

Dani snorted. "Typical overachiever profile. So tell me, Mr. Flash," she said in a news anchor's voice, "when you got changed into a tiger, were you a little less obnoxious?"

"Since you mention it, yes. I changed a lot."

"Next question is a little personal," she went on. "Were you concerned that wearing all-over stripes would make your butt look big?"

"Uh, no."

"Well, I'd have to agree, Jack. You have a bodacious butt. Killer tan. Love the fur coat, too. I want to thank you for being my guest this morning and we have some lovely parting gifts—"

"Ugh, TV talk shows," he laughed. "Forgot about those. I've forgotten about a lot of things. A sense of time, for one. One day flows into the next."

"Interesting," Dani yawned.

"Yeah, you sound fascinated."

"Let's talk about your love life. Any cute tigresses in the picture, Mr. Flash?"

He shook his head. "Not in the Himalayas. I guess there used to be, but not anymore. You see them in Tibetan art and those great rugs, but that's about it. The abbott conjured me up out of an old wall painting."

Dani waved a hand airily. "No one to play with, huh?"

"I've met a few clouded leopards, and a snow leopard once—small cats. They didn't want anything to do with me. No, I'm alone."

"Do you think I could shapeshift into a tiger?" Dani's question was impulsive but she suddenly wanted to know.

"Interesting idea. I don't know. Why would you want to?"

"To see what it's like to be you."

Jack shook his head. "You wouldn't like it. I mean, I've gotten used to it now, but I hated it at first. Being invisible is just so goddamn lonely. Some of the Tibetans can see me, though—like the guy who built this bed. We're pals. He likes *Playboy*. Wants to know if I can introduce him to Miss October." He reached up and clasped one pole of the carved frame. "But Westerners can't see me or talk to me. Except for you."

"Hmm," Dani said. "That was a good reason to learn Tibetan right there. Otherwise it would be like being in solitary."

"You got it." His expression was faraway and sad. "I try to keep busy. If I don't have anyone to rescue, I follow trekkers and climbers around just for laughs, chase a few blue sheep, things like that."

"Blue sheep?"

"Yeah. Not domesticated. They look more like goats than sheep. Their heads and part of their bodies have a slate-blue color in the right light."

"Oh. I was imagining something like Marge Simpson but with four legs."

"Who's Marge Simpson?"

Dani looked at him curiously. "You have been here a long time, haven't you?"

"Yeah. Like I said, the time just flows by, especially when I'm in tiger mode."

She reached up and stroked his hair. "If you could go home to the U.S., what's the first thing you'd do?"

"Call you," he said softly. "That's assuming you make it back. Go out on a date. Order a humongous hamburger with Heinz ketchup. For some reason, I crave Heinz ketchup. Why is that?"

"It's really sweet," she said, laughing. "Make that two humongous hamburgers with Heinz ketchup. I could eat one right now. What else?"

"See a movie. A stupid, insane, guy-type, Hollywood action movie. Share a giant-size bag of dyed yellow popcorn with imitation butter sauce with you."

"And I thought you were going to say have sex."

"Nah. We've done that. You didn't waste any time, sweets."

Dani grinned. "I couldn't help myself. I heard the call of the wild and you looked too good to be true. I didn't know I was getting a magic tiger into the bargain. Hell, I'm not sure I want to return to reality."

Jack gave her a look that she couldn't quite read. "But Moe will. We'd better go see how he's doing. His arm should be healed by now."

"In less than two hours?"

He nodded. "Seeing is believing. Let's go. You can ride on my back."

Dani bounced off the bed. "Morph, please. I'm ready."

Jack stood up, shimmered into nothingness and the tiger appeared in his place, saddled up and ready.

They took a different route back, through deeper tunnels carved from the living rock. The walls dripped a crystalline liquid that the tiger paused to lick.

"Thirsty?"

Yeah. You?

"I am but I don't want to lick rocks, thanks."

Look in the pouch on the right of the saddle. There's a thermos of cocoa in it.

"I'm impressed, Jack. You're a very smart tiger. How'd you make cocoa?"

Swiss Miss. Boiling water. It's not rocket science. I made it before you woke up back at the monastery.

"So you knew I'd force you to come get Moe," Dani laughed.

The tiger nodded. *Always prepared.*

She pulled out the thermos, managing to unscrew the cap and take a few swigs as they padded along. "Whoa. Hold it. Who are they?"

The tiger stopped without making a sound and swung its massive head to where she was pointing. *Gods. Young gods.*

"How young?" she asked mischievously.

Definitely over the age of consent. I think they were carved about a thousand years ago. Does it matter? They're not human.

She clung to the saddle horn with one hand and put the thermos away with the other as they approached the carvings in the wall. "There're some dakinis in there too. Looks like spring break."

Guess they sneaked in.

"I thought you said they had to stay on the wall."

They're supposed to. But they have their ways. The dakinis like sex and they like men.

"I can see why." Dani's gaze swept over the sinuous stone bodies of the young gods on the wall. They were much taller than the naked dakinis they clasped, looking down at them with celestial lust. One, the tallest, the caramel color of old ivory, had lifted his goddess by her round buttocks, holding her in a position of tantric sexual union. Dani could clearly see his long rod thrusting deeply into her and the sensual perfection of the pendulous balls between his sculpted thighs.

Impulsively, she reached out a hand to touch the carving there . . . and felt the balls grow warm in her hand. The stone god smiled down at his consort, as if the dakini had done the touching.

You have the same powers I do, the tiger murmured. *Careful. The statues can pull you into their world.*

Dani didn't answer, awed by the sight of stone coming to life, in hues of flesh that seemed not quite human. Yet the sensual gods and their divine consorts writhed in a loving orgy, imbued with very human passion by their creators centuries ago.

A nearly naked dakini, clad only in a wisp of veil, lifted her slender legs to her lord's bejeweled ears that he might penetrate her more deeply from above, and cried out with pleasure when his shaft filled her.

Her twin kissed him, flicking her tongue over his lips and offering up her breasts for his delectation, while another god parted her golden labia and entered her, an expression of heavenly bliss upon his handsome face. The others, and there were many, were joined in a hundred different erotic positions with the fluid grace of dancers, completely interconnected and constantly in motion.

The sight was breathtaking. Even the tiger looked on with reverence, forgetting all about his animal instincts for a few minutes.

One by one, each god reached climax with his consort—there were a few dakinis who achieved their bliss with a female companion, Dani noticed with a secret smile—and imperceptibly became stone again, frozen upon the wall until a future moment of release.

"Awesome. I will never forget that, Jack. They make human sex look kind of ordinary."

But we can do it whenever we want. They only get to do it, oh, once every hundred years. No one takes this shortcut any more.

"Are you saying I should count my blessings? Yeah, you're right. Okay, looks like the show's over. Let's go get Moe."

Yeah.

"I wonder why I could bring them to life like you did," she mused. She realized, feeling afraid, that it might be because she was becoming, imperceptibly, more like Jack. If she was between two worlds . . . she would have to choose one eventually.

You'll be all right, Dani. I promise I'll get you out of here and it'll be good-bye and good luck. No hurt feelings or crap like that. Just good-bye.

The tiger padded on, turning right at an intersecting tunnel. Even telepathically, his answer sounded a little grim to Dani's ears. Like someone who didn't want to say good-bye.

They found Moe sound asleep on his silken bed, watched over by a cooing demi-goddess with a peacock feather fan. The sling was gone and his arm had healed. The tiger interpreted the green Tara's advice for Dani's benefit: he was to stay asleep for the journey up and out of the mountain. Moe stirred slightly and smiled when the goddess pressed a kiss to his forehead. Dani and the tiger exchanged a look.

He never had it so good, Dani.

"I know. Too bad he won't remember." She attempted to thank the green Tara in the few words of Tibetan she knew, and the goddess of mercy inclined her head with a gracious nod, a glint of amusement in all her eyes.

"Did I say something stupid?" Dani whispered to the tiger.

He shook his heavy head. *Don't worry about it. She understands what you really mean.*

Then Dani fastened him to the tiger's saddle as before, and walked beside them through the caverns and tunnels that honeycombed the mountain. They came out into the fresh air at a different place from where they had entered, near a mountain pass and—amazing sight—a paved highway.

Not far away from where they were standing, thousands of prayer flags on thin poles fluttered in the unceasing wind, left there by pilgrims and travelers to send blessings over the landscape. The tiger batted at a prayer wheel, making it spin and sending out a hundred more.

"What are you doing?"

Gaining merit. Spinning a prayer wheel is a very efficient way to get your divine two cents in.

Dani laughed and paused to take in the awesome view. The descending crags opened up to a limitless view of the brown Tibetan plains, with a few grazing yaks making infinitesimal dots on it.

She untied Moe and grabbed him under the arms, strong enough to wrestle him off, but not strong enough to hold up his full weight for long. She let him slump to the ground, where he stretched out as if he were still ensconced on the Tara's silken bed.

Now that they were out in light that seemed agonizingly bright, Dani checked him quickly for signs of injury. No emergency room ever had illumination this good. But Moe wasn't going to need emergency care. His arm was sound and he didn't flinch under her expert touch. His color was good and his breathing was regular. Moe had probably never been this healthy, Dani thought, given his climber's penchant for running himself ragged. The green Tara really knew her stuff.

Moe mumbled something she didn't understand, then opened his eyes and looked at her groggily. "Dani? What the hell happened to you? That storm . . . I shouldn't have gone on ahead. I found the rope wrapped around a rock and saw the crevasse—and I thought—well, I kept on looking. I tripped over some goddamn thing I didn't see and broke my arm." He rubbed his temples with gloved hands. "How'd we get here? Jesus, do I have a headache." He peered at her. "And visual disturbances. You know, it's like I can look right through you."

Dani nodded, seeing the tiger shimmer into nothingness and Jack appear in its place. "Take it easy," she said. "We're going to flag down a truck and hitchhike into Lhasa. Got to get you back to civilization. You need a thorough physical."

Moe probably didn't, but explaining that she was now between two worlds *and* fooling around with an invisible tiger just seemed like more trouble than it was worth.

Moe groaned. "Gah. I'm a climber. I fucking hate civilization. But ohhh—this sure as hell feels like altitude sickness." He rubbed his right arm. "Did you take off the sling? Weird. I know that I—I mean, I dreamed that I broke my arm. Guess I didn't."

Dani patted his arm. "No, it's fine. You have quite an imagination."

"I also dreamed that a beautiful lady with green skin was taking very, very good care of me. And hey—where's our gear?"

"Gone," she said simply.

"Um, you never did say what happened to you, Dani. Or how we got here. I know you didn't carry me—" He broke off, hearing the rumble of a truck making its laborious way up the mountain road.

"I'll explain later," she said. She walked to the middle of the road and peered down the high pass. The truck appeared—and disappeared—around several bends in the road, then finally began the ascent to the pass.

Jack went with her, speaking in silent tigerese so Moe wouldn't hear even though he couldn't be seen. *I'm coming with you. That looks like a Chinese army truck. They're going to ask questions. This part of Tibet isn't open to foreigners.*

Dani shrugged. "Nothing we can do about it. You can't fly me and Moe to all the way to Lhasa on your back, can you?"

He smiled slightly. *No. But I'll make sure you get there safely.*

The truck ground to a halt, but the driver didn't shut off the engine. Their luck was holding. The man at the wheel was Tibetan, his wife and several children crowded into the front seat, brightly dressed in traditional garb and weighed down with offerings. They looked like they were on their way to a religious festival.

Thanks, Tara. Jack winked at Dani. *Nice to have friends in high places.*

The family broke out into smiles, and motioned them into the back. Moe clambered in. "Going to be a bumpy ride, but it's a ride." He moved stacked crates and piles of bulging burlap bags aside to make them a place to sit as Dani stood on tiptoes to look into the cab.

She thanked them profusely in guidebook Tibetan and offered to pay, but they laughed uproariously.

"Why are they laughing?" she whispered to Jack.

You said that the pink yak is your sister, I think. Or something like that. But he won't accept payment. This guy probably works for the Chinese Army and he's not allowed to pick up foreigners anyway.

"Does he gain merit?"

Of course. But Tibetans are kind people, Dani. He would've picked you up no matter what.

"Okay, I'm coming," she responded to Moe's call, waving at him. With a boost from Jack, she got into the truck, swinging her leg over the tailgate and dropping down next to her climbing partner.

"It's getting worse," Moe grumbled. "I saw the sky right through you, Dani. You're right, I'd better get back. This truck is heaven sent."

"Seems that way, doesn't it?"

"But you *gotta* tell me how we got here. Where the hell are we? I don't know this pass—"

Jack leapt over the tailgate and knelt before him, unseen, moving a hand in a pattern over his head, drawing a mystical diagram. Moe's eyes rolled back and he lost consciousness, lolling against a burlap bag stuffed with something soft.

There. No more questions.

"Is he all right?" Dani asked nervously.

We're going to get him to Lhasa, sleepwalk him onto a plane, and all he'll remember is that you're off to explore Tibet with some women trekkers you just met.

"Did you hypnotize him?"

Mind meld. Now come here and cuddle up. It's a long way to Lhasa.

"And it's cold." They moved a little distance away from the burlap bag where Moe slept. Dani settled down next to Jack, who put his arms around her and let her rest his head over his strongly beating heart. She knew at that moment that nothing had ever felt so right.

4

Once Moe was safely on a plane, Dani took in the sights of Tibet's capitol for the second time since she had come overland from Nepal with him. It seemed like a very long time ago, though it had been only a little over a week, all told, since they'd set out to the remote western plateau for their ill-fated climb.

Thrumming with that glad-to-be-alive feeling, even though Jack had made it clear that she wasn't alive, strictly speaking, Dani admired everything, from the towering white walls of the immense Potala Palace to the trinkets in the bazaar.

An upcoming festival, the ones their Tibetans had been going to, crowded the streets with a fascinating mix, from tall Khampa tribesmen to Buddhist monks in maroon and saffron robes, to ordinary Lhasans, interspersed with the sunburnt faces of tourists, trekkers, and climbers.

The dry, dusty air made her cough and Dani noticed she wasn't the only one. On two feet but still in tiger thought patterns, Jack read her mind.

Respiratory disease is common here. Nowhere near enough

doctors or nurses in Tibet, even in Lhasa. Most people hardly ever see one.

She nodded. The Tibetans, ruddy-faced and strong, seemed generally cheerful all the same, carrying burdens and doing heavy work that would make Westerners croak at this altitude. They often smiled, and not as if they were seeing through her.

You could do a lot of good if you decided to stay.

"Oh, right. Dani Fairweather, Traveling Nurse, and Dr. Jack Flash. Step right up, folks." A passing trekker, gaunt and wild-haired, laden with a backpack that probably weighed close to what he did, gave them a hopeful look. She smiled but looked away. "Oops," she said to Jack. "How come he could see us?"

Been in Tibet too long, I guess, he answered. *Anyway, we could do rescues. And basic health care. Outreach programs for Tibetans. Stuff like that.*

"You have it all figured out, don't you?"

I've been thinking about a lot of things. And like I said, you might not be able to go back. If you decide to stay—

"That's a pretty big if."

He shut up about it by the time they reached the Crazy Yak in downtown Lhasa. The Tibetan waiter was friendly, but the Americans and other foreigners gave her puzzled looks, as if they literally couldn't make her out.

Dani ignored them and ordered. She savored every mouthful of her freshly grilled burger when it arrived, just about licking her chops after the first few bites.

You look like a tigress. Jack, still invisible, sat in the opposite chair, down to a T-shirt. He'd put his parka over the back of his chair, just as she'd done. The restaurant was stuffy and crowded and a little too warm.

"This is so good. You have no idea." She hadn't even taken a sip of her Coke.

Yes, I do. I like watching you enjoy it. Very sexy.

Dani licked a trace of ketchup from the corner of her mouth. "Not Heinz, but it's good. So when are we going back?"

He put his elbows on the table and propped his chin with one big hand. Was it the slatted blinds on the windows or did she see ghostly stripes on his skin? He seemed to be lit from within, but that was probably just another optical illusion.

To the monastery? As soon as I can get us a ride. He looked at her steadily, his beautiful blue eyes on fire.

She would have to call that color Unfair Blue. And speaking of fair, how come the one man she'd had the best sex of her life with, shared the most amazing adventure with, flown off into the wild blue yonder with, was trapped in a magic spell?

With no way out. Talk about living for the moment. Every second she spent with him drew her deeper and deeper into a world she didn't want to leave. There was only one word for that feeling.

I'm glad you're coming back, Dani. More glad than I say.

She shrugged and polished off her burger. "Seems like I don't have a choice. And I might be falling in love with you." At his astonished look, she held up a hand. "Whoa. Not sure about that." She put a paper straw into her Coke, and slurped it vigorously.

Good enough. It's a start. He beamed at her like a high school kid with an almighty crush on an out-of-his-league cheerleader.

Which Dani had never been, she reflected. Just a tall, skinny jock who ran faster, hit a tennis ball harder, and climbed higher than most of the boys. They really hadn't paid attention until the awful day her big boobs had appeared, something that had taken her a while to get used to.

But Jack seemed to love all of her, in a wholehearted way that could be just sex starvation, of course. Maybe not. Maybe she'd met Mr. Right at last. Of course, it was a crying shame that he was also Mr. Dead, but Mom would have said, with a wicked little wink, that you can't have everything.

Funny she should think about her mother liking Jack. But Mom would've, no doubt about it. Dani grinned back at him, then pulled a handful of yuan from her daypack to pay for the burger and sorted through the bills.

Let's go. Tuck it under the plate.

"I'm trying to calculate the tip."

Jack sighed, took the paper money from her hand, and picked out the right amount. The young Tibetan waiter arrived just as the bills were fluttering in midair but he didn't bat an eye.

It took nearly two days to get back to the western plateau and the isolated range of mountains where Jack lived. Dani craved a bath. The dust that blew over the arid plains covered travelers—covered everything—with a thin layer of grit. Her eyes itched. Her butt was sore from riding in several trucks with no shocks. The seasonal thunderstorms rolling through had made it unsafe to fly any part of the distance, but he had put her on his back for the last bit up the mountain.

"Welcome home," Jack said gallantly. "My monastery is your monastery. Make yourself comfortable."

"Thanks," she said, heaving a weary sigh. "I just wish I could do magic." They walked in to the pillared, gorgeously painted hall inside the carved doors, their footsteps echoing.

Her footsteps, anyway, Dani noticed. As usual, Jack made no noise at all. "I want a bubble bath. And then I want to get a pedicure and loll in bed and read stupid magazines. I want to be a total girl, not a trekker. I feel like I'm a hundred years old."

Jack nodded. "Done complaining?"

"Yeah. Sorry. It's not your problem, is it?"

"I have the solution. Come this way."

Dani dropped the bags of stuff she'd bought in Lhasa, wondering if she would ever actually need the engraved brass teapots or demon doorstop that she'd bought. He gestured her over to a door that led to an endless, winding staircase of stone. "Oh, no. Not the nine thousand steps to heaven. Spare me."

"If you want a bath, you've got to go up to the room under the roof. I built a cistern to catch meltwater."

"You never told me there was running water here."

"More like an improvisation on that theme. An engineering degree comes in handy in a country like Tibet."

"*Hot* running water?"

"I take the edge off the cold with a blowtorch, put it that way. Not hot. More like kinda warm. And the room has a southern exposure, so there's a passive-solar effect—"

"Okay, okay. Sounds good." She followed him up the narrow stairs with a definite bounce in her step. Catching her breath at the top, she peered around a carved doorjamb into a small, sunny room that held, incongruously, a huge, claw-footed bathtub.

"The last lama ordered it sent from India in 1959, just before most of the Buddhist monks got kicked out of Tibet by the Chinese. Took two months to get it here over the passes, according to the monastery records. It was a great event locally."

"Wow. I'm impressed. Hey, where'd you get all these?" She patted a stack of neatly folded towels on a gilt table. "Don't tell me that trekkers left 'em behind."

"From the Hilton. As in the Autonomous Region of the People's Republic Hilton." He grinned. "Meaning that I, uh, I liberated them from a Chinese army barracks."

"Oh. What a luxury to have so many." Dani picked up the one on top. "They're a little scratchy but they are new. Cool."

He waved a hand at a padded table. "How about a massage to start off?"

"Sure. I wouldn't say no to that, ever."

Jack knelt and started to unlace her dusty boots, pulling them off one by one, slipping off her mismatched wool socks with sensuous care.

Dani had to laugh. "You make me feel like I'm wearing high heels and stockings."

"That's the idea." He smacked her butt. "Keep your pants on for now."

Dani looked closer and saw that the table had been put together from various bits and pieces of scarce wood, and padded with toweling nailed on along the edge. "How strong is that thing?"

He swept her off her feet and settled her on it. Dani stretched out on her side, patting the padding. "Comfy. I like the Jack Flash Spa. You're full of surprises."

"We aim to please."

"Got any herb tea? That would warm me up."

"Probably. But I think it's downstairs with the freeze-dried meals and canned goods in the kitchen. I leave that stuff there in case people take shelter in the monastery. But I've got something else to warm you up." He went to a cupboard and swung open the doors with a flourish, revealing a row of liquor bottles with distinguished labels. "My secret stash. Care for a Manhattan? I have maraschino cherries, believe it or not. Brandy? Forty-year-old Scotch? Tequila? No limes. Sorry."

"Don't tell me trekkers left maraschino cherries behind."

"No, I swiped this stuff," he said. Dani raised an eyebrow. "Corporate climbing teams buy duty-free booze in Hong Kong and bring it with them. They think they're going to climb Everest"—he snapped his fingers—"just like that and have a cocktail afterward. But the mountain kills one out of every four."

"Don't be so cold."

"It's a fact."

"Let's think of happy things." She sat up and made a regal gesture. "Brandy, please. Got any peanuts?"

He grabbed a handful of airline snack packets from a carved wooden bowl. "As a matter of fact, I do. And pretzels."

"Hog heaven." She caught the foil-wrapped snack he tossed her way and ripped it open, pouring the contents into her mouth and crunching blissfully.

"I hope you don't mind drinking brandy out of a plastic cup."

"Not at all."

He poured out a healthy slug into a cup that said Souvenir of Hong Kong. Dani took a sip of the amber-colored brandy and coughed. A feeling of heat began in her stomach and permeated her entire body. "Ooh, that's good. Tastes different at this altitude. A lot stronger."

"And it'll go to your head faster, believe me." He stood by the table, taking the cup from her and inhaling its fragrance, then giving it back.

She took another sip and lay back on the table, contemplating the ceiling. "Uh-oh. You're right. The room is spinning."

He began to lift her sweater, revealing her bare breasts, which he caressed slowly and lovingly. "Mm-hm."

"Do my nipples," she said, feeling brandy-bold.

"Okay." He caressed her all over, making Dani even dizzier with desire. His touch, his voice, his nearness, all conspired to make her crave more from him. It had been a few days since they'd had sex—or had it? She was beginning to feel as he did: that time, here in Tibet, passed in an entirely different way. Like a magical river, it flowed at its own pace—and sometimes seemed to be holding still or moving backwards.

She struggled out of her sweater, and rolled over, bare to the waist. But not before she saw the longing in his eyes as he reached out to help her—a longing that was not sexual. She didn't want to think about it and closed her eyes as his big hands rested on her back.

With long, slow strokes, he began to give her a massage, easing the tension of their journey home with an expertise that seemed divinely inspired. In the warm room, the highest in the monastery, Dani felt an odd sensation of floating, as if she were hovering over the vast plains outside, able to see far into the distance.

But not into the future, she told herself. You have to go home. Her conscious mind was kicking in. Fighting a magic that was older than the mountains that cradled the monastery.

Another, deeper part of her consciousness took hold. *Home to what? Your home is here now. Stay.* Was that her mind or was it . . . Jack?

He was all business at the moment, concentrating on the massage he was giving her. "How does that feel?" Jack murmured, his voice low and soothing.

"Fabulous," she said, almost unwillingly. She relaxed, becoming boneless, as he continued his ministrations. Had any other man ever been this good to her? Not even remotely. Had she ever felt this happy with anyone? Not at all . . . she drifted into a blissful half-sleep.

"That's all for now, Dani. You need some rest."

She lifted her head when he lifted his hands from her back. "But that was very restful. More, please. And what about my bath?"

He leaned down and scooped her up from the table. "Later. No whining. You're going to get everything you want. All part of my master plan."

The feeling of being cuddled and carried was unbelievably seductive. Dani gave in to it and leaned her head against his chest to listen to the solid beat of his heart. "Okay," she whispered.

He brought her to the bed in the stone room, letting her reach down to pull the patterned silk comforter back and settling her on the worn sheet beneath. He kicked off his boots and stretched out beside her, the wool of his sweater pleasantly rough against her bare breasts as he drew her close to him.

"Not going to get undressed?"

"Nope. This is just a nap. Sleep, Dani. You need it more than I do." His voice was lulling, almost a purr. He stroked her hair and her back, then pulled the comforter over her shoulders, cocooning them in its deep warmth. The combined effects of his TLC and the shot of brandy made Dani's eyes drift shut. She could get used to this. She could *really* get used to this.

She slept . . .

And dreamed of a white tiger, moving through clouds of fragrant incense, before it came to sit peacefully with a group of monks clad in maroon and saffron robes. Their sonorous chanting resonated within an ancient temple, echoing with the unearthly bass drone of a Tibetan trumpet eight feet long. She was there with them, sitting apart, wearing the traditional dress of a Tibetan woman of high rank, meditating before an altar filled with the images of familiar gods.

The white tiger turned its noble head to look at her with eyes the piercing blue of the Himalayan heavens.

You have been here before, the tiger said. And that is why you have come here again. Please stay . . .

Dani stirred, came back to full consciousness, and realized that she was being carried by Jack, back down the hall, the way they had come.

"How long was I asleep?"

"Hours. It's tomorrow again."

"I'm not even going to try to figure that out."

"I told you that time in Tibet is different."

His heartbeat echoed in her ear, pressed against his chest. "Oh, Jack, I had the weirdest dream. You were in it . . ."

"Really?" he said indifferently. Dani began to suspect that he had mind-melded himself into her dream. And that she was being slowly, inexorably seduced by him into staying in Tibet.

The idea was beginning to seem ... entirely natural, even if his powers of persuasion were supernatural. And sexual, she thought ruefully. Very, very sexual.

Not that there was anything wrong with that.

"Really," she answered. "But I don't want to talk about it."

He kicked open a door to the small room at the top of the monastery. "Ready for your bath?"

She looked down from his arms into the gleaming, empty tub. "Sure. But water would be nice."

Jack set her on her feet, giving her nipples a friendly tweak. "Your every wish is my command. Water's coming up." He picked up a rubber pipe that snaked along the floor and used a makeshift contraption to pump water into the tub.

"Was that here yesterday?" she asked.

"Yeah. You were too tired and cranky to notice." He pumped and the tub slowly filled.

The water was perfectly clear. Dani dipped a hand into it. And cold. At least the room was warm. He was right about the passive-solar effect.

Jack picked up Tibet's answer to piped gas. "And now ... the blowtorch." He fired it up and applied to the sides of a large metal jerrycan already filled with water. It took a while to heat it to the boiling point while Dani watched nervously. "That's the best I can do."

He put the torch down and used one towel to swaddle his hand and another to grip the handle of the jerrycan, pouring it into the porcelain bathtub while Dani looked on, amused by his ingenuity. She noticed another jerrycan in the corner, heating over a small but brightly burning portable stove.

"That's my backup tank," he explained. "Nothing worse than running out of hot water."

"I couldn't agree more," Dani said.

"And now ... I get to make you insanely happy. Totally

turn you on. Be your bath attendant and devoted slave. Give you another massage, if you like. World-class pussy worship. Whatever you want."

"Sign me up." Dani began to unfasten the pants she'd slept in. "Are you doing this to gain merit?"

He gave her a wicked smile. "I'll gain a hard-on, I can tell you that. I'm going to enjoy this as much as you will."

Dani grabbed the bottom of his sweater and lifted it. "Take this off, pal. I prefer my slaves half-naked to start."

"Okay with me." He yanked off his sweater the rest of the way and his undershirt too, pulling them over his muscular arms. His small nipples hardened as she ran a hand over his chest. "Mmm. No."

"What do you mean, no? Slaves don't get to say no."

"This one does. I want this to be all about your pleasure. Any objections?"

"No. Outside of the smart mouth, you make a great slave." She slid her unfastened pants down to her ankles, but before she could step out of them, he kneeled and planted a kiss right on her pubic curls.

"Thanks for not wearing underwear."

"I gave you my last pair. The ones I got myself off with, remember?"

His semi-erection instantly got a whole lot larger. "Do I ever. Now get in the bath while it's still warm."

She kicked the pants into a corner and stepped into the sparkling water. Not quite *ahhhhh* temperature but it sure as hell would do. She was still a bit stiff from her long sleep. Dani sat down, wriggling her toes and splashing water over her shoulders and front.

"Allow me the pleasure of scrubbing your back." Jack took a folded towel and knelt by the side of the tub. "Only the softest bristles for my lady." He picked up a brush from a table with several resting on its top, and tested it on his palm. "Perfect."

Next to the brushes, Dani noticed small, old-fashioned ginger jars, which probably held lotions and potions. The yellowing labels were written in flowing Tibetan script. "Where'd you get this stuff?"

"The green Tara's handmaidens. They come by now and then with care packages."

"You're pretty popular with otherworldly babes. Dakinis and handmaidens and what not."

Jack tried to keep a straight face. "You think so?" He dipped the brush in the water, then popped off the lid of one of the small jars, tipping it and letting a fragrant soap flow out onto the dampened bristles. He dripped water onto it, then lathered it up, splashing water on Dani's back before scrubbing it gently with long strokes. And side to side short strokes. And massaging circular strokes.

"Oh . . . my . . . God. That feels soooooooo good."

"Thought you'd like it. I like it when Tara's girls do it to me."

She felt the warm, soapy water trickle down her spine and shuddered with pleasure. "Aha. So it's not just care packages."

"Well, no." He lathered up the brush and did her back again. "Hey, I have to have a few pleasures. And it's not like they ever spend the night. They're too busy. Tara's the goddess of mercy, and we all know the world needs it. She's got more important things to do than hang around with a bored tiger."

"Mm-hm. But you say her handmaidens do. Interesting."

He smirked as he scrubbed her. "It does get interesting sometimes."

"Don't tell me. I don't want to be jealous. But back up a sec—you *want* them to spend the night? You mean you're not one of those here-today-gone-tomorrow climbing studs?"

"It gets lonely. And the wham-bang, unh-unh-unh, light-up-a-smoke routine gets old."

"A cigarette afterwards? How unhealthy. I'd rather have an energy bar."

"Got 'em. Downstairs."

"You seem to have everything an imaginary man needs."

"Maybe so."

But I don't have you. Had he said that or had she imagined it?

"Could you scrub a little lower?" She wriggled forward in the bath and reached over her knees to show him her back.

"I can see your gorgeous ass. Get on all fours, Dani. Let me take care of you."

She obliged instantly, scrambling onto her hands and knees, and wiggling her wet ass at him. "How's that?" she cooed over her shoulder.

"Nice. I especially like the big pink polka dots where you were sitting. Very nice." He ran the soft, lathered-up brush over her butt and down the back of her thighs. "Enjoying yourself?"

"Hell, yeah."

Jack brought the brush around and caressed her belly, making her giggle. He touched it to her breast and tickled her nipples with the soft, soapy bristles, then dropped the brush in the water, and used his strong hands instead, lathering her body all over.

He took a washcloth, sopped it in the water, and began to rinse her with generous strokes, squeezing the cloth out and repeating the process, taking care to hit every hot button she had all over again. Nipples. Ass cheeks. The nape of her neck. The sensitive spots where her thighs ended and her buttocks began. Everything got rubbed with the dripping cloth.

Had she ever been treated this well? Dani knew she hadn't. And there was more to his TLC than just a warm-up for sex. His hands communicated his feelings in a way that words could not. Jack made each stroke linger, appreciating every inch of her, as if . . .

I'm memorizing you. In case you go back.

"No mind-melding. You're a man at the moment. Talk to me."

He sloshed the washcloth in the water and trickled a warm stream along her spine. "How can I persuade you to stay?"

"I'm here, right? But what do you mean by stay?"

"You know. Like forever. Have my cubs."

Dani clutched the edge of the tub and pulled herself up halfway. "I am so not ready for this discussion. Could we go back to the giving-me-intense-pleasure part?"

"Why not?" he said in a silky voice, his eyes glittering. Then he fastened his lips on one wet nipple, and his fingers on the other. The sensual thrill made her arch back and thrust her breasts out. She stroked his spiky blond hair as he sucked her expertly, moving his mouth to the other nipple and his hand between her legs.

"That's pretty persuasive," she said softly.

His head rose and he captured her lips, parted in a silent moan when he played with her clit. He broke the kiss and reached into the water for the soap, lathering her up all over again. Then Jack pulled back to admire her dripping, soapy pussy. "Oh, yeah. Squeaky clean. Time to rinse." He splashed warm water between her legs, grinning when she giggled with each splash.

Then he picked up the washcloth again, tucking a fingertip into the cloth and giving her clit a tender little scrubbing of its very own. Dani opened her mouth in an *ooh*.

Jack grinned. "I love it when you make noise. And do I have a sex toy for you. Sit back."

She obeyed, lolling her head against the sloped back of the huge tub, and listening to him open and close a cabinet door. Sounds of this being connected to that followed. He came back with a tube in one hand, keeping his thumb over the end, then let clear, warm water spurt from it into her bath.

"Oh," she breathed. "Like my shower massager. Oh, those pulsing jets . . . yes, yes, yes." She opened her legs.

Jack swished the light bubbles on the surface of the water away. "Mind if I look?"

"No." She closed her eyes. "Do it."

She heard his hand enter the water and felt the first pulse of warm water against her clit. He concentrated on arousing her, keeping the flowing rhythm steady with on-offs of his thumb. It felt like a strong tongue moving over her most sensitive flesh, with the intensity of a private masturbation session in the shower.

Dani knew he was watching but she didn't want to open her eyes. Her hands slid down into the water, pulling on her clit as Jack sprayed it with pulsing jets.

"Don't come yet," he said softly. He brought the tube up and used it to pulse jets of water onto her erect nipples and she parted her lips in ecstasy. His mouth came down over hers as she moaned, capturing the sound she made and mingling it with a tense, very masculine moan of his own.

"Get up," he breathed. She opened her eyes at last, clasping the rim of the porcelain tub and rising, dripping wet. He steadied her with one hand and helped her turn around slowly with the other, sluicing warm water over her back and ass, shoulders and breasts. Her long, dark hair soaked it up, and rivulets flowed from it, as if she had turned into a naiad before his eyes.

"Look at you," he murmured. "More beautiful than any goddess. I could watch the water roll down your velvet skin for the rest of my goddamn life, if I had a life . . . do you know what you do to me, Dani?"

"No," she said softly. She looked into his eyes, almost frightened by what she saw there. That longing look had intensified a hundredfold.

"Stay with me, Dani. Please. If you go—"

"I'm not going anywhere," she whispered. "Don't you know that by now?"

The water slowed to a trickle and stopped. He embraced her, wet as she was, as if he had never touched her before.

"Do you mean it, Dani?"

"I can't promise I'm always going to be here. But right now we have each other. And it feels incredible. Let that be enough."

He released her with a sigh and Dani stepped out of the tub. He swaddled her in one huge towel and made a clumsy wrap out of a small one for her hair. Dani smiled and fixed it so it stayed.

She clasped his hand, grateful for the strength in it. Her knees were wobbly. Fully aroused, totally unsatisfied. Dani had no doubt, judging by the tigerish grin on his handsome face, that more pleasure was in store.

He pulled off the big towel and rubbed her down briskly with another one. Dani sighed. In this extremely arid climate, she could feel her skin tightening already. But Jack had opened a third jar and was pouring a golden liquid that looked like buttered honey into his hand. He sat down on a low chair, put his legs together and patted one thigh. "Come on. Over my knees."

5

"Another spanking?" Dani came over, letting her hips sway as she walked. Two could play at teasing.

"No. Something just as good. Maybe even better. I want you to really open up to me."

She bent to her waiting lover, turning his face up to hers for a long, sensual kiss, letting him use his free hand to play with her nipples. "That goes right where it counts," she whispered into his mouth. His touch made her pussy tighten and throb. They kissed for another minute, while Dani enjoyed the anticipation, looking down through her half-closed eyes to assess his hard-on through his pants.

Huge. Good. She straightened, then kneeled to one side, and eased herself over his lap. Jack widened his legs to support her as much as possible and Dani relaxed, completely naked and deliciously clean.

The towel turban fell off her hair and Jack smoothed the long, wet strands to one side so it wouldn't trickle down her back. She felt his cupped palm rub the warmed lotion over one of her ass cheeks and then the other. Then he used both hands and increased the pressure, massaging her butt and the tight back of her thighs, all the way down to her knees.

Dani let her arms go to the floor, hanging her head and raising her bottom for his sensual ministrations. He didn't make a move to finger fuck her this time, seeming to like what he was doing now just as much. But she parted her thighs anyway, giving him a good look at her swollen, slick labia just for the hell of it.

"Showing off?" he said softly. "You know I like looking at your pussy, don't you? But not right now. Keep your thighs together and your ass high."

She obeyed.

Jack put a hand on each cheek and squeezed them softly, then pushed her oiled buttocks together and squeezed again. Then he gently opened them, which made her labia open a little too. Squeeze. Open. Squeeze. Open. He kept her open the last time, using his warm hands to spread her buttocks apart and look his fill.

Jack sighed roughly. She knew that he was aroused beyond belief. She began to move her hips, but stayed spread open, putting on a tempting display of succulent feminine flesh.

"Yeah," he growled. "Roll around. Rub my leg if you want to. Make yourself feel good, Dani."

She stopped. "Did I tell you to stop? Some slave you are." He drew in a ragged breath and resumed his incredibly stimulating treatment of her bare behind. He rubbed the honey-thick lotion into her skin while he was at it.

His cock was so big it was about to burst out of his pants. Wickedly, Dani wriggled on it, thrusting her hips down on the muscular thighs that held her so comfortably, making him gasp.

"Dani, don't. I'll come in my pants, I swear."

She held still. "Keep rubbing in that oil. I love it."

"Yeah? Good. Wait until I do the same thing to your tits."

She rolled over in his lap, holding on to his shoulder with

one hand and scratching his bare chest gently, dragging her short fingernails over one nipple. Jack winced. "I don't want to wait. Do them," she said, thrusting her breasts up.

He eased her down to the floor, grabbing folded towels from the stack and using them as pillows under her hips, head, shoulders, feet, kneeling beside her to make her comfortable, getting off on playing slave.

Dani twisted around and grabbed the elastic waistband of his pants, pulling them halfway down, running her fingertips over the fine golden hair on his muscular thighs. He wasn't wearing underwear either. Jack's cock sprang out, right where she wanted it—near her lips.

She raised her head and took his full length in her mouth. He had the presence of mind to tuck three more folded towels under the back of her head, so she could relax and really suck him. Then he held himself up over her with ease—rock jocks had amazing, totally amazing arms, Dani thought blissfully.

Jack moaned as she pumped his throbbing cock with her mouth, teasing the sensitive part under the head with a fluttering tongue action, tasting the first drops of cum that he couldn't keep back.

"Stop it . . . stop it," he gasped, pulling out and staggering up to his feet. He forced his stiff erection down and pulled his pants over it.

Dani lay on the floor, looking up at him with her mouth open. "Why?"

"Just not yet, okay? Not yet." He plopped into the chair and caught his breath. "When I say this is all about you, I mean it."

She rolled over onto her belly, her chin propped in one hand. "Scratch my last comment. You are the worst fucking slave there ever was. But you're also the hottest."

He swiped a hand over his sweaty face. "Whatever. I want this to last and you're getting me too hot." He drew in several deep breaths. "The monks were right. Desire keeps me here. But the way I want you—I never felt this alive. I want to lose control and take you with me. Make you mine. You okay with that?"

"Yeah. Totally." She rolled onto her back, feeling playful in an animal way. His eyes were glowing, she noticed, and he looked hot all over, with faint tiger stripes on his skin that seemed to be lit from within. The same thing she'd seen at the restaurant in Lhasa, only brighter now, maybe because he was naked. The fine, pale gold hair on his body heightened the contrast of the dark stripes.

His breaths came more slowly and he leaned back, letting the chair tip so he could stretch his long, powerful legs out all the way.

"Do I have to knock you over to get my tits done?" she asked, arching her back.

He tipped the chair back on the floor with a thump. "No. Sorry. I zoned out for a few secs." He picked up yet another jar and uncapped it, sniffing the contents. "Yeah, this is the stuff."

"What do you mean?" Dani tugged on her own nipples, which made his cock stand up straight all over again.

"The good stuff." He poured a thin liquid in his hand and rubbed it over her breasts, pushing her hands aside.

Dani cried out. The magic was going deeper still. Like a supernatural fire, the golden liquid heated her skin and made it tingle, made her ache with exquisite longing for his touch.

She couldn't tease him a moment longer, couldn't play coy, couldn't do anything but desire him. Her arms reached out for him, drawing him down to her to feel her breasts. The sensation of his hands on her skin was so strong that she almost reached orgasm then and there.

"Do you want me, Dani?" he whispered. "Body and soul?"

"Yes! Oh, God, yes . . . don't stop! Don't ever stop!"

Jack bent his head down and suckled one nipple, holding it

in his teeth but not biting. He let go and did the same to the other one, then caressed her tits with his palms, increasing the sensual friction that the liquid made so pleasurable.

She let her legs fall open, thrusting her hips up helplessly. Dani was dying for the sensation of a big cock rammed inside her. His cock.

Jack put a hand on her belly and pushed her gently down. "Like I said, this is the good stuff." He dipped a finger into the jar and dripped a little of it onto her clitoris.

Dani felt erotic electricity shoot through her. But she couldn't come, not without him. Not without touching herself. She reached a hand down but he grabbed her wrist.

"Makes you lose control, doesn't it? Makes you want whatever you can get . . . as far in as it can go. You want your pussy fucked, I know you do."

She pushed up against his hand but again he forced her gently down to the floor. He began to caress the curved line at the bottom of her belly. "Beautiful. Like the curve of the moon." His gentleness made her tremble, and she trembled even more when his exploring fingers parted her labia. "I have something for you, Dani."

Too swiftly for her to see where it had come from, he produced a large dildo made of some smooth material. Not wood. Maybe ivory. There were thin straps running through a hole in one end. He touched the other end to her lips. "Lick it."

She opened her mouth and licked it thoroughly, wanting only to obey him and please him, so he would please her. The strange stuff in the last little jar had made her half-crazy with lust and longing for Jack's body, Jack's cock. But if he wanted to watch her suck a dildo, then that was all she wanted to do.

He watched her deep-throat the thing, his eyes glittering darkly. "That's enough. Get on all fours. And spread yourself. Think about something really hot and wild. Me and another guy double-fucking you. Lesbian pussy-pounding party. Young studs in bondage, hands behind their backs and cocks up. I don't care. Just stay wet."

Dani set the slick dildo to one side, kneeled down with her face on a folded towel, and reached around to pull her ass cheeks so far apart it almost hurt. He had to see pink. Her pussy was totally open. "Please," she whispered. "I want you in me . . . deep inside . . . fucking me until I scream . . . please!"

He didn't answer, just picked up the dildo and put the head of it inside her pussy, sliding it in a fraction of an inch at a time. "Take it slow. Have your hot fantasy inside your head and feel this thing inside your body. Here it comes." She gave a guttural moan when he thrust the rest of it in suddenly and hard. Then he tied the straps around each of her thighs, like a harness. "I want you to keep it in, Dani. Just let me look at you fully penetrated."

Feeling the big dildo all the way inside her, not fighting him when he tied the thin straps of the improvised sex harness tight, very aware that his eyes were on her every second, Dani felt a gigantic wave of pleasure pulse through her. He reached underneath and cupped her breasts, then took her nipples between his fingers.

Exquisitely sensitized by the liquid he'd smeared on her breasts, her nipples became even more erect. "I know how much you like this," he said softly, growling into her ear. "You said it goes right to your cunt. And right now your cunt is filled with something big and thick, and you want to be fucked, don't you? Like an animal. Mounted by your mate. Feeling a hot, stiff shaft deep inside you, moving hard and fast. I want you to turn into an animal . . . but not yet, Dani. Not yet." He tested the straps and tightened them a little, bringing the ends around her waist and tying them just under her navel.

With her face turned to one side, resting on the towel, she didn't see the next toys he brought out. But she felt them. He placed tiny, velvet-padded clamps on her tender nipples. Dani moaned, feeling his hands clasp her breasts and touch the clamps. His low voice reverberated against her neck.

"Wow. That is so fucking hot. You . . . totally aroused . . . on your knees. Strapped in a sex harness . . . hot nipples clamped. Doesn't hurt when it's done right, does it? Just makes you wild with desire. I have to tie you to tame you." He flipped her onto her back with careful strength and shucked his pants at last, kicking them into a corner. "Got you where I want you."

Too charged up to talk or even whisper, Dani put her arms around her thighs and lifted up her hips. Feeling simultaneously helpless and strong, she wanted to be shameless, wanted him to be excited by her submissive display, wanted to arouse him to the very limits of his self-control.

Jack stood over her, his heavily muscled legs apart, and stroked his cock. She felt a few drops of cum fall onto her belly and then he stopped stroking. His erection was so hard that his cock was right up against his tight lower abs.

"Give it to me," she breathed. "Please . . . please. I don't want this thing in me. I want you. Only you."

"Yeah. Now it gets real. Now it's nothing but your body and mine."

He reached down and pulled off one nipple clamp, pulling her tender flesh into a soft point before the softly padded clamp popped off. An erotic thrill flashed through her breast but before it was over, she felt the same thing happen on the other side. Dani let out a cry of pure pleasure. Jack squatted, letting his heavy balls and cock bump against her side. She wanted desperately to suck him and writhed until his big hand on her belly stilled her.

He untied the thin straps of the dildo harness and rubbed the red marks on her skin, using a little more of the liquid in the jar until the marks disappeared. As before, he flicked a few drops onto her exposed clitoris. Dani screamed under her breath. She had never known that sexual sensation could be so intense, never known that she could want a man so much.

"Pull out the dildo yourself," he said. "I want to see you lick your juice off it. Don't touch your clit. Just pull it out really slowly."

Dani grabbed the loose straps and pulled, feeling her pussy lips open to release the huge thing, looking up at Jack with half-closed eyes and seeing his slight smile as it came out, dripping. She opened her mouth and tongued it eagerly.

"No more," he growled. "My turn." He took it from her and set it aside, putting his mouth on hers and kissing her wildly. Then he stretched out on top of her and thrust his cock deep into her pussy, pinning her to the floor, fucking her for all he was worth, wrapping his arms around her shoulders and burying his face in her neck.

He stopped and caught his breath, rising slightly to look into her eyes. Jack stroked the damp hair back from her face with utmost tenderness, staying quietly inside her, so erect and so swollen that she couldn't move.

The sensation of his powerful body dominating her, filling her, was overwhelming. She felt tears rise without spilling from her eyes. Jack seemed to shimmer through them. "Don't morph," she whispered.

"I'm staying human." He still didn't move and Dani wondered how close he was to coming. He dropped his head again and rode her hard, giving an anguished moan that tore at her heart. He was holding her like he never wanted to let her go and never would.

Dani surrendered to him at last, enfolding him with all her womanly strength, pulling him inside her body, wishing she could soothe the rawness in his lonely soul. "Shh. Don't talk. Let's make love."

He rose up on his elbows but kept her pinned with his big cock. "Isn't that what we were doing?"

"That was outer-limits fucking. Hot and hard. No holds barred."

"Did you like it?"

"You know I did, tiger. You know just how to get to me. But now . . ."—she caressed his face tenderly—"it's time for some loving. The real thing."

She stroked his back, feeling a strange heat radiating from him.

"Do you love me, Dani?" The tiger stripes on Jack's skin were glowing intensely now, the difference between the black and white sharply clear.

"Yeah. Just as you are. Sexy beast."

"I love you . . . but . . . do you really want to stay here?" His growl held a potent joy. "Be mine for real?"

"I do." She turned her head and looked with wonder at her arms. The transformation was happening to her too.

The fur that stole over his body, soft and thick, was just like hers. The face of a great cat—a tiger—that stared down at her showed her own face mirrored in its blue eyes—a tigress.

We are one . . . and the same.

With a roar, the tiger pulled back and let his female, nameless now, arch and howl. She turned over on all fours, ready to be mounted. He grabbed her with unsheathed claws and penetrated her, deeply and completely. Like an animal. Like her mate.

There was no going back. She was his . . . forever.

Night of the Jaguar

Vivi Anna

1

Low rumbling growls sounded from the trio of jaguars as they slunk through the dense bush of the Amazon jungle. Rays from the sun streamed through the thick foliage, making erratic beams of light that reflected off their shiny fur as they crept around each tall tree. The beasts' muscles rippled through their lean bodies as they pounced over fallen rotting logs. Powerful and elegant, the giant cats possessed the jungle like great warriors protecting their land.

The leader, his solid black coat shimmering like polished onyx, bounded in front of the other two. Silently, he crept forward, his belly low to the ground as if hunting some unsuspecting prey. The other two jaguars lay on the forest floor, in the shadows, poised and ready to leap up if needed.

Each step the beast took, his muscular legs quivered with strain, and he growled softly in his throat. Pressed close to the ground, he inched forward on his stomach, his paws out in front. Claws extended, finding purchase in the dirt floor. Low pants came from his open mouth, and it looked as if the mus-

cles under his fur were moving, undulating, rearranging themselves into something else, something unnatural.

The beast started to change. Its body shifted, elongated. Its
paws stretched and narrowed. Claws retracted into flesh, and
pointed ears curled into themselves, disappearing from atop its
large square-shaped head.

The low rumbling growl became a pain-filled moan.

A great wind blew through the jungle, shaking trees and ripping leaves from the branches. The sound of the screaming wind
drowned out the deep cries from the beast writhing on the forest floor. Leaves, sticks, and debris swirled around in a growing
dust devil.

Just as quick as the wind erupted, it died. Eerie silence en-
cased the jungle. No other animal stirred in the surrounding
trees or the low dirt burrows. Time stood still for a few brief
moments.

Movement from the shadows disturbed the air and the scattered leaves on the ground.

A form strode into a ray of light. It was no longer a beast
with midnight fur and yellow glowing eyes, but a man. Stretching
his rangy limbs, he pushed his long black hair away from a
sharp angular face. Eyes that still glowed amber searched the
jungle with a keen awareness.

Taking a step forward, his lean muscular body rippled with
the movement. Sweat sheened the golden skin of his defined
chest, his flat stomach, and the dark coarse hair between his
powerful legs. Two jagged black markings, like lightning bolts,
lined his hips on either side, diagonally swooping down to a
point just above his groin.

He was as sleek and powerful as the black jaguar, a warrior
protecting his land.

Mara . . .

He crooked his head, as if to listen. Lifting his nose, he
scented the air.

Mara . . .

A low snarl rumbled in his throat as he took another step forward. The two spotted jaguars behind him stood and came to his call, rubbing up against his slick glistening thighs. Turning his head, he stared straight in front of him as if something or someone lurked there in his path.

His lips twitched. "I see you."

Fear invaded Mara's body as she struggled against the ropes binding her wrists and ankles to two trees. Spread apart in the shape of an X and naked, she felt laid out as if in sacrifice to an ancient god. Which was possible. For surely the golden-skinned man must be a god?

She'd never seen such a man. Long, lean, and darkly sexy. The sight of him, naked and glistening with sweat, with the two beasts at his sides took her breath. Despite her fear, she stared in awe.

He stopped a few feet away and scrutinized her with an intense interest. As his gaze traveled from her feet to her face, she had the distinct feeling of being caressed expertly by firm rough fingers. Her fright soon abated, and shivers of pleasure radiated through her body to gather in a ball of heat right at her center.

Mara reasoned she should be afraid and not aroused. Held captive and bound to the trees, with no way of escaping, she was at the mercy of the man in front of her. He could do anything he wanted to her and she couldn't stop him. Part of her, the primal and unexplained element deep within her, didn't want to stop him.

He took another step forward until he stood so close she could smell him. Wild and earthy, like a thunderstorm. Involuntarily, she licked her lips, tasting sweat on her tongue.

Without touching her, he scented her skin, nostrils flaring. Her eyes fluttered shut as his hot breath on her flesh sent shudders of delight over her. Goose bumps rose on her skin, and her nipples tightened into aching rigid peaks.

When she felt him pull back, she opened her eyes. She watched as his eyes dilated in lust, and he licked his lips as if the scent of her had made him hungry. She gasped when he dropped to his knees.

Desire gathered deep within her sex and she let her head fall back in rapture. He wasn't touching her yet, but the mere thought of him doing so sent her spiraling into bliss.

A far corner of her mind whispered that she should be scared, that she should scream for help. But the hushed sounds couldn't be heard over the hammering of her heart and the thundering throb in her sex.

The teasing was driving her insane. She hungered for him to touch her, even wanted to beg him to caress her skin, to trail his tongue over and into her flesh. The scent of her own lust floated up like musk perfume. She was hot and wet, anticipating the feel of him feasting on her juices.

At last Mara felt his hot breath brush over the intimate folds of her flesh. Her clit swelled in response, aching for attention.

Please, she wanted to beg. *Please touch me, taste me, take me.* But the words would not come. All she could do was moan her encouragement, will him to touch her throbbing pussy. She watched as he opened his mouth, the tip of his tongue peeking out from full sensuous lips. She gritted her teeth preparing for the sizzling whip of electricity she knew would come the moment he touched her . . .

Mara, wake up . . .

Mara Galas came awake with a jolt, nearly hitting her forehead on the seat in front of her. Just in time, her cousin Hector put his hand out to steady her.

"Wake up sleepy head. We're at the park entrance," he chuckled.

Yawning, Mara glanced out the bus window. They had arrived at the Manu Reserve in Peru. The gateway to the beautiful and mysterious Amazon rainforest. Mara had scrimped and saved out of her meager teacher's salary for two years, but had been dreaming of this trip for even longer. Something about the Amazon called to her. Now she was here in answer to that summons.

Hector tapped her on the head playfully. "You were twitching there pretty good. What were you dreaming about?"

Mara smiled, remembering the majestic creatures that stalked through her dream. Then she thought of the man that had transformed from the beast in the shadows. The tall, bronzed god who made her salivate with desire and quiver with pleasure. She remembered all too well the way his body rippled when he moved, and the impressive organ between his legs. Thinking about stroking her hand over his body, made her thighs tighten and tingle with lust. The dream had seemed so real.

"Jaguars," she coughed, putting her hand over her mouth to hide her heated cheeks.

"Jaguars? I can't promise we'll see any on this trip. But you never know." He patted her on the back and then moved to the front of the bus while the other passengers disembarked.

She watched him for a brief moment, chuckling at his bumbling efforts to help an elderly couple with their overstuffed packs. She was surprised that Hector had chosen to be a tour guide. He wasn't the friendliest person she knew. As a kid, he had been a bully, and constantly tormented her and his younger sister Ginessa. Thankfully, he had grown out of it.

Hefting her pack over her shoulder, Mara was relieved that she'd packed light. Hector had sent her a list of things to bring, and of items *not* to bring. She read in travel books that people, especially those on their first trek, tended to overpack. They were going to be hiking over uneven terrain, through dense foliage and possibly through muddy waters, and Mara didn't want to be carrying more weight than she absolutely needed. She may be green when it came to exotic travel, but she had prepared well for this trip.

As she shuffled down the narrow aisle of the tour bus, Mara's thoughts shifted to her ex-boyfriend, Clint. He was supposed to have been with her on this trip. They had started planning it after only six months of serious dating, as a way to celebrate their blossoming relationship. After another eight months of planning, and Clint's wandering eyes and hands, Mara told him to take his own hike, because he definitely wasn't going anywhere with her.

She knew she had made the right decision calling it quits, but sometimes, on important occasions like this one, Mara felt the lonely pull on her heart. That she had no one intimate to share this with saddened her.

The moment she stepped off the bus and inhaled the moist fragrant air of the land, Mara forgot about everything but the majestic sight before her. She knew it would be green and lush, but didn't expect the deep rich color to move her to tears.

Hector stepped up next to her and put his arm around her shoulders. "Beautiful isn't it?"

She shook her head, unable to assign words to her overwhelming feelings. "Beautiful? Hector, I never thought anything could be so spectacular."

"For a biology teacher, I imagine this is like an adolescent wet dream," Hector chuckled.

She laughed with him as she took in the majestic surroundings. Soon her thoughts strayed back to her dream, and the hot naked man stalking through the jungle. The jungle she was now standing in front of.

Sweat trickled down from under her ponytail of long, sable-colored hair and past the collar of her white T-shirt. Her skin began to tingle as a light perfumed breeze blew over her sweaty goose-bumped flesh. Thoughts of sultry sizzling sex popped into her mind as she viewed the forest. In her head, she imagined her body writhing naked and slick with sweat on the forest floor, a golden-skinned man with black hair mounting her from behind.

The firm hold of Hector's hand on her shoulder jerked her from her carnal images. She tore her gaze from the trees and glanced at him. He was looking at her expectantly.

"I'm sorry, what?"

Smiling, he tapped her head again with his index finger. "I said, are you ready to go?"

Turning back to the jungle, Mara took in a deep breath, cleansing her body with the clean crisp air. Tingles of anticipation made her knees weak and her belly clench. "Yes, I'm ready."

The seven-mile hike into the Acjanacu Pass was exhilarating. Mara identified various plant and animal life that she had only been able to read about before. She made notes in her travel diaries and took pictures, so she could share the experience with her class the next school year.

By the time the small tour group reached the campsite, in the high forest nestled in a thick cloak of clouds, exhaustion settled over Mara. Her T-shirt and shorts stuck to her skin as the humidity wrapped its sticky tendrils around her. After pitching her small tent and unrolling her sleeping bag, Mara wandered to the communal dining tent. She would get a small bite to eat, and then crawl into her sleeping bag for a long, deserving sleep.

Hector waved to her the moment she stepped through the canvas. Smiling, she walked over to him as he continued to converse with the young couple from Ireland.

After Mara greeted them, Hector put his arm around her and steered her back out of the tent. "How about some tea?"

"Sure."

"I have something I want to show you."

After brewing a pleasant herbal blend, Hector opened his pack and took out a small covered bundle the size of a man's wallet. Sitting down beside Mara on his bedroll, Hector carefully unwrapped the colored material.

Mara watched his face as he pulled on each piece of cloth. He looked like a man possessed. Whatever lay within the fraying fabric was something of incredible value, or Hector would never be so enthralled.

Mara remembered a time during summer holidays, when they were kids, when Hector had found what he had thought was a gold coin. It turned out to be a game token from one of those places like Chuck E. Cheese's, but he cherished that coin, polishing it every day, stroking it like a pet.

He had that same glassy look in his eyes as he finished unwrapping his new prize.

"Isn't it spectacular?"

Mara looked down into his hand. It was spectacular. She'd never seen anything so remarkable, except possibly in history books or archaeology texts.

The object Hector held was made out of jade. Shaped like a Mayan temple, with a flat roof and staggered steps on the sides, there was an open door at the top of the pyramid. Rays of gold shot out from the doorway like beams of light. At the bottom of the amulet, an animal crouched as if ready to attack any moment. It was a black jaguar, fashioned from onyx or some other black stone.

Mara gasped at the sight of the beast, staring at her, like an omen. Her stomach clenched, not in fear, but in anticipation. Of what, she couldn't fathom. The thought was right there at the edge of her mind like a clinging fog.

Her fingers itched to touch the talisman. "Where did you get it?"

"At one of the old ruins near the Yucatan." He sighed as he traced a finger over the exquisite markings. "About a month ago, I went digging at night. Something urged me toward a particular temple, and there it was laying in the dirt."

"Did you show it to anyone? Like the archaeological society?"

Hector closed his hand over the amulet and cradled it to his chest, a frown crinkling his face. "No. They'd just take it from me."

"Hector, that piece should be in a museum. It's too important to keep as a prize."

He scrambled up to his feet. "It's mine, Mara. I found it. It belongs to me."

Mara got to her feet, concerned with the rage in Hector's voice, and the way his brow glistened with sweat. "You'd get credit for the find. You know that. This isn't the first artifact you've dug up."

"But this is different." His eyes looked strange as he stared off into the distance. "I can't let go of it. I can't, not until . . ."

A rustling sound near the tent drew their attention. Mara looked toward the side of the canvas, but saw no shadows of anyone approaching. She turned back to Hector. He was staring at her with a mixture of anger and anguish on his face.

"You want the amulet," he stammered.

"What? No. Hector, are you all right? You look . . . frightened. Is something going on? Something you're not telling me?" She reached for him, but he pulled back clutching the amulet tight to his chest.

"No! You can't have it. I'm waiting until he comes."

"Who? What are you talking about?"

A loud thrashing noise came from outside the tent, near the tall bushes on the side of the camp. As Mara flinched at the violent sound, Hector brushed by her and out the tent flap. Worried about his erratic emotions, Mara followed him.

He was spooked about something. He didn't act like a man in control, but one running scared. She'd seen it before. In grade-school children, mind you, about to go to the principal's office, but the look was still the same. Frightened and nearly pissing their pants.

Hector stood a few feet away from the camp staring wildly into the surrounding trees. Dark shapes played across the ground like shadow puppets as the sun set. Mara came up to him, intent on touching his shoulder, to soothe him, give him some support. Maybe then, he would tell her what was really going on.

The beast came out of the jungle before she could reach Hector.

In a horrible flash of black and yellow, the animal was on Hector and ripping him apart. His screams echoed in her ears as she witnessed teeth and talons sinking into his flesh. Blood sprayed over her like a warm misty rain.

Without thinking, Mara rushed forward. She could not let Hector die. Reaching down to her leg, she unsheathed the small pocketknife she always carried on hiking trips. Leading with her weapon, she advanced on the snarling, savage scene in front of her.

Time stopped. Everything was a blur. Mara couldn't tell one thing from another. More screams echoed in her ears. But whose? Hers? She couldn't decipher the sounds as they resounded in her head.

Colors swirled in front of her eyes. Red. Black. Yellow. Always yellow. Amber eyes staring into her. Eyes of an animal, but solely aware. The beast looked into her. Into her soul, and memorized everything about her.

Before Mara spiraled down into a deep dark chasm, she heard voices around her. They were speaking, yelling, all at once. Different voices, different dialects. She couldn't understand what they were saying.

As the black swallowed her whole, she heard someone speaking, whispering in a desperate hush.

"She won't make it. It nearly tore her heart out."

2

The incessant beeping in her head finally forced Mara's eyes open. She blinked up at the white ceiling and realized instantly where she was. There was no mistaking those sounds or those pungent smells. She was in a hospital. St. Mercer's, in her hometown.

She tried to turn her head, but found it too stiff and sore to move. Licking her dry lips, she glanced to the side. Her mother, Lee, sat slumped in a chair, asleep.

"Mom?" she croaked. Her throat felt like crinkled paper.

Her mother jerked awake. Eyes wide and teary, she leaned on the bed and grasped Mara's hand.

"Oh, my baby. How do you feel?"

Mara concentrated on her body, feeling it, gauging it. She started at her feet and worked her way up. Nothing hurt immediately, more like a throbbing or dull ache. Surprisingly, she found that she felt tender, but on the mend.

"All right. A little sore in my chest and my neck."

Her mother sobbed and put her head to their joined hands.

The door to the room opened, and her sister Selena walked in carrying two cups of coffee.

"Ma, I got you . . ." She startled and sent coffee sloshing over the sides. "Holy shit, you're awake." She rushed to the bed, setting the coffees on the little table. "The doctors thought for sure you'd be out for days."

"Selena, your mouth," her mom chided.

Selena waved her slim jeweled hand at Lee. "Mara's awake Ma, who gives a rat's ass what comes out of my mouth."

Mara nearly choked as Selena bent down and smothered her in a fierce bear hug. Her perfume, overpowering as always, wafted up Mara's nose and nearly made her cough.

"Lena, you're choking your sister. Be gentle."

After she released Mara, she snorted at her mother. "What, I can't hug my sister? She nearly died, Ma. She's lucky to be alive at all. One hug isn't gonna kill her. Is it Mara?"

Mara wanted to chuckle and scream all at the same time. But the meaning of Selena's words sobered her instantly. She had nearly died. The attack had been real.

"Where's Hector?"

Selena glanced at Lee and raised her brow. Her mother clenched Mara's hand tightly.

"He didn't make it honey," her mother said, her voice tight with emotion.

Sighing, Mara closed her eyes. She had suspected as much the moment she woke up. Images of too much blood invaded her mind. She was sure that the animal had torn out his throat. No one could survive that. Her heart ached at the thought of his brutal death. His younger sister, Ginessa, would be devastated.

"We didn't think you were going to make it either," Selena commented.

Opening her eyes, Mara stared at her sister.

"The cat ripped open your chest."

"Selena!" her mother exclaimed.

Mara brought a shaky hand up to her breast. She touched her flesh through the thin cotton of her hospital gown. She could feel the ridges of stitched-up flesh under her palm. Taking a deep breath, she felt a tight pull on her skin like someone was yanking off a Band-Aid.

"Well, it's true, Ma. She might as well know the truth."

Mara raised her hand toward her sister. "It's all right. I do need to know." Selena stepped forward and grasped her hand tightly.

"How long have I been here?"

"Three days. They flew you in from Cusco. You spent a day there so the doctors could stitch you up. You lost a lot of blood, and they weren't sure . . ."

Mara squeezed her mom's hand when she couldn't finish the sentence. She had almost died. The doctors in Peru weren't sure she would make it.

The door opened again, and a doctor carrying a clipboard walked in. He looked shocked when he saw that Mara was awake and lucid.

"Well, Ms. Galas, you've decided to give us a major surprise and finally wake up. Ahead of schedule, I see," he joked as he glanced down at his clipboard. But Mara saw the concern and surprise in his eyes before he bent his head.

He came around the side of the bed, took her temperature, and checked her eyes with his little penlight. "I'm Doctor Zerner. How's everything feeling? Any pain?"

Mara shook her head. "I feel a little tight in my chest, but that's it."

Nodding, he glanced at her mother and Selena. "Could you ladies give us a few moments? I'd like to talk to Mara alone."

Her mother leaned forward and kissed Mara's cheek. "I'll see you later, honey."

Selena squeezed her hand, but said nothing. Mara could see

the emotions welling up inside her. She knew her sister used humor to cover her pain. They had been through enough together to figure that out.

After her mother and Selena left the room, the doctor helped Mara sit up a little, so he could untie and pull her gown down over her breasts to her stomach. When she was lying back, Mara risked a peek at her chest.

Nothing could prepare her for what she saw.

Three long, dark pink, puckered wounds ran diagonally across her chest. The longest had to have been around eight inches, starting at the top of her right breast and ending at her second rib, under her left breast. Tears filled her eyes as she stared at the disfigurement. How did she ever survive?

"Believe it or not, you're healing very well. It's fantastic how fast your body is regenerating." He covered her back up and patted her shoulder. "I'm extremely pleased with your progress, Mara. You'd never know that this happened only five days ago."

"When can I go home?"

Picking up the clipboard, he wrote some notes on her chart. "Another few days. You need to be up and moving around before I can consider it. Your body could still go into shock." He touched her hand. "I'll have a nurse come by and see if you're up for a walk."

Nodding, Mara smiled as the doctor left. Moving her arms, she pushed herself up against the pillow. Her stitches pulled and pinched, but she sucked in a breath and gritted her teeth. She wanted to go home. She suddenly felt the need to be in the security of her house. Maybe then, she could digest what exactly happened to her in the jungle.

And why she felt like it had a meaning beyond her comprehension.

After several aided walks around the hospital, and badgering the nurses to let her move on her own, Mara was exhausted and sore. Instead of sitting vigil at her bedside, she convinced her mom and sister to go home and get some decent rest. She assured them both that she would not drop back into a coma. She was wide awake and aware. Very aware.

The attack on her was a blur, but she could still vividly picture the beast on top of Hector and feel the desperate need to save him. Guilt that she had failed slashed through her heart. Reflexively, she wiped at her arms, still able to feel the blood that had sprayed there.

Climbing back into bed, Mara nestled into the warm wool blankets. As she lay her head back on the plumped-up pillows, her eyelids shut. They were hot and heavy, impossible to keep open. She didn't fight it. She knew she needed the sleep. A healing slumber.

She also knew the darkly erotic images would come, but she was too tired to care.

The dream came almost immediately.

Dusk settled over the trees. The waning sunlight played through the canopy of leaves, forming long dark shadows on the forest floor. A fresh scent perfumed the air, as though any minute it would rain. Mara loved that smell.

She ran through the jungle. Her heart thumped in her chest like the rhythmic drumming of a tribal ceremony. Sweat trickled down her back and from her brow. She was naked, her hair unbound and blowing freely around her face. The light breeze played over her skin, eliciting shivers from her flesh.

Someone was chasing her. But she wasn't afraid.

In fact, she felt vibrant and excited. Arousal drew her nipples into hard tight buds, and sent ripples of desire between her thighs. Her sex dripped with ravenous need. She knew what he would do to her when he caught her. And she hungered for it.

As she jumped over a fallen tree, Mara glanced over her shoulder at her pursuer.

Wet with sweat, his long black hair brushed back from his gorgeous, sharply angled face. His full sensuous lips parted in a snarl. He looked wicked and dangerous as he chased her, his chiseled naked body heaving with the effort. The dark tattoos lining his pelvis flowed like black water when he moved.

Mara wanted to trace her tongue down those black lines to the large cock hanging between his muscular thighs. Already she could feel the full, ridged length of him in her mouth. She hungered for it. For him.

She kept running, but slowed. This was the game. Catch me if you can. She knew he could. He was powerful and graceful, and had no problem capturing his prey.

He seemed tired of the pursuit, because in two long strides he was upon her. Nipping her at the waist, he lifted her off the ground and spun her around to press her roughly against a tree. The bark bit into her back as he moved into her, possessing her completely with his body.

"I have you now, *mi gatito*. You cannot escape."

His voice, low and gruff, made little quivers race up and down her skin. She struggled against his hold, wanting to feel his power over her. His hand moved up along her side, up her arm, brushing lightly against the side of her breast, to her face. He cupped her cheek with his palm and tilted her head up toward him.

Suddenly, a sense of dread washed over her. She didn't want to look him in the face. She didn't want to see his eyes. Because she feared what color they would be.

But she couldn't resist. With a sigh of relief, she saw that his eyes were dark, almost black, and dilated with desire. Not the glowing yellow she had been expecting.

Bending down, he took her mouth roughly, entering her lips with his tongue.

He tasted wild, like the earth. Diving her hands into the wet silk of his hair, she savored his flavor with her own testing and teasing. Nibbling his lips, she swept her tongue over his, sampling him.

As they kissed, he moved down her body and cupped her breasts with his palms. He squeezed and molded them, flicking his thumbs over her nipples. Mara groaned into his mouth as he pulled each pebbled bud between his thumb and forefinger and twisted them. Exquisite glorious pain shot through her body, straight to her center. Her pussy started to throb. She parted her legs in response to ease the ache. But only the full length of his cock would satisfy her burning need.

After one final nibble on her bottom lip, he pressed kisses to her chin and over to her ear. While licking the lobe, he whispered hungrily to her.

"I smell your lust for me, *gatito pequeno*. Do you want me to fuck you?"

Her knees buckled at the sound of his harsh words. She liked how he dominated her, not only with his body, but also with his words. He was in control. She knew it, as did he. There was no mistaking the possessive way he moved his hand down her body, feeling her skin as he traveled to her sex. Slowly he slid his fingers between her swollen labia, and parted her.

She knew she was wet and dripping along the insides of her thighs. She'd never been this lusty before, this wanton. She felt liberated and vulnerable at the same time. The conflict only made her hotter.

Moving his fingers back and forth over her soft folds, he found her clit and pressed on it. Gasping, she dug her nails into his shoulder to prevent her body from falling to the ground. It would not take much to push her over the edge into orgasm. Already her body vibrated in ecstasy. Her thighs tingled, and her belly tightened in anticipation.

With ease, her lover slid two long fingers into her. He moved them up and down and swirled them around to feel every inch of her inside. Slowly, he pushed another finger into her and spread them apart. Moaning from the intense pressure in her sex, Mara raked her fingers down his shoulders and over his chest.

He groaned loudly and bit the flesh over her collarbone. The pain surprised her, and Mara jerked back trying to get away. But he held her still, immobile, with his mouth and his hand deep inside her, moving up and down, his thumb flicking over her aching clit. Abruptly, pain transformed into pleasure, and Mara pushed against him, asking him for more. To do what he wanted. Anything to keep the hot flow of sensation surging through her.

"You are mine, *mi gatito*. No one may possess you but me."

Slipping his hand from her pussy, he grabbed her around the waist and pulled her away from the tree. His other hand moved around her back and down to her ass. He caressed one cheek, and slid his fingers into the valley between them. He turned her in his arms so that her backside nuzzled into his groin, against the solid length of his cock.

As he rubbed his throbbing organ against her, she could feel him grow hotter and harder. Swallowing, she didn't know if she could handle the full length of him. He was big and thick and like steel against her cheeks.

One hand gripped her breast, and the other cupped her as he nestled in behind, licking the back of her neck.

"I want you, *gatito*. I want you on your hands and knees."

Yes, she thought. Yes, whatever you want. The ache between her legs pushed at her tolerance. She'd never felt a throb of desire so intense, so passionate, that it made her grit her teeth to stop from begging. To beg him to release her from her craving, to push her past that point of pleasure and into rapture. Never in all her years had she hungered for a man, for him to take her, to fuck her until she screamed.

Mara knelt on the ground. Spreading her legs, she tilted her ass up to him, tempting him to take her. Before he covered her with his body, he watched her. She could feel his stare on her open, glistening sex. His scrutiny of her intimate flesh made her groan. She wriggled her ass, enticing him to take her now. She felt like a whore waving her wares in his face. And that made her hotter, wetter, hungrier for his cock deep inside her.

"Please," she begged. "Please take me. I am yours."

With a fierce growl, he was on her, nestled against the cheeks of her ass. One hand braced on her back, he guided his cock into her. He went slowly, although she could tell by the vibrations in his arms and legs that he wanted to ram into her. Gritting her teeth, she spread her legs farther apart, opening for him. She could feel her pussy stretch wide to accommodate the girth of his cock. He kept pushing into her and still she stretched until she could feel his balls hanging against her mons, tickling her with their coarse hair.

"Oh by the gods, *gatito*, you are deliciously tight."

He started to move. Sliding slowly at first, letting her adjust to his thick throbbing penis deep inside her sex, the tip touching the door to her womb. With each thrust, Mara gasped. Her whole body burned with need. If she didn't reach orgasm soon she was sure she'd combust from the inside out.

Gripping her hips, her lover increased his rhythm, his sac smacking against her with each thrust. The sounds of their flesh slapping together echoed through the jungle.

Mara could also hear quick gasping mewls around her. She soon realized that they came from her own mouth, as he pounded into her again and again. She shook her head, and moaned. She couldn't take any more. It was too much; he was too much. With each thrust, she thought she'd rip in two. If only that would ease her ache. She had to do something or her mind would burst. Already she felt light-headed and out of breath. Reaching down between her legs, she found her clit. It throbbed painfully, and she flinched when her fingers touched it. Pressing down, she pushed through her pain and found that sizzling whip of pleasure coiling through her body.

Grunting, he rammed into her, falling over her back to nuzzle into her neck, his hands finding her breasts. While he continued to slide in and out, he squeezed and pulled her nipples.

Mara was almost there. Her orgasm hovered just on the edge of her body. One more flick on her clit and she would free fall over. Turning her head, she wanted to look into his face as she came. Her dream lover, the man that she hungered and lusted for like no other.

His yellow, glowing eyes pierced her sanity.

Mara bolted up in the bed, gasping. Cold sickly sweat slicked her skin and hair. Shaking, she clutched her blanket to her breasts. Her heart hammered painfully under her ribs. She could feel it thumping through the thick fabric of the wool and through her wounds.

Taking in deep cleansing breaths, Mara tried to calm herself. Her body still quaked from fear and desire. She still could feel the throb of lust between her legs. It pumped in sync with her racing heart.

She'd never had a dream so vivid before, so painfully real. If she moved her hand down to her sex, she imagined that she would find him still embedded inside. That was how real he felt. His wild smell still lingered in the air. Still slicked her skin.

Closing her eyes, she laid back down on the pillows. She needed to calm. She needed to reason that it was only a dream. A figment, although vivid, of her fertile imagination. Moving her hands over her chest, she felt her erect nipples. They tingled and ached, rubbing against the fabric of her gown. Shifting her legs, she felt the sticky residue of her lust on the inside of her thighs. Never had she been so wet. Not even after having an orgasm.

Taking in more calming breaths, Mara tried to reason through her dream. She was still suffering from her attack. Naturally, she'd been transported back to the Amazon. It was the presence of her dark dream man that puzzled and unnerved her. The dark sexy man with glowing yellow eyes.

Licking her lips, she noticed how dry her mouth was. She reached over to grab the plastic cup of water on the little side table. The movement shot jolts of pain down her arm. Sitting up again, Mara untied her gown and slipped it off her arm. She looked sideways at her shoulder where the pain seemed to be radiating from.

In between her shoulder and neck was a red mark. A deep crimson impression of teeth. She'd been bitten.

Staring at the mark, she tried to stay calm. Her dream man had bitten her in her dream. *Her dream.* So why was she staring at his teeth impressions on her flesh?

As Mara unlocked the door to her house, she breathed a sigh of relief. She needed to be home. Surrounded by her things, she thought she would be able to heal much faster. Although, according to Dr. Zerner, he'd never seen more rapid rejuvenation. He said it was a miracle.

Miracle or not, Mara didn't think it was her body that needed the most therapy. She hadn't had another vivid dream like the one in the jungle, but her thoughts were . . . disturbing.

Padding into the entry, Mara glanced around at her quaint home, taking in her small but cozy living room. Everything looked normal, in its place. Vases of flowers spotted the room. Well wishes from family and friends.

Kicking her shoes off, Mara wandered into the kitchen, tapping the glass of her freshwater aquarium on the counter. It was her way of saying hello to her fish. They probably didn't appreciate it, but it was the only way to get any acknowledgment from the little buggers. Fish weren't the friendliest pets to have.

After watching them swim for a moment, Mara wandered into the living room and looked at each of the vases, reading the little notes that went with them. Sympathetic messages from co-workers and neighbors, relatives she never saw. And one luscious bouquet of tiger lilies from Clint.

Taking the card, she plopped down on her deep green sofa and read it. *I miss you. Love, Clint.* Even now, it was always about him. How he felt, what he wanted. A wishing you well would have been appreciated. Ripping the card in two, she let the pieces flutter to the floor. Bastard. If she ever saw him again, she'd . . . she'd rip his throat out.

Mara gasped as a gory scene slammed into her mind.

Clint lying on the floor of her bedroom. Mara crouched over him, licking at his torn, bloody neck.

Mara buried her head in her hands. Rubbing at her eyes, she tried to erase the gruesome images. More of what she had suffered in the hospital. Several times, she had glanced at people, the nurses, the orderlies—even Dr. Zerner—and saw them at her mercy.

Most of her thoughts had been sexual in nature. This image of Clint was all fury and violence.

The shrill ring of her phone startled her. Reaching to the table alongside the sofa, Mara picked up the receiver.

"Hello?"

"Mara? It's Ginessa."

Mara closed her eyes and let her head fall back on the sofa cushions. Hector's sister. And her friend. Her heart ached for her cousin, for the grief she must be suffering.

"Ginessa. I'm so sorry."

"Thanks." There was a long pause, and then, "How are you doing? Lee told me you were on the mend."

Mara rubbed her hand over her chest where the wounds were quickly vanishing. "I'm getting the stitches out in a couple of days. My doctor's in shock at how fast I'm healing."

Another silence filled the void. Mara wanted to say so many

things, but didn't know how. Without hurting Ginessa all over again.

"Ginessa . . . I tried . . ."

"Don't. You don't need to torture yourself, Mara. There was nothing you could have done. Understand? Nothing. You did too much already and almost died because of it."

Sighing, Mara felt tears running down her cheeks. "I wish I could come for the funeral."

"Don't worry about it. It's going to be small, low-key." Ginessa paused again. Mara could tell she wanted to say more. There was something in Ginessa's tone that told Mara there was a whole lot more that she wasn't saying. "Listen, did Hector say anything or do anything to lead you to believe that he was in some sort of trouble?"

The amulet.

The moment Mara thought of it, shivers ran up and down her back, and beads of sweat formed on her upper lip.

"He found an artifact of some sort. He was acting weird about it, right before . . ." Mara paused. She didn't want to think about the attack again. "Why? What's up?"

"I don't know. Hector and I weren't close anymore. He started pulling away a few years ago. I hardly saw him, or talked to him. But about a month ago, he called me and said that he wanted me to see something. Something he found. He said it would make him rich, powerful."

"It must have been the amulet he showed me."

"Do you have it?"

"No. Wasn't it in his . . . personal affects?"

"No. I have his stuff, and there doesn't seem to be anything of real value. Nothing he would be so . . . intense about."

Mara could hear Ginessa's voice waver. There was something she was keeping inside, unsaid. It almost sounded like she was afraid.

"Ginessa, what's going on? Are you all right?"

"I don't know. I feel strange. Like I'm being watched. Everywhere I go, I feel a presence. Like I'm being stalked."

A black jaguar ran through the trees into a shadow. As it stepped out of the gloom, it was no longer a cat, but a man. Her dream lover.

Mara shook her head to jar the image from her mind. The phone trembled in her hand.

Ginessa sighed. "I'm being silly, I know. Mom's taking Hector's death hard. So I'm in charge of everything, you know. I'm just tired."

"I know."

"Well, I've probably tired you out. Get some rest. I'll talk to you soon."

Before Mara could respond, Ginessa hung up the phone. A sense of alarm crept up on her as she set the receiver back in the cradle. The amulet was somehow important. But how could it be related to Hector's attack? An animal killed him. Not a person.

Despite her concern, a yawn escaped her lips. Mara got up from the sofa and shuffled down the short hall to her bedroom. She was tired and achy. More than she wanted to admit. Dr. Zerner told her to take as many short naps as she needed throughout the day. It would still be some time before she was fully recovered.

Still, after Ginessa's phone call, she didn't think she could sleep. Too many images filled her head. Memories of the attack, and of something else. Dreamlike thoughts of the majestic jaguars running through the jungle, but she found them to be more substantial, more real than just nightly imaginings. As if they were a message of some kind.

Looking around her room, she noticed everything to be neat and orderly. She knew that her mom and sister had come over before her release from the hospital. Wanting, needing some space and solitude, she had asked them to drop her off at home without coming in with her.

Her bags from the trip were on her bed, untouched. She would unpack and then get some rest.

Picking up her daypack, Mara upended it on the bed. Her camera, notebooks, water canteen, pack of gum, and pocket-knife fell out onto the flowered quilt. Swallowing, she looked away from the knife and focused on her notebooks. There were two of them. She picked one up and thumbed through it. Only five pages had been written on; the others were painfully blank. As she neared the last few pages, something heavy and green fell out from between the paper.

With a cry of dismay, Mara dropped the notebook onto the bed. Her hand shook as she reached down toward the blanket to what lay there.

The amulet.

How did it get in her pack? She remembered Hector still cradling it in his hands when they had left the tent. Did one of the tour group discover it on the ground after the attack and put it in her pack, thinking it belonged to her?

A tingling crept through her fingers as she picked it up. The jade was smooth and cool in her hand. She rubbed her thumb over the markings, feeling the skill and artisanship of the artifact. It was stunning. How it had managed to stay in its flawless form, she didn't understand. It had to have been close to two thousand years old.

Wherever she touched it she felt pins and needles in her extremities, as if from falling asleep or clenching them too hard. The sensation spread up her arms like electricity.

Panic speared through Mara as her shoulders and neck started to prickle. But she couldn't let go of the amulet. It was as if it were glued to the palm of her hand.

As the shivering sensation spread down her torso and into her legs, she sat down on the edge of the bed. Fear seized her when her vision started to fog. Things in her room became blurry and unrecognizable.

Her head began to swim, and the light in the room faded. Mara was suspended in the dark. She didn't know if she was awake or unconscious.

Suddenly, bright blinding light flashed before her eyes and she felt like she was floating in the air like a helium balloon. Blinking away the white spots, she found herself standing in a courtyard of emerald green grass, and looming before her was an ancient Mayan temple, like the one on the amulet.

It couldn't be possible. She closed her eyes and opened them again. The temple was still in front of her. Only now, people were walking up and down the stone steps. Dark-haired, golden-skinned people in sarongs and waist wraps.

She could feel soft grass under her feet. She glanced down and saw that she wore no shoes, and, to her shock, no top either. She was bare-breasted and unscarred, with only a cloth wrap around her hips that barely covered her crotch.

Lifting her hands, she cupped her breasts, running her thumbs over her nipples. Two gold hoops pierced both pebbled peaks. Slipping a finger through one, she pulled. Jolts of pleasure shot through her body, aiming straight between her legs. She cried out in surprise at the intense sensation.

These were not her breasts. In fact, when she looked down at herself, she was not in her body. This form was fuller, more voluptuous. And the skin darker. She smoothed a hand over her hair and grabbed the ends to inspect them. This hair was darker and longer, with beads woven into the strands.

What was going on? Where was she? Was this a dream? If it was, it was the most intense, vivid dream she had ever had. She could smell the sweet scent of orchids in the air, and could feel the warm breeze brush over her flesh, the weight of the jade and gold cuffs she wore on her wrists. Cuffs that bore jaguar insignias.

Mara glanced around uncertainly. Before she could decide on what to do next, two other women, dressed in similar garb, approached her, broad grins on their brown faces.

One of the women took her arm, pulling her toward the temple stairs. "You must come. He is waiting for you."

"What? Who?"

The other woman took her other arm. "He summoned you. You must not keep him waiting."

Mara struggled against their grips, but both women were very strong. "I think you have the wrong lady."

Both women chuckled, and one of them said, "You always fight the summons, but you know that Xalvador desires no one but you."

Xalvador. The name seemed to soften something inside Mara as the women pulled her up the steps. It was somehow familiar to her, yet she could not discern from where.

As they neared the entrance to the temple, a mammoth of a man stepped out into the sunlight. He wore a similar wrap at his waist, and metal cuffs on his wrists. But Mara's eyes were riveted to the black tattoos that started just above his hip bones and swooped down under his cloth, just like the dark man in her dreams. He also had similar tattoos circling his biceps.

"I will take her from here." His deep voice rumbled over her like thunder.

The women bowed their heads and scurried away, giggling.

Mara could do nothing but stare up at him, frozen on her spot. He was one of the biggest men she'd ever seen.

"Are you going to come quietly this time, or do I have to carry you again?"

On a soft cry, Mara turned to run back down the steps. Maybe if she ran fast enough she could transport back to her room. Where it was safe and secure.

Before she could even reach the first step, the giant grabbed her around the waist and lifted her off the ground. As easy as lifting a child, he spun her around and hefted her over his right shoulder like a duffel bag. As he marched into the temple, Mara kicked and screamed. But he just laughed.

"I hope one day to find a woman as spirited as you. Xalvador has picked well."

As they crossed the room, Mara could hear female squeals and giggling. Mara couldn't see what was going on, but she could hear it, smell it, and feel it.

"I found her, Xal."

The mammoth flipped her up and set her on the ground. She fumbled when she turned. The sight before her was not something she ever expected to see.

"Come, kitten, we have been waiting for you."

He was there, her dream lover. Lying on a soft rug on the floor, surrounded by five naked, writhing women and another equally gorgeous man, he held out his hand toward her. She stared into his eyes, drawn to him. Mara gasped when she felt her feet move, stepping into the throng of naked people. Smiling at her, he stood and grasped her hand.

He was unclothed and glorious. As he pulled her close, she noticed his erect cock. The first pangs of desire flared between her legs. He wrapped his arms around her, and nuzzled into her neck. She could feel the iron length of him digging into her hip. While he pressed kisses to her neck and ear, she was immobile, as if she had no control over her body. She couldn't push away from him. And if she looked deep into her heart, she found she had no desire to.

If this was real—and lord, it certainly felt real—she wanted to experience it. Wanted to experience him. Before she had only thoughts and distant feelings of him, but even then she had never burned so greedily for anyone. The mere press of his lips on her skin nearly brought her to her knees in surrender.

"I love how you taste," he breathed into her ear, and lathed her lobe with his tongue.

Shivers of delight surged over her, traveling at light speed directly to her sex. Instantly, she started to drip with desire.

As he nibbled on her chin making his way to her mouth, Mara could feel a second pair of hands on her. She flinched in shock as someone removed her wrap from around her hips. She glanced down and saw another woman at her feet, slowly caressing her calves and making her way up her legs.

Mara would have protested but it felt too good to argue. She felt languid and pliable, like clay. Helpless to do anything but to take pleasure in the hands and mouth on her flesh.

On a sigh of pure bliss, Mara parted her lips as Xalvador pressed his mouth to hers. His wild taste was no surprise to her, and she relished it with her tongue on his. His kiss was almost savage as he nipped and tugged at her lips with his teeth, plundered her mouth with his tongue. Giving in to him, she wrapped her arms around him and held on for the wild ride.

Xalvador leaned back for a moment and stared into her eyes, his brow furrowing. "Something is different about you. You have given in too easily. Where is your fight, kitten? I was looking forward to your claws."

Mara paused, unsure what to say. Bringing a hand up to her face, she rubbed her fingers over her lips. It was not her mouth, but that of the woman's body she occupied. Could he taste the real her inside? Did he know that she was not truly his "kitten"? That somehow she had been transported into this woman's body. Because surely, that was what had occurred. Mara had no other explanation for what was transpiring. What would happen to her if he found out?

"If you do not kiss me again, you will find out where my claws are," she said haughtily, hoping she sounded like his woman.

Moving his hands up, he cupped her cheeks, keeping her face still, and stared hard into her eyes. He smiled. "Hmm, not the answer I was expecting. Where oh where, has my little Lareina gone? Let us find out."

Without warning, Xalvador bent her backward, forcing her down to the floor. She was lying back on the soft fur rug, Xalvador kneeling on one side of her, and the other women gathering around her brushing up against her body.

Leaning down, Xalvador kissed her cheek and then her chin, teasing her with the soft press of his lips. She parted her lips in invitation, but he kissed around her open mouth, chuckling when she turned her head to find him.

"I see you want to play a new game."

He moved his hands over her, molding her breasts, flicking the hoops up and down. The slight movement sent a sizzling crack of electricity through both nipples. Writhing from the sensation, Mara could feel her sex moisten even more in response. She parted her legs to lessen the throb, but the cool air against her skin just increased the ache deep inside her pink folds.

He caressed her arms and down to her fingers. He linked them with his and lifted her arms up and over her head, to press her hands against the floor.

With a nod from Xalvador, one of the women took hold of her arms, pinning them tightly above her head. Mara struggled, but could not move. Two other women spread Mara's legs wide apart, holding her ankles firmly to the ground.

Mara cried out while her legs were yanked apart. She felt open and vulnerable, out of control. Xalvador stood and stepped in between her parted legs. He looked down at her, taking in his fill of her exposed form.

"So beautiful you are, my pet. I love to look at you, to watch you. You are most enchanting when you are deep in the throes of passion. So hot and wet, dripping for me."

Mara squirmed under the hold the women had on her, but she couldn't deny her increasing lust. She liked what he was doing; she liked that she had no control, and that he could command the other women to touch and taste her. She would revel in it. Enjoy it. Just thinking about the possibilities made her nipples tingle, her pussy gush in anticipation.

Kneeling between her legs, Xalvador placed a hand on each of her thighs, pressing his fingers into her flesh.

"Let me see if we can make you come."

Before deserting her, the two remaining women hovering on either side of Mara touched her body. Starting with her shoulders, they caressed her skin lovingly. Moving down, they soon touched her breasts. Skilled fingers caressed and molded her nipples, coaxing low moans from her lips.

While the women played with her breasts, Xalvador slowly made his way up her thighs. Rubbing his hands in circles, he inched closer and closer to her sex, all the while watching her face.

Mara's breath hitched in her throat, as his fingers brushed over the light sprinkling of hair over her mound. Like a soft breeze, his hands swept over her, careful not to touch too much too soon. He was teasing her, and it was driving her insane.

The throb in her pussy intensified, hovering right on the line between pleasure and pain. If she had free reign over her hands, she would have slid them in between her nether lips and eased her own suffering. But she couldn't. He wouldn't let her. She was at his mercy.

As Xalvador continued to tease her sex with light brushings of his fingertips, the women at her breasts leaned down to suckle on her nipples. At her right breast, the woman slid her tongue into the gold hoop and flicked it up and down. Jolts of pleasure whipped through Mara's body. She gasped at the sudden sensations coursing through her and in her.

While the talented tongues of the women continued to lap and suck on her aching buds, Mara writhed on the floor, arching her back. She pushed her pelvis up, in hopes that Xalvador would ease her torture. That he would lick and suckle her clit, and fill her with his fingers, his tongue, anything to push her over the edge to orgasm.

Her wishes did not go long unfulfilled. Lying down on his stomach between her spread legs, Xalvador parted her with his thumbs. She could feel his hot breath on her intimate flesh as he nuzzled his face into her. Lightly at first, he trailed his tongue up and down her slit, swirling the tip as he reached her opening.

Heaving, Mara thrashed about against the hands that held her still. The torment of his tongue sent her spiraling under waves of pleasure. Each time he neared her throbbing pearl she thought she'd drown from the agony of near release.

"Oh God, please," she moaned.

As if bowing to her wishes, Xalvador nudged her clit with the tip of his tongue. Mara jerked up in response to the hot lash of pleasure that whipped over her. With one hand, he pressed her down to the floor, keeping her still while he continued his assault on her flesh. He lapped at her sex, concentrating on her clit, suckling on it in between strokes of his tongue.

With ease, he slid two fingers into her opening. Instantly, her sex slurped at his digits, eager for more. He didn't disappoint, as he slipped in another, swirling them around in circles. She could feel him pressing against her velvety flesh, as if in search for just the right spot. She prayed he'd find it and end her pleasurable agony.

The scorching heat between her legs was quickly nearing unbearable. Mara was close to climaxing. The muscles in her belly and thighs tightened, preparing her for the overwhelming rush of ecstasy. A few more flicks on her aching nub and she'd tumble over the edge.

As he continued to thrust his fingers in and out, pushing as deep as he could go, Xalvador suckled on her clit. She could feel his teeth scrape against her sensitive flesh as he sucked on her, and she cried out from the delight of it.

With one final lunge of his fingers as deep as they would go, he probed them around, feeling her. All of her. Clamping her eyes shut against the sudden rush of pleasure, she screamed as he found her spot, the fleshy mound on the inside of her vagina. He pressed hard just as he clamped down on her clit with his lips.

She came like a volcano. White blinding light flashed behind her eyes, and she couldn't get her breath. Thrashing about, she finally was able to pull her arms free. Instinctively she grabbed onto Xalvador's head, pulling on his hair, to release her from the electrifying hold he had her in. But he didn't succumb to her attempts. He continued to lick her clit and move his fingers inside, prolonging her orgasm.

Another powerful wave of pleasure crashed over her. Again, her body tightened and writhed on the floor. She couldn't take any more. It was too much. She was certain to go insane as sizzling hot flicks of pleasure assaulted her body one right after another, until she could not think beyond the sensations deep in her sex.

Finally, she stopped fighting, and rode the waves of pleasure until she was spent.

After several minutes, Mara was able to move. The women had relinquished their hold on her. Slowly, she opened her eyes. Xalvador was still in between her legs but sitting up watching her. His mouth glistened with her juices.

He grinned at her. In between his full lips, she saw his teeth. They were straight, white, and elongated like the fangs of an animal.

Mara screamed.

The high-pitched sound echoed in her ears, jolting her from her reverie. As if sucked out by a powerful vacuum, Mara was no longer lying on the floor in the temple but curled up in a ball on her bed racked with violent shivers.

She threw the amulet across the room. Then her stomach

rolled over. Moving to the edge, she threw up on the floor. After heaving until she was dry, Mara rolled over back into a tight ball and rocked herself.

Although sweaty and shaking, Mara still felt the pangs of desire through her body. Thighs tingling, nipples achy and sore, and her sex still weeping with intense need. Had it been a dream? Did holding the amulet induce an imagining so vivid and real that she could still taste it in the air and on her lips? Closing her eyes against tears, she wanted to scream. She couldn't go on like this. Her body could not possibly take the torture on her senses for much longer. She either had to exorcise her dream lover from her mind and body or somehow find him, and fulfill all her carnal hungers.

4

As Dr. Zerner clipped the last of her stitches, Mara stared at her face in the full-length mirror on the inside of the doctor's door. Dark circles lined her sunken eyes. She couldn't sleep. Her dreams were keeping her awake, thrumming with nerves, just on the brink of total climax. Never in her life had she reached such heightened sexual awareness. About herself and others. She desired more, but knew her cravings would be her undoing. She could feel not only her body, but also her soul unraveling with each passing day.

Something more than a savage attack had happened to her that night in the jungle. Her chest had been ripped open as well as her sexual appetites.

"There, last one." Dr. Zerner stood back and admired his handy work. Smiling, he looked up at her. "They look great, Mara. It won't be long before they start to fully heal. Eventually they'll fade enough that we could use a laser to make them completely vanish."

"Thanks, Dr. Zerner."

He turned to set his clippers on the table, while Mara was

able to button up her blouse. Because of the stitches, she'd been going without a bra. Made things easier.

"Is there anything else you want to talk about? Any other issues you've been having?"

Mara hesitated. Should she tell him about her dreams?

Dr. Zerner furrowed his brow. "Mara, is there something?"

"I've been having vivid dreams. Extremely vivid."

"About what?"

"Jaguars."

Nodding, Dr. Zerner patted her hand. "That's not uncommon. One attacked you. It's only natural that your fears are materializing in your dreams."

"Yeah, but they're turning into men, and men are turning into jaguars. I'm also hallucinating during the day. Seeing things that can't, or shouldn't be there. I can feel things, see things, and smell things. Things that can't possibly be real."

Narrowing his eyes, Dr. Zerner scrutinized her. If he could read her face, he would know that she was scared. Terrified that she was slowly losing her mind.

"Okay, let's have a look at your eyes. Maybe you sustained a head injury we didn't pick up the first time."

Picking up his penlight, he leaned forward and lightly touched her head. The press of his fingers on her skull sent delicious shivers racing down her neck. Instantly she perked up, wanting more of that touch. While he looked into her eyes, Mara pushed at his hand with her head, like a cat rubbing against its owner for attention. A low purr started in her throat.

Startled, Dr. Zerner pulled back. "Mara, what . . ."

With incredible speed, Mara jumped off the examination table and had Dr. Zerner pushed up against the door, her body pressing intimately into his. Growling low, she nuzzled her nose into his neck and rubbed her body over his.

"Mara, stop."

She didn't want to stop. He smelled good, like spiced rum. If she could, she wanted to run her hands all over his body feeling his warm flesh against her skin. Knowing that his heart raced because of the way she rubbed up against him.

Moving her face all around, she sniffed at him, and knew he was afraid. His fear heightened her arousal. She wanted to taste it upon his lips.

Lifting her head, she stroked her cheek against his. As she shifted, Mara caught sight of her face in the mirror behind him. What she saw reflected sent her spiraling back into reality.

Her eyes, elliptical like a cat's, possessed a soft yellow glow.

Pushing back from Dr. Zerner, Mara put a shaking hand to her face. "Oh my God, I don't know what . . ."

With his hands up in defense, Dr. Zerner took a hesitant step toward her. "What happened, Mara? Did you have a hallucination?"

"I'm so sorry."

Unable to look him in the face, Mara brushed past him and opened the door. Hugging herself, she swept into the waiting room and out the door. Selena, who was waiting for her, jumped up from her chair and rushed after her.

Selena caught up with her outside near the car and grabbed her arm. "Mara? What's the matter? What happened?"

Mara's body was shaking. She couldn't control it. What had happened in the doctor's office shook her foundations. Foundations of sanity. She had lost her restraint. The overwhelming desire to touch and taste Dr. Zerner had overpowered her will and forced her off that table and on him. She knew what she was doing, but still felt powerless to stop it. It was as if another entity had possessed her body.

Her eyes. Why had her eyes changed? Had that been another part of her delusions?

"I don't know." She pulled from Selena's grip and paced in the parking lot beside the car. "All I know is I don't want to go home, Selena. Something's going on and I have to think and walk it off." She started across the lot toward the large park across the street.

"What should I do with this?" Selena held up the wrapped amulet Mara had given her.

"Put it somewhere safe. And don't unwrap it Selena. Whatever you do, don't touch it."

"Mara, you're scaring me."

Mara rubbed her hands over her face and sighed. "I know. I'm scaring myself." With that, she turned and jogged across the street to the large-treed park.

Adrenaline raced through her body. She needed to work it off. A long walk through the park and to home should ease her body and her mind. She needed to think, clearly. What was happening to her challenged all she knew to be rational and sane. Could she be suffering from a psychosis that forced her to take on the traits of her attacker? Did she believe, for all intents and purposes that she was turning into a jaguar?

Oh God, she thought as she rubbed a hand over her face, she was going insane. Soon, they'd have to commit her to an institution before she started peeing in the sandbox and chasing rabbits through the trees.

Laughing out of frustration, Mara lifted her face to the warm summer sun. It was starting to wane to the west but still the hot rays felt like heaven on her skin. Maybe that's what she needed, to sit in the sun and relax. Glancing around, Mara spotted a nice sunny spot in the open field of green grass. She sat down cross-legged and raised her face to the sun.

As the rays beat down, Mara could feel her body starting to loosen and relax. Moving her shoulders in circles, her limbs softened like rubber bands. Yawning, Mara stretched out onto the grass to lie on her side, her arms tucked under her head. For the first time in days, she felt like sleeping.

She didn't question the sudden change, but accepted it. Too tired and confused to do anything else, she closed her eyes on a sigh allowing her body to float in her tranquil state. She felt like she was in a renewal stage. As if the sun was healing her body and soul. She'd never felt so cozy and comfortable in all her life.

Grinning, as if drunk from too much alcohol, she slowly opened her eyes to take in her surroundings. Toddlers ran around screaming, their mothers chasing them, birds chirped, dogs barked, old men sat on benches feeding the birds.

And her dream man with long black hair was leaning against a tree, watching her.

Sitting up, Mara's heart began to beat like a drum. Shivers raced up and down her back, causing the little hairs on her arms to stand up on end.

Run. That was her first and only thought.

Pouncing to her feet, she jogged back through the park toward the street. When she reached the sidewalk, she glanced over her shoulder. He was following her.

Mara picked up the pace as a new surge of adrenaline flowed, giving speed and strength to her legs. Running down the street, she easily maneuvered around objects and people. Her strides were fluid and graceful. She had been a jogger for years, but never a sprinter. She never thought she was fast enough. Not until now.

As she turned a corner and raced down a busy downtown street, she risked a peek over her shoulder. He was right there behind her, matching her stride and pace. If she slowed any, he'd be right on her. She needed to lose him, or find a place to hide.

Ahead at the corner, Mara noticed the old city library. It was big, dark, and populated. A perfect place to lose her pursuer. Without thinking, she ran into the street. Cars honked their horns as she weaved through traffic. The person in the small sports car wasn't even looking as she ran right in front of him. Tires screeched as he stepped on the brakes.

Without hesitation, Mara jumped. As she soared through

the air, the toe on her runner scraped the roof of his car as she passed over it. Landing on the other side, she didn't even break stride, but ran, full out, to the library steps.

Taking the steps two at a time, she pushed through the revolving door and rushed inside. Glancing around, Mara searched for the perfect hiding spot until she could make her escape. Upstairs. It was dark, and crowded with multiple rows of books. Several little nooks and corners to hide in.

She glanced over her shoulder. He hadn't come in the library yet. There was only one entrance and he hadn't passed through it. Not yet. Trying to avoid unnecessary attention, Mara quietly walked up the long staircase to the second level. She found the darkest most obscure corner to hunker down in and wait it out.

As she leaned against the back wall, she tried to slow her breathing. Surprisingly, she wasn't that out of breath. Her lungs didn't burn with a need for oxygen and her legs didn't ache. More like a warm tingling after a good solid workout. And how the hell did she manage to jump over that car?

A sudden change in the air sent shivers of dread and something familiar over her skin. Mara turned her head toward the long row of books in front of her. Between the books, she could see a dark form moving toward her. Holding her breath, she slid along the wall, away from the approaching shape.

"I know what's happening to you."

Mara froze. His voice was exactly like from her dreams. Low and musical, like a Spanish guitar.

"What do you want?" she managed to breathe out.

"I can help you. The changes can be controlled."

He stepped out from behind the row of books. His long dark hair was pulled back in a ponytail, highlighting the lean sculpted plains of his golden face and the dark depths of his eyes. He looked just as sexy and dangerous as in her dreams. More so, as she could feel the heat wafting off his body as if she had been standing next to a fireplace. Something inside her called to him. She could feel it building up into a hot ball of liquid desire. Shaking her head, she averted her eyes, not wanting to look upon him and question her sanity.

He took a step closer to her. "Don't be afraid, Mara. Don't fight it."

Vibrating with a hearty mixture of fear and arousal, Mara slid along the wall away from him toward the stairs. "How do you know me? Who are you?"

He kept in pace with her, walking alongside, not any closer but near enough to unnerve her. She could smell his wild, tantalizing scent.

"I am Xalvador of the Itzamna pride, and I have been called to protect you."

Xalvador. His name was like melted chocolate on her tongue as she whispered it lowly to herself. It couldn't be. He couldn't be. Her realm of reality was slowly shrinking with every passing moment.

Shaking her head, she moved toward the stairs, circling around him. "Who called you?"

He met her gaze, his eyes intense and knowing. "You did."

Her dreams. Of the jaguars and the jungle. Had she called him somehow?

"What? Now I know you're crazy. What are you supposed to be protecting me from?"

"From a dark evil that wants to possess you."

She smirked. "The only dark evil I see is you. So I suggest you back off."

Other patrons turned and stared as she continued to step away from him. Eventually her back pressed up against the railing.

"Mara, come with me." He held out his hand. "I can see in your eyes that you sense the truth. Come with me and I will explain what is happening to you. Why you see things. Why you feel things foreign to you."

She wanted to reach out to him. Her fingers twitched in response to the need to feel him. Searching his face, she saw truth in his eyes, but also other emotions. Desire. Need. Hunger. These things caused her belly to clench and her thighs to tingle. What she saw in his face were her own emotions reflected back to her. She wanted to go with him.

Before she could hold out her hand, hot blinding light flashed behind her eyes. She closed them and shook her head, trying to dislodge the images flashing there. Glowing yellow eyes in a man's face. A handsome man. Like the one standing in front of her.

Crouching down, Mara then sprang up in the air and landed on the thin railing, balancing precariously like a tightrope walker. Perched like a cat, Mara glanced down to the ground below. If she fell, she would die. The floor of the library was old but expensive blue slate. There was nothing to break her fall.

"Don't be afraid." He took a step toward her.

Mara flinched and pulled back. But there was nothing to pull back into. She fell off the railing.

He reached out and grasped her hand before she could plummet to the floor. Mara screamed as she dangled from the second floor balcony. Other people rushed to the railing, but there was nothing they could do.

Her life was in his hands.

"It's okay, Mara, let go."

She stared up at him in shock. Let go? Was he mad? She'd die for sure, or at the least break every bone she had.

Sweat slicked her skin and she could feel her hand slipping from his hold. "I'm slipping!"

"It's okay. Trust me. You can let go."

Shaking her head vehemently, Mara knew she was going to fall. He was barely holding her. Slowly, she started to slide from his hold, until he had her fingers, and then they, one by one, slipped from his hand.

As if she was in slow motion, Mara watched him as she fell backwards. With each passing second, he moved farther and farther from her. Her stomach flipped over as the sensation of free falling surged over her.

Instead of crashing into the slate floor, Mara landed on her feet and on the pads of her hands, in a crouch, her knees bent to absorb the pressure of the fall. Shocked gasps resonated around her, as she slowly stood up straight and looked around.

Slowly glancing up, she saw him still crouched down, his hand hanging through the railing spokes staring down at her. He had a small smile on his lips.

People started to crowd around her, asking her if she was all right. Their questions sounded muffled to her, as if she was underwater. She couldn't think straight. Everything was too confusing. Too surreal. What happened could not have possibly occurred. It was impossible. Wasn't it?

She couldn't think here, surrounded by others, everyone talking to her at once. And his presence only confused her more. She needed to get out, and now, before she had a mental breakdown.

Turning on her heel, she ran out of the library without looking back.

5

By the time Mara unlocked the door to her house, the sun had set and darkness had shrouded the sky. Instead of returning immediately to her home from the library, she had ended up wandering around her neighborhood in a numbed state of shock and bewilderment. Questions continually went through her mind. Who was the dark man? And what was happening to her? As she padded through her front door and locked it behind her, she was still no closer to any answers.

While she slipped off her runners, her stomach clenched tightly in hunger. The last time she'd eaten was a quick salad at lunch, more than eight hours ago. Wandering into the kitchen, Mara tapped the glass on her aquarium and then opened the door to the refrigerator. Nothing was appealing. Another cramp in her stomach caused her to double over in pain. She needed to eat something now.

Sniffing the air, she found a scent that made saliva pool in her mouth. She rummaged through the shelves of her fridge, pushing things aside, but couldn't find the source of the delectable smell. Shutting the door, she turned and surveyed her kitchen. Another agonizing cramp seized her belly. Her knee buckled, forcing her down to the floor. Sweat popped out on her brow and upper lip. She was ravenous and couldn't think past her rumbling stomach.

In a panic, she looked around her. She needed to eat. Something. Anything. Her eyes rested on the aquarium.

Struggling to her feet, she walked to the glass, watching as the little fish swam in circles aimlessly. The brilliant colors swirled around in her mind confusing her. Taking a deep breath, Mara smelled the inside of the tank. Instantly, her stomach clenched again and saliva dribbled out from between her lips.

Without another thought, she dipped her hand into the water and scooped out one fat orange fish. She opened her mouth and dropped it in, swallowing it down in one gulp. Plunging her hand in again, she scooped out another fish, and then another. Until her tank was empty, and she sat staring at it wondering why there were no more little fishes she could eat.

Realization hit her like a boulder to the forehead. Her stomach started to roil over at the thought of what she had done. She managed to reach the sink before her gorge rose and she violently retched. After she emptied her stomach, Mara ran the tap and lapped at the water. The cool liquid settled her stomach.

Turning off the faucet, she wiped at her mouth with a paper towel. She couldn't turn around and look. She didn't want to see the empty aquarium and know that she had deliberately eaten her pets. What was she turning into? What would have happened if she had had a hamster, or worse, a cat? Just thinking about it again made her stomach flip over in revulsion. She closed her eyes and rested her head against the windowsill over the sink.

A soft scratching sound raised her head. Turning toward the front door, she strained to hear the sound again. There. Again, a soft scratching like nails across wood. Was it at her door? Whatever it was, the sound definitely came from her front veranda.

Stepping softly, Mara approached her front window. Lifting the curtains, she peered out onto the porch. Although it was dark, she could still see shapes in the streams of moonlight. Nothing. She couldn't see anything on her porch. No lost dogs or cats, no squirrels or rodents trying to gain access to her house.

She let the curtains drop. A louder sound at her door turned her head. She watched in horror as the doorknob began to jiggle back and forth. Someone was trying to break in. Sprinting to the door, she grabbed the knob to keep it from turning.

"I'm calling the cops!" she yelled.

The knob stopped turning. Breathing a sigh of relief, Mara relaxed against the door.

A dark shape passed the front window.

Heart pounding, Mara jumped up and ran to the glass. Peeking out, she couldn't see anything. A loud banging sounded at her back door, causing her to jump. Sweat trickled down her back, and she could hardly breathe. Taking a step back from the window, Mara moved toward the middle of the living room.

More sounds came from her porch. Sounds she couldn't distinguish. Someone walking. But more than just one set of feet padded across the veranda. A loud bang came at her front door again.

Mara jumped, gasping at the violence of it.

Now, more scratching. More banging.

Glancing around her in a panic, Mara grabbed the phone from the side table. There was no dial tone. She set it down and stared at her door. The knob jiggled again, and a pounding sound resonated from the frame. It almost sounded like it was breaking, the wood splintering from excess pressure.

She ran into the kitchen and grabbed the biggest butcher knife she had from the wooden block. Holding it tightly, she went back into the living room. Her heart was fluttering in her chest like a hummingbird's wings. Taking another shaky step, she tried to swallow down the lump forming in her throat.

There was more pounding. More feet scrambling across her porch. Dark forms passed her windows several times.

Mara couldn't handle it any longer. The noises, the shapes. Everything was too fanatical, too confusing. With the knife still in her hand, Mara put her hands over her ears then opened her mouth and screamed.

Except the sound that came out wasn't exactly a scream, but a loud guttural growl.

Within seconds, the noises stopped.

Taking her hands from her ears, Mara stared at the door, expecting any moment for the pounding and scratching to continue. It didn't.

Cautiously she stepped toward the door. She put her ear to the wood and listened for sounds and movement outside. Nothing but the wind, and a yowl of an alley cat down the street.

Unlocking the door, Mara took a step back and opened it. As the hinges squeaked, she took in a ragged breath. Fear making her vibrate.

Nothing menacing framed the doorway. Looking down, she took in the frame. It was splintered and broken. Long slash marks cut through the wood. It looked like someone had tried to pry the door open with a knife.

She stepped out onto her porch, shaking with apprehension, and now anger. Angry that someone would vandalize her home this way. All thoughts of something strange and otherworldly vanished from her mind. This was a group of teenagers playing around and being stupid.

She walked down her porch and checked alongside the house. No sign of anyone. Shaking her head at her pumped-up suspicions, she turned to walk back to the front door.

All thoughts and reason left her mind. Dropping the knife,

she brought her hands up to her chest to somehow stop her heart from breaking through her ribs.

He was there, standing on her porch. His hair was free of restraints and the wind blew it around him like a menacing dark cloud. And he wasn't alone. Two other men stood behind him. Too men just as dark and just as dangerous. She remembered them from her mind trip back to the ancient Mayan temple.

Before she could react, her stomach cramped painfully, bringing her down to the knees. The pain blasted through her like a small bomb, and she couldn't move, couldn't think past the agony.

In seconds, he crouched down next to her. She didn't even see him move. When he picked her up in his arms, she wanted to protest but found she couldn't form the words. He carried her into the house, the two other men following behind.

"Lock it," he commanded as he swept her into the living room.

He marched through the room, down the hall, and into her bedroom, setting her on the bed. Shaking her head back and forth, she tried to tell him to leave, to stop touching her, but nothing came from her mouth. She couldn't make the right sounds, only short pants of breath.

Dark pain made her head swim, and she closed her eyes. But that only made her nauseous, so she opened them again. He bent over her to brush the hair from her sweaty brow.

The other two men stood off to the side of the bed looking on in interest.

He motioned to the taller man. "Tito, stand guard. Make sure Jago doesn't come back."

With a curt nod, the big man marched out of the room.

"Get me a wet cloth," he commanded.

The other man went into the small bathroom adjacent to the bedroom. Mara could hear the water running, but she couldn't turn her head. She couldn't look away from Xalvador. She stared at him, taking in every feature. The way his brow crinkled in worry, the laugh lines around his eyes, and the way his full sensuous mouth moved when he spoke.

Mara flinched when she felt the cold cloth on her forehead. Her skin was burning. She felt like an inferno was raging inside her body.

"It is the change, Mara. It is upon you. Your beast wants to come out."

Beast? Mara shook her head. "No, I . . ."

He put a finger over her lips to stop her words. "Do not try and speak. It will only hurt more. You have to make a decision. Let your beast out or . . . or we can suppress it for now." He glanced up briefly at the other man in the room then back to her. "It will not be a permanent thing, but at least you could still function."

She stared into his eyes. What was he talking about? And why was she so hot? The heat searing her flesh was staggering. She couldn't think past it. She needed to get cool. Lifting her hands, she started to pull at her shirt.

"I'm hot. Help me. I'm so hot."

He raised the washcloth and wrung it over her face. Water dribbled over her skin. The relief was insignificant. She'd need a waterfall to relieve her agony.

"The burn is from your body trying to change. Your muscles are going to change, your bones are going to lengthen and tear, everything about you is going to shift, Mara. Do you want to turn? Do you want to change into a jaguar?"

Jaguar. She was turning into a jaguar. How was that possible? She couldn't wrap her mind around the notion. It was too inconceivable even to ponder.

But the heat. The heat was going to burn her alive.

She grabbed his hands. "Help me."

He nodded. "I will help you Mara, but you have to trust me. Can you do that?"

"Yes," she panted as another wave of heat scorched her body, forcing her to writhe on the bed in agony.

He pushed her hands away and grabbed her shirt. With one pull, he rendered the blouse in half, buttons popping off to land on the floor. He glanced down at her scars. She thought she saw a flash of sorrow cross his face. If it had been there, it was gone just as fast, as he sat her up and pulled her shirt off.

Mara didn't fight him as his hands moved down to her pants. The moment her shirt had come off, she felt some reprieve from the sizzling heat burning her inside and out. Within minutes, he had her pants undone and down her legs. The only thing left on was her panties.

When he reached for them, she swatted his hands away. He glanced up at her, annoyance clenching his jaw.

"You said you would trust me. Now do it."

The force behind his voice gave her pause. She lowered her hands and let him do what he wanted. She could see his jaw tighten in determination, as he gripped the band of her blue cotton panties and yanked them off.

She was now lying there completely naked, vulnerable. But as the heat kept spearing through her, she didn't care. She just wanted the pain to go away.

After a brief nod to the other man, Xalvador stood up, pulling his shirt up over his head. "Kemen, take off your clothes."

Kemen hesitated. "Xal, she's your—"

"I can't do this alone. Her beast is too wild, I can't tame it by myself. I need you."

Kemen nodded, and then started to remove his clothes.

Mara watched as Xalvador stripped off his dark T-shirt and black pants. He looked just as delicious as in her dreams. Even down to the black tattoos lining his narrow hips and pointing down to his crotch. His cock was no disappointment either.

Desire, hot and hearty, surged over her. Like a bolt of lightning hitting her right between the legs, she wanted him. No other thought occupied her mind, except him. Touching him, tasting him, feeding on him. She could think of nothing else.

She reached up for him, and pulled him down to her. Instead of covering her with his body, he nestled in alongside her, pressing his body to hers, and wrapped his arms around her waist to hold her still.

"Kemen, hurry."

The other man nestled in behind Mara, spooning her with his equally naked and gorgeous body. He was leaner than Xalvador, but possessed the same tattoos and the same impressive endowment.

They pressed into her, sandwiching her in between them. Xalvador nestled his face into her neck and up to her ear, whispering words she didn't understand. But she felt her body starting to calm. The heat lessened, and the pain swirling in her stomach started to diminish. She could almost think again. If it hadn't been for the two svelte naked bodies pressed up against her.

She closed her eyes against the other feelings stirring in her body. An ache deep and intense started at her center. Her nipples were erect and tingling. A groan formed on her lips.

Mara started to move her body. She couldn't help pushing her ass into Kemen, and streaking her hands over Xalvador's chest. It was like walking around in a chocolate factory without being able to sample the sweets. Their bodies next to hers were too much of a temptation. She didn't possess that kind of willpower.

"Lay still," Xalvador commanded, but she could hear the strain in his voice. She knew he was having a difficult time keeping his hands immobile.

She glanced down between them and noticed his cock swelling in size. He was as responsive to her as she was to him. Behind her, she could feel Kemen's cock twitching in between the cheeks of her ass.

"I can't," she hissed between clenched teeth. "You feel too good. Both of you."

Mara let her hands roam down to Xalvador's cock, and wrapped one hand around his shaft. Instantly, he started to harden like rock.

Cursing, he reached down and pulled her hand away. "Let us calm your beast first, Mara. A cat needs her pride to soothe her soul." He set her hand on his chest, over his heart. "Feel my heart. Feel my breathing. Feel the rhythm of it." He took in a deep breath and let it out slowly. "Match yours to mine."

Mara squirmed against them. She didn't want to breathe slowly; she didn't want her heart to stop pounding like a drum in her chest. She wanted to touch, taste, feel, and take what they could give her. The heat intensified in her body, but it concentrated with fierce need between her legs, deep inside her pussy. If she didn't fill herself up with something soon, she thought she'd go mad.

A growl rumbled in her throat. She wanted them now. Merciless desire for them both clawed at her body. Mara no longer felt in control. All reason and rational thought abandoned her. She was alone with her ravenous hunger. And nothing but brutal fast sex would satisfy her.

6

Desperation clawed at Mara. Something inside her bubbled to the surface, ravenous with lust. Hungry for both these men.

Reaching behind her, she slid her hands over Kemen's thighs and nuzzled her fingers against his cock. "I want to fuck you both. Now."

"I think she's lost control, Xal," Kemen groaned, as Mara continued to rub her fingers up and down his growing erection.

Xalvador cupped her face with his hands and stared into her eyes. "Mara, your beast is trying to control you. We can appease its appetites, but you must be willing."

She looked into his face. He was beautiful. The most beautiful man she had ever seen. And she wanted him like no other man before. She was more than willing.

"Mara wants to play," she purred. "Play with her, Xalvador, make her growl with ecstasy."

This time when her hands roamed down to his cock, he didn't stop her. He was rock-hard and scorching hot when she touched him. Gripping him tightly in her palm, she tugged him closer. Damn the foreplay, she wanted his cock in her now. Already her pussy was on fire and sopping wet. A delicious contradiction. The insides of her thighs were moist from her lust.

As she stroked him, nestling the velvety tip of his cock against the soft folds of her sex, he pressed his lips to hers. The kiss was electric, sending jolts down her body, firing her nerve endings, waking up every part of her body inside and out. Moving his hands, he buried them into her hair, pulling her even closer to him.

As they kissed, Mara could feel Kemen's fingers exploring her. He squeezed and molded her breasts, flicking his thumbs over her tightened peaks. One hand continued to tweak her nipples, pulling and pinching, while the other moved down her torso. Sweeping his hand down her outer thigh, Kemen grabbed her leg and raised it up so he could nestle his leg in between her thighs. As he did that, his knee brushed up against her pussy. She moaned into Xalvador's mouth as quick flashes of pleasure burst through her.

Pulling on Xalvador, Mara settled his cock into her inner folds. She moaned as he slid back and forth along her silky slit to her opening. With slow careful thrusts, he inched into her.

Kemen put his hand behind Mara's knee and raised her leg, pulling back on it to spread her wide, giving Xalvador easier access to her.

The new position allowed Xalvador to slide, nice and tight, into her. Moaning as he filled her up, Mara raked her nails over Xalvador's back, hanging on as he stretched her. He felt like heaven pulsating inside her. She began to move her pelvis to encourage him to start thrusting. She didn't want slow, easy, and gentle. She'd had that her whole sexual life. Now, with these two men, she hungered for it to be fast and rough. And she'd have it no matter what they said. The increasing appetite inside her wouldn't settle for anything less.

"I won't break," she groaned while nibbling on Xalvador's

neck. She pushed on his chest to roll him onto his back. She wanted the control. She didn't trust them to give her what she needed. They both seemed to think she was fragile. A woman to handle with kid gloves. Well, the gloves were off, and she would take what she craved.

Hands on his shoulders, Mara pressed him into the mattress and spread her legs wide to straddle his pelvis. Without pause, she drove down on him, completely impaling herself to the hilt of his cock.

A loud groan expelled from his parted lips as Mara started to move over him, sliding up and down with long languid strokes. He was so hard and unyielding in her pussy as she pumped her hips. He fit inside her perfectly, as if they were two pieces of the same puzzle. Except it wasn't enough. She wanted, needed more.

Glancing over her shoulder, she saw Kemen kneeling on the bed behind her, watching her slide up and down on Xalvador's stiff cock. She could read in his eyes that he was uncertain of his actions. She could tell he wanted to join in; his erection bobbed up and down with the movement on the bed. But something about his manner showed he had mixed feelings on how to, and if he should do anything about it.

Right now, there was no room for conflict, for chivalrous behavior. She needed his cock, too, if she was going to satisfy this nagging, voracious ache between her legs. Mara no longer felt in control. The ravenous need inside her body and soul was calling all the shots.

"Get over here, big boy. There's always room for two." She slid her hands over the cheeks of her ass and spread them apart in invitation.

Mara had never had anal sex. She'd wanted to, but her past lovers had always been reluctant and too prudish to try. When she masturbated, she'd often slide a dildo in and out of her tight pink bud. Orgasms came fast and furious when she did.

And right now, she could think of nothing but reaching climax. Her insides tightened just thinking about the wicked possibilities.

She let out a joyful gasp when Kemen finally snuggled against her back, sliding his cock between her spread ass cheeks. He reached between her thighs and slid his fingers into her sex, nudging his knuckle against her engorged clit.

Leaning slightly forward, Mara braced her hands on Xalvador's chest. She watched his face as she slammed up and down on him, pushing against his cock and Kemen's fingers.

He clenched his jaw in determination as he reached up and cupped her breast. Pulling on her nipples, he smiled when she cried out. Oh, he was an arrogant one. Thinking that he was in control of her pleasure. She would have to show him how wrong he was.

Gripping his wrists, Mara pulled his hands away from her breasts, and, leaning forward, pushed them back over his head.

"I say what goes. I'm in control." She nipped his chin with her teeth, and then dragged her mouth down his neck.

A low and rumbling growl sounded from his throat. She watched as his eyes dilated in desire and his lips parted on a groan. That was better, she thought. Now, she needed to get the other one in line.

"I'm wet, but not wet enough for what I want," Mara said as she glanced behind her. "I have some lubricant in the bedside table. Something to help you fuck my ass."

She turned her attention back to Xalvador as she felt the bed move with Kemen's departure. Trailing her tongue over his throat, she continued to move her pussy up and down on his cock. A tight ball of heat started to form deep in her belly. She was vibrating furiously from the jolts of pleasure zapping through her. It would not be long before she orgasmed. But she needed that hard push. Nothing but rigid thrusting in her ass would send her over the edge.

Moments later, she could feel a cool liquid sensation between her cheeks. Kemen was rubbing lube into her crease, massaging her inner folds with firm strokes. Watching Xalvador's face, she wondered if Kemen's hand near his cock was turning him on. If Kemen feeling where they joined sent delicious shivers up and down his spine. Because it did to her.

On a groan, Mara pushed back when she felt a finger sliding into her ass. With the lubrication, Kemen's finger slid in with ease. With each thrust on Xalvador's cock, Kemen matched it with his finger in her anus. Already, Mara could feel both her vaginal and anal muscles tightening, readying for the big climax. But she wasn't quite ready for it. She wanted to feel both men in her at once. Feel their cocks nearly touching, with only a thin membrane separating them as they drove into her repeatedly.

As if sensing her feral needs, Kemen slid another finger into her tight hole. At first, his movements were slow and easy, but with her pants of encouragement, he picked up his pace, pumping them out vigorously. She was ready, damn it. She wanted to scream for him to hurry. To plunge his cock into her now. She had no more patience for going slow.

Pushing back on his fingers, Mara snarled, "Now! Fuck me now!"

Kemen withdrew his fingers, and replaced them with his cock. Collapsing on Xalvador's chest, Mara gritted her teeth as Kemen slid his thick pulsating erection into her tight virgin ass. He went slowly, and she was glad for it. She wanted him, but realized that her body needed to adjust to the intrusion. She tried to relax her muscles, opening up for him. Little licks of pain radiating up her body forced her to take in a deep breath.

Xalvador moved his hands down to her ass. He kneaded her cheeks and spread them farther apart to aid Kemen. Then he found her mouth, and kissed her. Nibbling and sucking on her lips and tongue, inhaling her quick pants.

After a few moments of pain as the head of Kemen's cock pushed into her, Mara could only feel excruciating pleasure as he slid all the way in. Tears rolled down her cheeks as intense mind-blowing rapture surged over her. The two men held still, waiting for indication from her to move. She wanted the control; they were giving it to her.

Taking in a deep breath, Mara let go of Xalvador's arms and sat up, forcing herself farther down the length of Xalvador's cock. As she moved, she could feel both penises throbbing within her velvety walls. She'd never felt so inflamed before. Like nothing could douse her lust. But damn, she would definitely try.

"Ah, you feel so good moving inside me." She shuffled her ass, pushing down on both of them. Both men groaned in unison. "More please. Fuck me till I scream."

Xalvador slid his hands down to grip her hips. Digging into her flesh, he started to move his pelvis, pumping into her. At the same time, Kemen placed his hands above Xalvador's and drove into her.

Mara cried out as pangs of savage pleasure zipped through her body like lightning bolts. Her breath heaved from her lungs and she thought she'd die from the surges of scorching hot ripples radiating inside her pussy. Could someone die from being fucked too hard? She hoped to find out.

Whimpering mindlessly, Mara could do nothing but hold on for the ride. As Xalvador plunged into her, Kemen retreated. They worked in unison to give her the best, wildest, hottest fucking of her life. Held in place by both their cocks, Mara couldn't even reach down between her legs and rub her clit to aid the mind-shattering orgasm that was building. Gasping for breath, she dug into Xalvador's chest with her nails and let him decide her fate.

As if sensing her desperation, Xalvador moved one of his hands around her thigh to slide his fingers into her cleft. The moment he touched her clit, Mara jerked, as a white-hot explosion went off in her pussy. Simultaneously, they buried their cocks into her as her climax slammed into her.

Crying out, Mara shut her eyes against the sensory assault on her body. Waves, whips, jolts, and hot flows of agonizing pleasure surged over and through her all at once. She couldn't distinguish one feeling from another, or where the sensations were coming from or ending.

All thoughts left her. The only thing she could do was ride the wave and let it wash over her into bliss. Shutting her eyes, she collapsed onto Xalvador in total exhaustion. Finally, she could feel the inner flame inside her, the one that nearly burned her alive, subside. It had been satisfied. For now.

7

Something woke her. A thought, or a feeling that she couldn't quite place.

Stretching, she opened her eyes. She was in her bed, naked under the covers. Rubbing her face, she looked around the room. The light was waning outside, but beams of it streamed through the curtains, piercing the dark of the room. She turned from the window and glanced around her unlit room.

In the shadows, she saw Xalvador sitting on a chair at the end of her bed, watching her and drinking from one of her coffee cups.

She sniffed the air. Coffee. But not anything she had in the kitchen. The smell was rich and bitter, heavenly.

"Do you want some?" He gestured with his cup.

Sitting up she gathered the sheets to her chest and leaned against the headboard. She nodded, embarrassed to do anything else. She couldn't remember everything that happened last night, but the soreness of her limbs, and the raw throb between her legs told her much more than she wanted to know.

Tito, the giant, wandered into the bedroom as if summoned

on a thought, with a steaming cup of coffee in his hand. Without a word, he handed it to her, then disappeared back into the living room.

She took a sip and sighed in delight. The taste was delicious, and potent.

"It's Venezuelan. A special blend."

She lowered her cup and looked at him. She knew he was watching her. Could sense his eyes scrutinizing her. Mara looked away and back at the bedroom window.

"What time is it?"

"Six o'clock."

She whipped back to him. "In the evening?" she sputtered.

"You needed your sleep."

Rubbing a hand over her face, she sighed. "I guess so."

"How do you feel?"

She blushed. How did she feel? Like she'd had sex for four hours straight with two powerful men. That's how she felt. What did he want her to say?

"Um, fine, I guess."

"We must talk about last night." He got up from the chair and walked over to the bed. He sat down on the edge, next to her feet. A beam of light streamed over him, and she saw the marks on his chest. Long, red, angry scratches.

"Oh my God . . ." Shaking, she set her cup down on the night table. "What—?"

Grinning, he traced his fingers over the wounds. "You were very . . . playful."

"I . . . I did that?"

"Si, gatito. I have more of them on my back."

She bunched her hands at her waist, but they itched to reach out and touch him, to trail her fingers over the marks.

"Does it hurt?"

He shrugged. "Only a little. It is a good pain. You know what I mean?"

She thought of the flare of tenderness between her legs. Yes, she knew exactly what he meant.

"I'm so sorry."

He chuckled. "Don't be. I'm honored to have your marks on my body. That you would be so aggressive with me. It's our way."

"It's not my way."

"But it is, Mara. You have changed. There is no going back to who you once were."

Then she remembered his words . . .

Do you want to change into a jaguar?

"But people can't change into animals. It's not possible."

Xalvador reached over and set his cup beside hers on the night table. "More than two thousand years ago in the city of Cerros, the king and a few noblemen sacrificed many people to the gods, in exchange for warriors that would forever protect them from those that would seek to supplant them from the throne. Because of the people's fear of the giant cats that roamed and hunted in the jungles around them, the gods breathed their power into four of the beasts, transforming them into men. The four *balam,* or knights, protected the people of Cerros, and did their masters' bidding in whatever form, be it jaguar or as men, that they wished."

Mara glanced from him and noticed that Tito and Kemen had entered the room and were listening intently to the story Xalvador was weaving for her.

"Over time, the knights began to question the things they were ordered to do. Too many people were dying for a few men's twisted desires. So they rebelled against their masters. With the gods' help, the four knights were able to banish the king and his nobles to the underworld. The city of Cerros fell and the people fled from it in fear. The *balam* went back to the jungle, but were forever changed."

Mara looked from Xalvador to the other men, then back to Xalvador. "You said four *balam*, four knights. I only see three of you."

Xalvador glanced briefly at the other men. She didn't know what passed between them, but she could tell it was serious and painful, and she wasn't sure she really wanted to know.

"Jago is our fourth. But he has taken a different path."

Mara leaned forward. She didn't like the tone in his voice. It sent a surge of dread over her, as if someone had walked over her grave.

"What does that mean? A different path?"

Standing, Xalvador stared down at her, his face a stern mask. "He is after you. I don't know why, but he has come to your city specifically to seek you out."

The amulet . . .

"Hector, my cousin, he found something near one of the temple ruins . . . near Cerros I think. It was a jade amulet."

Mara could feel the change in the room. It was as if electricity was surging from some exposed outlet. The hairs on her arms stood up on end.

"What does this amulet look like?"

"It's shaped like a temple, with a black jaguar standing guard at the bottom. The entrance at the top is open, and it looks like beams of light are coming out of it."

"The Amulet of Xibalba," Kemen spoke, a quiet awe in his voice.

"If he should use it . . ." Tito's words trailed off, as if he was afraid to voice his suspicions.

Xalvador looked at the others and rubbed a hand over his face and through his hair. "Si, that would explain many things."

"What's wrong? What's so important about this amulet?" Mara questioned, fear quickly washing over her.

"It is the amulet of the underworld. With it, Jago could unlock the prison doors and release the ancient kings. Their power would be too terrible to comprehend." Turning, he advanced on Mara. "Where is the amulet? Do you have it?"

She tried to pull back from him, but he grabbed her arm to hold her in place. "I gave it to my sister."

As his eyes bored into hers, she had the distinct feeling that he was probing her mind, her feelings.

"It made me feel weird so I told her to find a safe place to hide it. And told her not to touch it." Shivering, Mara remembered what had happened when she held the amulet. She looked away from Xalvador's intense stare, remembering it too well from her dreams. Despite her concern, desire new and fresh flared once more between her legs. "I didn't want to touch it again . . . I saw things."

Xalvador pulled her arm, forcing her to face him again. "What things?"

Anger flared alongside her lust. She was tired of being grabbed, and pulled, and questioned. She had the questions, damn it! They were interfering in her life. Not the other way around.

She pulled her arm back, and glared at him. "Just weird things. Now if you would all mind, I would like to get up and get dressed. I'm tired of being questioned, especially since you're wearing clothes and I'm not. You're crowding me, so please get out of my room."

Xalvador nodded to the Tito and Kemen. They left without a word. But Xalvador turned and stared down at her as if he had every right to be there. His arrogance was starting to grate on her fraying nerves.

"You too."

"I will stay."

Leaning forward without having the sheet fall away from her chest, Mara tried to muster her dignity. She raised her chin, and met his gaze evenly.

"You will go, or I'll scratch you in much lower, harder to reach places."

She expected him to argue with her, comment that he would do as he wished. What she did not expect was the slow easy grin that lit up his devilish face. Her belly tightened instantly, and her nipples peaked as if a rush of cold air blew over them.

"Teasing me is not going to make me leave your bedroom."

Mara blushed as other lower parts of her body grew hot and tingly with need. He had an effect on her, like no other man. The way he looked, the way he smelled, the way he spoke, constantly drew on her sexual hunger. Licking her lips, she could still remember how he tasted. Wild and sultry. Like the way the air smelled after a rain.

She clamped her legs shut, as memories of him between them popped up in her mind. Sex with this man was not going to solve her problems.

Reining in her lusty notions, Mara relaxed. "Please, I need a few moments alone. This is all very . . . overwhelming."

She witnessed him soften, and it tugged at other things beside her loins. Her heart skipped a beat or two.

He nodded, then turned and walked out of her room.

Throwing back the covers, Mara swung her legs over the edge of the bed and stood up. She stumbled once, but remained standing. Her legs wobbled like rubber as she walked toward her dresser to acquire some clothes. She passed her full-length mirror and caught a glimpse of her body in the glass.

She took a step back and really looked at herself.

The scars across her chest were almost healed. Only thin pink lines marred her skin. She traced them with her fingers, marveling at how quickly they had vanished. She knew it to be impossible, but the truth lay scratched across her body.

There were other things different about her. Muscles she didn't realize she had rippled under her skin, as she twisted back and forth. Her legs were leaner, more defined; even her ass seemed to be rounder, firmer than ever before. She'd always been fit from years of jogging and eating healthy food, but now she possessed an athlete's form. A svelte body made for sprinting and jumping.

Behind her, reflected in the mirror, Mara spied her old wooden dresser. It was as high as her chest. The thought made her remember jumping onto the railing in the library. How easy it had been, how instinctive. Turning, she sized up the heavy dresser. Could it hold her?

Without another thought, she crouched down then sprang into the air. She landed squarely on top of the dresser in a squat. If she stood, her head would scrape the ceiling. She looked around her room. From this height, she saw things differently. The sensation was dizzying but exciting.

Mesmerizing. That's what Xalvador thought, as he watched Mara from the doorway, crouching on her dresser. He found he could not tear his eyes away. Her body was perfect, the way it flowed like water when she moved. He'd never seen a creature so enchanting. Not since his late wife, Lareina, had died more than two thousand years ago.

They shared similar physical traits, Mara and Lareina. Long lustrous dark hair, deep-set brown eyes hooded by long black eyelashes that could heal a man with one look. Soft sun-kissed skin, and a lean and agile body that could bring a man to his knees. Their one main difference: Lareina was not a shopeshifter. She had no inner beast to control, to tame.

No, it was in Mara that he found his match. Mara's spirit summoned him. She was a fighter.

From the moment he saw Mara in the park, his body grew feverish with desire. He had recognized her instantly. Something about her compelled him. It wasn't only the beast raging through her that drew him, but something familiar. A quality in a woman that he had been missing for more years than he could care to admit. Passion. Fierce animal passion.

Watching her over the past few days was like viewing a caged animal. He could see the beast trying to break free. Struggling against its human restraints. But he was uncertain if she was ready to release it. He didn't know if she was prepared to embrace that feral part of her soul.

She fought the beast hard last night. With his and Kemen's support, she was able to battle it back, push it back down into its most primal condition. Back into her heart where it had seeded and started to take root.

Eventually she would lose the fight, and the beast would claw its way out. For now, he would help her keep it subdued with her sexual hungers. But lust and desire would only work for so long. If the jaguar wanted free, it would not pause to think just whom it was destroying for that liberty.

The doorframe creaked when he shifted to get a better view of her. Her head whipped up and met his gaze. Her eyes were glowing.

She shifted to turn and fell off the dresser. She landed hard on her ass.

Chuckling, Xalvador wandered over to her and offered his hand. "You're supposed to land on you feet, *mi gatito.*"

She paled as she took his hand. He wondered what she was thinking to look so frightened. Was she still afraid of him?

He kept her hand in his and squeezed. "Are you all right?"

She nodded but pulled her hand away. "I'm fine. Just knocked the wind out of me when I fell."

He stared at her, searching her face for the truth. She was hard to read. Several conflicted emotions seemed to darken her face. He nodded to her, to try to relieve some of her anxiety. "Get dressed. We need to get that amulet from your sister before Jago figures out the same thing. He won't ask for it. He'll take it."

Xalvador could feel the shivers that raced over her. She was justified in her fear. Jago was ruthless. He had been when he was a jaguar knight, and now that he had turned rogue . . . he was a nightmare that the whole world would endure if they didn't stop him.

As Mara pulled up along the curb in front of Selena's condominium, Xalvador unclenched his hands and relinquished his fierce hold on the dashboard. Glancing in the rearview mirror, she noticed the others had the same pale white-knuckled looks on their faces.

Pulling on the parking brake, she looked over at Xalvador. "Let me guess, you don't like to ride in cars?"

"It's not my favorite type of transportation. I'd rather walk twenty miles with blisters on the pads of my feet than ride in a car."

"How about airplanes?"

He shook his head.

"Xal got sick on the one over here from Peru," Tito snickered from the back.

Xalvador turned in his seat and glared at Tito. Both he and Kemen started to laugh. Mara joined in. Eventually, the corners of Xalvador's lips twitched.

As she watched them, she could imagine that they weren't always serious and maudlin. According to Xalvador's story, they'd been together for more than two thousand years. Surely they'd had their fair share of good times. Suddenly, she had an overwhelming desire to witness and join one of those moments.

"So, Superman does have kryptonite."

Xalvador's brow creased in question. "What does that mean?"

"It means you have weaknesses."

"Everyone does."

"Good. Just making sure you're still human."

Something flashed across his face before he turned away.

Pain? Sadness? It had not been Mara's intent to hurt him, but to lighten the mood. Did he not think he was human any longer? Mara wanted to reach across the seat, grab his hand, and tell him that he was more human than any man she'd known before. That writhing in his arms had been the most basic human moment she'd had in her life. That she had felt more alive with him. But she didn't think he would hear that. Now was not the time to tell him.

Undoing her seatbelt and opening the car door, Mara asked, "How about boats?"

"Boats we can handle. We're very good swimmers."

They all got out of the car and walked up the sidewalk to Selena's condo.

"That's good to know, because if she's not here, she's on her way down to the docks, where she dances at the Mermaid Club."

Xalvador looked at her questioningly.

"It's a floating nightclub."

When they reached the door, Mara rang the bell. They waited but there was no answer. She knocked on the door and put her ear to the wood to listen for any sign that Selena was still at home.

"I don't think she's home." She stepped off the doorstep and put her face up to the living room window. She peered inside looking for any sign of her sister. Even through the gauze of the curtains, Mara could see that something wasn't right inside the condo. Her sister was messy, but not to the point where things were left laying scattered on the floor.

The sound of wood splintering jerked Mara from the window. She looked over just as Xalvador pushed open the busted front door.

"What are you doing?"

"Looking for the amulet. If we find it here, we won't need to make an unnecessary trip down to the docks."

He went through the door, Tito and Kemen following him.

Shaking her head, Mara trailed after them. She was angry that he had kicked in Selena's door, but he had a point. If they found the artifact, they wouldn't have to involve Selena any further. Maybe then, Mara could keep her safe and removed from the strange events taking place.

Once she crossed the threshold, Mara stopped dead in her tracks. The place had been trashed.

Sofa cushions torn open, their contents spilled on the rug. CD cases opened and tossed, their CDs scattered everywhere, on the shelves, on top of the stereo system, the floor. Glancing around, she couldn't believe the destruction. It looked as if a tornado had swept through.

She couldn't stop shaking as she moved from room to room. Nothing had been left untouched. Even the contents of Selena's refrigerator were strewn across the linoleum floor. Milk, from a slashed open carton, dripped from the kitchen counter.

With a strangled cry, Mara ran into Selena's bedroom. She feared the worse. She wouldn't be able to handle it if her little sister had been hurt, or worse.

Xalvador had beaten her there and was surveying the damage. The same destruction was evident in the room. Selena's mattress had been slashed open, pillows cut and emptied. Little feathers still floated in the breeze from the open window. Her dresser drawers were still open. Clothes, lingerie, personal affects lying on top and haphazardly scattered on the floor.

As she wandered aimlessly around the room, her gaze landed on the open window. And what she saw froze her blood. There were deep gorges in the window frame. Very similar to the ones around her door. Her head swam and she felt faint.

"Oh my God, Selena." Putting a hand to her chest, she stumbled and nearly fell.

Xalvador was there gathering her in his arms before she could collapse. He wrapped his arms around her and held her still.

"She's alive, I'm sure. There has been no blood spilled here."

He brought his hand up to her hair and brushed it from her face. "We will go to this club, find your sister and get the amulet. Then Jago will come to us, and we can finish what we came here to do."

She suspected that his words were meant to soothe her, but she could not stop her body from trembling. Although they would find her sister and protect her, Mara had a feeling that it wouldn't be enough. Fierce yellow glowing eyes still haunted her thoughts, and now she knew to whom they belonged.

Jago had ripped her cousin apart, and if given the chance, she knew he would try to finish what he had started with the deep gouges in her chest.

8

The Mermaid Club jutted out from the pier on a large floating platform. A long ramp connected the club to the dock. A huge bouncer stood at the entrance to the ramp, and the line to get in streamed down the dock for at least a block. It was obviously a popular nightspot.

After fighting to find a parking spot, this was the last thing Mara wanted to see. A long line to wait in. They couldn't wait.

With Xalvador in the lead, they approached the hulking bouncer. She could see the appraisal in his eyes as he surveyed Xalvador, Tito and Kemen. Most likely, he was trying to decide if he could take them. By the way he finally averted his eyes, Mara thought he came to a decision. No way in hell.

When they were within two feet, Mara stepped forward and approached the bouncer. "My sister dances here. I need to talk with her."

Smirking, he looked her up and down. "Yeah, my sister dances here too. Mom's real proud." He gestured toward the lineup. "Back of the line."

Mara glanced over her shoulder to see if Xalvador was going

to do anything. He and the other two just stood staring at the bouncer. She nudged him in the stomach with her elbow and raised her brow in question. He glanced down at her, startled.

"Little help."

Bending down, he whispered into her ear. "Ask again, this time let your beast out just a little."

Let her beast out a little? How the hell was she supposed to do that? Taking a calming breath, Mara reached down into herself, probing her heart for some indication of the cat that lay dormant. She wasn't sure what she was looking for.

When a low rumbling sounded in her throat, she thought that maybe she'd found what she was searching for.

Instantly she could feel a change. The nerve endings in her body started to snap. She was immediately on edge, aware of her surroundings. Scents smelled stronger, colors brighter, and everyone around her looked like they just might taste good if she bit into them.

This time when she approached the bouncer, there was no doubt that he was looking at her differently. Sweat immediately popped up on his broad brow, as she stepped forward to stand right in front of him. She put her hand on his forearm and smiled.

She could feel his heart start to hammer, and the blood race through his veins. The sweet smell of arousal tickled her nose.

"We need to talk to Selena. You're going to let us in, aren't you?" she purred as she trailed one finger down his arm, her nail marking her path in a pale pink line.

"Selena, of course. I should have seen the resemblance." He shot her a knowing look, and then unhooked the velvet rope blocking the runway path. "Go right in."

Trying not to gloat, Mara stepped past the bouncer and walked onto the ramp. She did glance over her shoulder at Xalvador. He winked at her, then smiled. Turning back around, Mara felt a warm glow surround her body. For the first time since the attack, she didn't feel distressed, or afraid. She felt empowered and strong.

As they neared the main door to the club, Mara could hear the rave music thumping. The vibrations swelled through the wood of the platform that the club floated on and jiggled the ramp under her feet.

The club looked unremarkable from the outside, just plain dark wood, but the inside was a virtual undersea adventure in sensual charm. The first thing Mara noticed when they entered was the colors. Blue and green everything. Iridescent and shimmering like water. The walls were lined with what looked like seaweed. The long curving bar was actually a giant aquarium full of coral, plants, and fish. Mara glanced away from the bar, remembering the night she ate all her pet fish. Her stomach gurgled in protest against the memory.

The next things she noticed were the six caged circular platforms dotting the club. Her sister was in one of them, but she had no clue which one.

Xalvador bent down to her ear. "Which one is your sister?"

"I'm not sure. From this distance, they all look the same."

All six dancers were wearing sparkling blue bodysuits, long blue wigs, and seashells covering their breasts and groins.

"Tito, Kemen, you take those two there." He pointed to the closest two dancers. "Ask if she's Selena, if she is, grab her and meet us at the door. Mara and I will check this one."

"It would be faster if we split up."

He clucked her under the chin. "Compelling one dumb brute is not the same as facing a Jaguar Knight. You and I stay together."

She huffed, but she knew he was right. She was no match for a shape-shifter of Jago's size and brutality. Actually, who was she kidding? She wouldn't be a match for a kitten-sized shape-shifter.

They wandered through the throng of people to the cylindrical dance platform along the right side. When they reached it, Mara peered up at the dancer. She was shaking her ass and flipping her hair around.

"Selena!" Mara yelled.

The dancer turned and glanced down at her. Blue eyes flashed in irritation. Nope, not Selena.

"That's not her," she said into Xalvador's ear.

He nodded and pointed to the next dancing platform surrounded by a gyrating mob.

While they were pushing through the thrashing group of party goers, Xalvador stopped, halting Mara with a firm hand on her arm. She looked up at him in question.

His brow was furrowed, and he craned his neck as if listening for something. Finally, he turned toward one of the other platforms on the opposite side of the club. Mara followed his gaze.

Tito and Kemen were standing by one of the platforms waving at them. Tito had his hand over his nose, blood trickling from between his fingers. The dancer was glaring down at them, her hand on her cocked hip.

Well, they located Selena.

When Mara and Xalvador finally made their way to the others, Selena was still ranting, her arms waving around madly. She stopped briefly when she spotted Mara coming towards her.

"What the fuck is going on?" She yelled as Mara approached the platform. "Do you know these brutes?"

Mara nodded. "Yes. I'm sorry, Lena, but can you come down? We need to talk to you."

"Mara, what the fuck are you into? This animal comes over, asks if I'm Selena, I say yes, and he fucking grabs me." She jumped down from the platform. "So I kicked him in the face."

Tito took a step back when Selena jumped down. Mara wanted to laugh at his reaction. The big giant was afraid of little hell-fire Selena Galas. Well, Mara couldn't blame him. She'd been on the receiving end of a few of Selena's rages. It was not a pretty sight.

Mara held Selena's arm and leaned into her. "I'm in some trouble, Lena. I need the amulet back."

"First, you need to tell me what's going on."

Xalvador stepped in between them. "There's no time for that. Tell us where the amulet is."

Mara sighed and shook her head. She knew what was coming, and wasn't the least bit surprised when Selena started poking her long blue fingernail into Xalvador's chest.

"Listen here, jerk, don't tell me what to do. Furthermore, who are you? And what are you doing with my sister? She just survived a terrible tragedy, you know. She's fragile."

Mara felt the change in Xalvador and the others almost instantly. She looked up just in time to witness Xalvador shift. Not into a jaguar but into the warrior knight he claimed to be. There was danger near, that she could feel on her own. It was like an electrical current running up and down her arms, making the little hairs stand on end.

She glanced toward the front door of the club. Jago had entered. Even without his glowing yellow eyes, she recognized him. He looked just like Xalvador, Tito, and Kemen, with long black hair, sculpted facial features, and sensual magnetism. Except there was an air of arrogance and violence to him that none of the others possessed.

And he wasn't alone. Four other large men flanked him on either side. They looked like gangsters. By the suit jackets they were wearing, it wouldn't have surprised Mara to find holsters and guns underneath the silk fabric.

Mara grabbed Selena, and spoke through clenched teeth. "Where is the goddamn amulet, Selena?"

Selena paled. She dug under her bodysuit and came up with a gold chain. "Right here." The amulet hung around her neck.

"Time to go," Xalvador commanded.

"I'm not going anywhere until . . ."

Xalvador nodded to Tito, and the giant picked up Selena and slung her over his shoulder. She didn't even have time to kick and scream.

"How do we get out? The front door's blocked," Mara asked, nerves thrumming through her body.

After one quick survey of the room, Xalvador looked at Selena. "Is there a back way out?"

"No, we're on a frigging platform in the water. Or didn't you notice that when you came in." Selena rolled her eyes.

"She sure is rude," Tito commented to Mara.

"Rude? I'm rude? Hey, Incredible Hulk, I'm not the one carrying you around on my shoulder without asking."

"Shut up, Lena. You're giving everyone a headache," Mara snapped.

Selena had the gall to look offended.

"To the back of the club," Xalvador ordered, as he herded everyone forward.

Tito took the lead, and like magic, a clear path appeared for him and his captive. Mara wasn't surprised. He was a formidable presence. Not easily dismissed or ignored.

Mara followed behind, with Xalvador and Kemen in the rear. Within minutes, they crowded into the corner of the club with no escape.

"Now what?" Mara asked Xalvador.

He was looking around at the walls, ceiling, and floor. Anywhere but at the approaching danger.

Mara nudged him in the ribs with her elbow. "What are we going to do? Jago and his grunts are coming this way."

"Anyone up for a swim?"

Before Mara could ask him what he meant, Jago and his cronies surrounded them, cutting off any chance of retreat. They were trapped with the walls behind them and the bad guys in front.

"Hola hermanos," Jago said with a nod, as if he were greeting old friends.

"We stopped being brothers, Jago, when you went rogue," Xalvador said, his voice tinged with menace.

"I want my life back, Xalvador. We were gods. We had everything we could ever desire. Gold, power, women, everything. You most of all had the world at your fingertips."

"It was not worth the price we had to pay, Jago. The sacrifices we made for their power. You agreed with that once; what has happened to change your mind?"

"I got bored," Jago smirked. "I'm tired of wandering the jungle, living half in and half out. I want it all back. I want the power that you once possessed. Once I release the kings, I will be in control."

"You can't control them, Jago. Listen to reason for once."

"Enough with the wise council. Give me the amulet, and I might let your pets live." Jago smiled at Mara.

The small hairs at the back of her neck rose as if a spider had crawled up her back. She shivered and had to stifle a gasp, as the malevolence of his smile surged over her like waves tinged in crude oil.

Xalvador took a step sideways to stand in front of her. She saw how his hands clenched into tight fists.

"I see you have become attached to my creation," Jago drawled. "And she is mine, Xalvador. You have no claim."

Mara put her hand up to her chest. The wounds there no longer ached. When she checked last, the scars had all but vanished. But as she moved, a twinge flared down her arm from her shoulder. *Her dream. The marking from her dream.* Xalvador did have a claim. On more than just her body. He claimed her heart and her soul.

She pushed past Xalvador. "He does have a claim. More than you ever could." She grabbed the collar of her T-shirt and yanked it down to reveal her right shoulder. The red bite mark was still there.

Jago stared at it, anger flaring in his eyes. Then his gaze lifted to her face. What she saw made her nostrils flare and her skin crawl. The man was pure evil. There was no other word for the vile emotions she witnessed swimming in his eyes.

"Get me that amulet from the other bitch," he barked. "Then kill them all."

Before Mara could take her next breath, Xalvador, Kemen, and Tito were moving. They each had one of the gangsters under their hands. Within minutes, bodies lay on the ground, and they had the guns.

Jago reached for Mara. Growling, she clawed at his hands.

Gunfire sounded. And the ground shook. The floor of the club cracked, splintered, and fell into pieces. The gangsters and Jago fell through the jagged holes into the water.

Suddenly, Mara slid in after them.

Jago had her by the leg, dragging her with him. She screamed for Xalvador as she went down.

The frigid water gripped her in tight icy tendrils when she went under. She kicked and flailed for purpose, trying to reach the surface, but something held her below.

Jago still had her, his hands wrapped around her neck, squeezing hard.

Mara beat at his hands, but they were like steel pressing down on her throat. Her lungs were burning for air, and her vision was quickly blurring.

Reaching up, she swiped at his eyes, digging into his face. But that did nothing but fuel his wrath. He squeezed her tighter and tighter until blood floated by her face. Her blood.

She could scent it even in the water. The smell made her hackles rise, and her stomach clench. And made something else deeper and darker in her start to boil and bubble to the surface.

Like a volcanic eruption, her beast burst free.

In a dark frenzy of talons and teeth, Mara broke away from Jago's hold. Everything was a blur in her mind. She saw nothing but red and black, and yellow. Always yellow. But now it seemed to be coming from the inside.

Rage consumed her. She swiped and tore at everything in front of her. Blood and gore swirled around her like a crimson typhoon. She could see nothing beyond it. Her mind was like a blender; mulching, crushing, and stirring all her thoughts into one mangled image. Killing Jago.

Her lungs ached, her head pounded, and she could feel nothing beyond her face. Even that was numb. Oxygen no longer fed her body. She felt adrift in a sea of nothingness. But before she could drift any further into the abyss, she had one single warm thought . . . Xalvador. If only she could live to love him.

Xalvador watched in horror as Mara splashed into the water. He had been too slow to grab her before she disappeared into the murky depths. He should have anticipated this. Jago was not an amateur. He was a man fueled by greed and power. Xalvador should have realized he would do something desperate and wrathful to spite him. Jago had always been jealous of Xalvador's status as leader.

As he surveyed the damage in the floor, all Xalvador could hear was Mara's screams. She had called to him while she went down. Even now, her calls echoed in his head.

"Mara!" Selena rushed toward the hole, yelling. Tito grabbed her before she could dive into the water.

"Get out of the club and meet me on the pier," Xalvador ordered, his eyes still on the churning water. "We can't afford any police attention." He turned toward his brethren and met each of their gazes. They knew what they had to do. Their duty would come first. Protecting the amulet was their first priority.

Turning, he dove into the icy water.

Instantly, he felt pressure on his lungs as he swam down. He could hold his breath for a long time, but the cold of the water would be his undoing. Already he could feel his blood start to slow. The frantic hammering in his chest dimmed to soft taps.

Thankfully, the water wasn't too murky, but because it was night, Xalvador could not see much that wasn't right in front of him. He swam down and then up, searching for any sign of her. Any sign.

Back down he went, and then up again. Still nothing. His lungs burned and he could feel the pressure on his chest. With a fierce kick up, Xalvador broke the surface of the water and sucked in much-needed air. He looked toward the pier. Tito, Kemen and Selena stood on the side surveying the edge of the break.

"Anything?" he yelled to them.

Tito and Kemen shook their heads. Selena just stared blankly into the wharf. He imagined she was in shock at seeing her sister disappear into the water.

Taking a deep breath, he dove back under. He would not give up until he found her. She was his responsibility. He had come all this way to protect her. She had called to him and he had failed her. He couldn't stand to lose another. The loss of his wife had sent him into a depression for many years. But losing Mara . . . that would nearly destroy him. She was his mate. They were connected in mind, body and soul. Without her, he would not be whole. His beast would be without its twin.

Something stirred near him. He swam toward the dark shape suspended in the water. As he neared it, dread pierced his heart like a spear. It was a hand. Jago's hand.

Abruptly, a warm feeling swept over him. Like a ray of sun through black storm clouds. Mara.

He turned. Just within reach, she floated up to him. Eyes

closed, hair floating around her like a dark cloud, she looked like an angel. Grabbing her around the waist, Xalvador kicked up to the surface. She was like ice in his arms. Like death.

Pushing the thought from his mind, he broke the water surface and swam toward the pier. Tito reached down and grabbed Mara's arms to pull her up. When he had her, Xalvador reached up for Kemen's outstretched hands. After Kemen dragged him up, Xalvador took Mara from Tito.

"We need to get her warm."

Selena hovered around the lifeless body in Xalvador's arms. Reaching out, her hands trembling, she touched Mara's face. "Is she dead?"

"Not if I can help it."

"But she's like ice. She's dead. My sister's dead," she wailed.

"We need to get her home, where I can get her warm. I can bring her back. I swear to you I can." Xalvador met Selena's gaze. He knew he shouldn't promise her anything. But he would do everything in his power to bring Mara back. Even through her frozen flesh, he could feel her beast clawing to get out. It was there—hot, flashing, and angry as hell.

It would be a fight, but Xalvador would bring her back. Or die trying.

9

It seemed as if time stood still during the drive back to Mara's house. Xalvador cradled her in his lap in the backseat as Kemen drove the car. Selena sat next to them, staring at her own shaking hands.

Although her heartbeat was weak, Xalvador just thanked the gods she still had one. The heater in the car was blasting out hot air, and sweat poured off Xalvador, but he didn't care. Mara needed to get warm. That was all that mattered.

When they arrived, Tito jumped out of the passenger side and opened the back door for Xalvador. He picked up Mara and rushed her into the house. Once inside, he ordered Kemen to run a hot bath.

As the water ran, Xalvador stripped off Mara's clothes and his own. He expected Selena to protest, but she just sat on Mara's bed, rocking back and forth staring at the rug. Shock had clearly settled in.

When the tub was full, Xalvador got in first. The water scalded his skin, but he barely noticed. All he could think about was Mara. He needed to get her better. He needed her to come back to him.

After Tito laid her in the water, Xalvador wrapped his arms around her and held her tight.

"See to the sister," he asked of Tito. "Give her some herbal tea, and see if she will sleep. This may take a while."

Tito nodded and then left the bathroom, shutting the door behind him.

As soon as he was gone, Xalvador placed his hands over Mara's chest, took in a deep breath, and then let it out. He took in another and another, until Mara's breathing pattern, although shallow, matched his. Her heart rate was still slow; he needed to speed it up, get her blood pumping through her veins. Only then could he bring her out of the suspended state she was trapped in. He just hoped her beast didn't come out first, untamed and hungry, and rip him to shreds. As he suspected had happened to Jago.

Closing his eyes, he ran his hands over her. First, down her arms to her hands, and then up again. He needed her to feel him. To feel his heat, to feel his heart beating for her. Again, he moved his hands down, over her breasts and down to her belly, and then up again, caressing softly. He continued this ritual several times until he could feel her skin start to warm and melt under his touch.

Her body heat was rising. As he placed his hands over her breasts, he could feel her blood starting to race through her system. Her nipples grew into tight buds under his palms. He sighed in relief as her body responded to him.

Xalvador nuzzled his face into her neck and spoke against her ear. "Mara, I know you can hear me. Fight for me, *mi amor,* I know you can. You're a fighter. You're tough, and strong, and the most enchanting creature I've ever known." He pressed a kiss to just below her lobe, and then whispered, "I could not stand to lose you, when I have only just begun to love you."

Closing his eyes against the pain that pierced his heart, Xalvador squeezed Mara tight against his chest. Love. This was not something he thought he would ever find again. The gods were cruel; he had always known this. But for them to bring Mara to him, a woman he could love for a lifetime, only to viciously take her away. That was beyond cruel. It was slow torture.

He would not give up. With every ounce of energy he possessed, he would bring her back to him. He believed she was in there, waiting. Waiting for something, for a reason to come back. He would give it to her.

Xalvador stroked his hands down her body again. This time he did it slower and with firmer caresses. Not to soothe but to arouse. Reaching her belly, he circled her navel with his fingers, and then dipped lower into the soft sprinkling of hair between her legs. Moving his legs between hers, he nudged them apart, giving him access to all of her. Slipping even lower, he slid his fingers into the soft folds of her sex. As he caressed her, he was rewarded with a low moan.

He pressed his lips to her neck and kissed her under her ear, where he knew she liked it best. "I hear you, *mi amor.*"

With deft strokes, he caressed her sex. Sliding up and then down, he circled her opening, then slipped two fingers inside. Even in the water, Xalvador could feel her juices flowing. Like liquid silk on his fingertips.

While he stroked her between the legs, he molded and squeezed her breasts with his other hand. He loved the way her pert flesh fit perfectly in his palm as he flicked her nipple with his thumb. Under his hand, he could feel the quickening of her heartbeat and her sharp intake of breath.

"Come back to me, kitten. I have so many things to show you," he whispered against her ear.

Continuing to slide his fingers up and down her cleft, but now pressing harder, Xalvador found her clit. He rubbed it in circles, while he moved his other hand down, inserting his fingers into her opening. While one hand pumped in and out, the other jiggled her hard bud of flesh. Within moments, her breathing quickened.

Xalvador could feel Mara returning. Life was beating inside her again.

After one more thrust inside her, Xalvador pinched her clit. Her thighs instinctively tightened and he knew that she was going to climax. He could feel it building to a crescendo inside her. Her velvety walls clamped down on his fingers.

As an orgasm slammed into her, Mara bolted up from Xalvador's chest and gasped, "Xalvador."

His name upon her lips sent shivers down his spine. With a sigh of relief, he slid his fingers from her sex and wrapped his arms around her.

"I didn't know if you would come back to me."

Turning in his arms, she met his gaze. "I heard you whispering to me. Did you mean what you said?"

"What part?"

"The part about loving me?"

Placing his hands on her waist, he turned her all the way around, so she straddled his lap over his swelling erection. He lowered her onto it, snuggling deep inside her. When they were face to face, he brought a hand up to her cheek, and tucked a strand of wet hair behind her ear. She was so pretty, his little kitten. He could be so lucky to love a woman like her.

"Si."

Leaning in close, rolling her hips over him, she pressed her mouth to his. "That is what made me come back. The sound of your voice, and the promise of your love."

He wrapped his hands in her hair, pulling her closer, and covered her lips with his. Sweeping his tongue over hers, he breathed in her flavor. She was like sugar to him. Sweet and sinful. He never wanted to be without her taste again.

When she broke the kiss, Mara leaned back and surveyed his face as if memorizing his every feature. "My sister? The amulet?"

"Both safe."

"And Jago?"

Xalvador frowned as he searched her eyes. Did she not remember? Maybe it was best that she didn't.

"Gone."

"Forever?" she asked, a slight quiver in her voice.

"I believe so."

With a sigh, she smiled and covered his mouth with hers again, nibbling at his lips. He held her close as they kissed. He never wanted to let go. But he knew that their love would come with a price. Nothing could be as simple and familiar as the kiss they shared.

Pulling back, Xalvador cupped her cheeks with his hands, to stare her in the eyes. "This will not be easy, Mara. Your beast has not gone away. It will burst free one day."

"I know," she said with quiet understanding. "But you can help me deal with it, right?"

"Si, but not here." He held her gaze hoping she could understand, hoping that she would know how much his heart would shatter if she turned him down. "Not in this house, not in this city. Only in the jungle, can I teach you what you need to know to survive."

"In Venezuela? In the Amazon?"

"Yes, my home."

He held his breath, waiting for her reaction, her answer to his unasked question. Would she leave everything she'd ever known for the chance of a lifetime with him?

"Can Selena come too? She's always wanted to see the jungle." She grinned.

Laughing, Xalvador kissed her hard. "Si, Selena can come. I'm sure Tito would be overjoyed to take her on a tour."

After another thorough kiss, Xalvador hugged her to him,

nuzzling his nose in the crook of her neck where he liked it the most. "Are you sure? I can't offer you much."

Mara leaned back and met his gaze. "Xalvador, you offer everything I have ever wanted. You."

Before they could kiss again, a hard knock came at the bathroom door. "Everything all right in there?" It was Tito.

"Everything's great. Tell Selena Mara is okay."

The knob on the door turned. "Damn it, I want to see for myself." Selena's voice sounded shrill and angry.

"I'm all right, Lena. You don't have to come in." Mara grinned as she slid up and down driving him in even deeper. "Actually, I'd prefer if you didn't."

As a fight ensued between Selena and Tito on whether anyone was going into the bathroom, Mara wrapped her arms around Xalvador's neck and started to ride him.

The minute he filled her up, he felt complete. His mind, body and soul had their perfect match. He found the woman he hadn't even realized he'd been looking for. Circumstance and fate had put them together. And he would do everything he could to keep it that way.

While he moved inside her, she nuzzled into his neck, trailing her tongue over his earlobe. "I was wondering, do jaguars mate for life?"

"I guess we'll find out." Wrapping his arms around her, he held on for their next wild ride.

GET NAKED FOR ME . . .

As assistant director of a Boston art gallery, Mercy Rothell has made some hot deals in her time, but none like this. In order to sign the impossibly sexy, brilliant, and successful artist Shamus Montgomery to do a show of his celebrated erotic sculptures, Mercy must meet his curious but absolutely non-negotiable demand—she must pose for him in the nude, night after night, or he walks. Never one to back down from a challenge, Mercy agrees. Burning under the intense gaze of the hottest man she's ever known, watching his hands work their magic, Mercy feels vulnerable yet liberated and fully aroused, desperate for the kind of satisfaction only a master like Shamus can give. In fact, she would beg him to cross the line. And once he does, mercy is the last thing she desires . . .

Turn the page for a thrilling excerpt from UNDRESSING MERCY by Deanna Lee. An Aphrodisia trade paperback on sale now.

I knew a lot about Shamus Montgomery as an artist. However, the need to know more about him as a man surfaced within seconds of seeing him for the first time. There was no mistaking the lust stirring in my body. My physical reaction surprised me. It had been a long time since a man had stirred my sexual interest.

I stood up from my chair and offered him my hand. I sucked in a small breath as my fingers disappeared in his. *Warm*, *calloused*, and *strong* were the first things I thought about his hand. "It's a pleasure, Mr. Montgomery. Holman is honored to be the first choice for your next show."

There, two whole sentences. I pulled my fingers from his and fought an overwhelming urge to crawl across the conference table and into his lap. I sat down.

I used the time it took Milton to greet Shamus to regain control. My thoughts had been scattered to the four winds by pure, unadulterated lust.

"I'm here because of you, Ms. Rothell. Your reputation precedes you."

Heat swept over up my face, and that pissed me off. Blushing was not part of the smart, modern-woman image I'd spent more than two years redeveloping. Therapy, self-defense classes, and determination had helped me carve out a place in the world where I felt safe and in control.

Settling back in my seat, I watched Shamus Montgomery pull out the chair directly in front of me. He was tall, at least six foot three inches, and had the grace of a big hunting cat. He sat down in the chair and focused on me as if I were the only person in the room. It was the sort of attention that I had enjoyed from men in the past, but felt uncomfortable with now. God, the man was breathtaking.

I waited until he was settled before speaking. "I understand you have twenty-two pieces ready for the show."

"Yes, but there are always twenty-three. It's what my audience will expect." He inclined his head and fixed his gaze on my face. "I need the right woman for the final piece."

"The gallery will help you find a willing model." I pulled out the contract and set it in front of me. *The right woman.* I fought a frown. Had I just promised to find this gorgeous and amazing man the right woman?

"I've chosen a model."

He's already found the right woman, I thought. *Lucky girl.* As soon as I found out who she was I figured I'd hate her guts. "Good. I've made the changes to the contract that your lawyer insisted on and have included the changes that you had previously agreed to. However, I must admit your breach-of-trust stipulation was a hard sell to the Board."

"I don't like sharing my work with people I can't trust. If exhibiting at Holman Gallery proves to be a pleasurable experience for me, I'll have no need to withdraw my work from your skillful hands." He paused, looked over my face carefully, and then asked softly, "Aren't you interested in knowing who'll pose for me?"

I forced myself to meet his gaze, taking in those dark brown eyes and thick, dark lashes. There was humor in his eyes and in the curve of his firm lips. Again, the desire to know what he tasted like surfaced. I let my gaze slide over the strong, angular features of his face. The man looked like a fallen angel. A profoundly naughty fallen angel.

Smiling back, I looked pointedly at the contract before speaking. "The gallery will secure the model you require for your last piece." I pushed the contract across the table with a pen.

Milton Storey grunted when Shamus picked up the pen and signed both copies with bold, deliberate strokes. He pushed the contract back across the table at me, but didn't lift his fingers when I reached for it. "I'll see you at six P.M."

I looked up and met his gaze, ignoring Milton's intake of breath at the statement.

My mouth dropped open. "Excuse me?"

"You're the model for my last project, Ms. Rothell." He stood as I signed the contracts. "You do know where my studio is?"

I nodded, overwhelmed. With hands that were surprisingly steady, I handed him his copy of the contract, then sat back in my chair. Dimly, I was even slightly proud of the fact that I had remembered to sign the contracts and give him a copy. I watched him fold the contract and then slip it into a pocket inside his jacket.

After a brief exchange with Milton, the damn man walked out, leaving me alone with the contract.

Trying not to shake, I placed it back in the folder with Shamus Montgomery's name on it and stood. "This should be filed."

Not bothering to look at Milton, I left the room and hurried toward my office.

Jane was in my office when I entered. She hopped up from

my desk and smiled. "I've answered all of the e-mails in your query folder. You have four meetings tomorrow morning before lunch, and I've confirmed the travel arrangements for Ms. Carol Banks. She'll be here on Friday as scheduled." She walked to stand in front of me and stared. "Well?"

I nodded. "He signed."

"Holy shit, Mercy! That's cool." She took the folder from my now-numb hand. "What's wrong?"

I swallowed hard and shook my head. "You won't believe me."

"Come on, spill it."

"Shamus Montgomery wants me to pose for his final piece for the show."

"Oh. My. God."

Oh my God, indeed. The blasted man had signed the contract after I'd assured him the gallery would secure the model he wanted. He'd backed me into a neat little corner. And it was a fascinating corner to be in. I was both excited and scared. It would've been foolish to deny that I found Shamus Montgomery insanely attractive.

"Mercy, this is awesome."

I turned and glared at her. "Tell me, Jane, exactly what part of this is awesome?"

"Come on! That sexy man wants to strip you naked and sculpt you. What the hell could be better?"

I was thirty pounds past my ideal weight, and pushing a size twelve. I've never been one of those women who dieted obsessively; however, I preferred being slightly slimmer. Also, I had no interest in getting naked for an artist. Shaking my head, I turned to find Jane staring at me. She frowned, walked to my office door, and shut it.

She turned and stared at me with a determined expression. "Mercy, you're a beautiful woman."

"Thanks, Jane." I didn't consider myself unattractive, and I had no way of explaining to Jane what I was really thinking.

"You have a lovely face and a great curvy body." She held out her arms to display the trim, tidy body I secretly envied. "I'm nearly a boy."

Laughing, I shook my head and sat down at my desk. "You don't look like any boy I've ever seen."

Jane leaned against my desk. "Look, a man like Shamus Montgomery doesn't make mistakes. He wants to sculpt *you*, Mercy. Not me and not Miss Perky-Fake-Tits Johnson out there."

I looked through the glass wall and out into the bull pen where Sarah Johnson worked. "You think they're fake?"

"Are you kidding? They can't be anything else," Jane snorted. "I've considered reporting her to the EPA."

"For what?"

Jane shrugged. "There is no way she's still biodegradable."

I laughed and looked back to Sarah; Milton was holding court at her desk. I personally found him tedious on most occasions, but it was obvious why Sarah feigned interest. She believed that he could help her get somewhere in the art world. Despite his upcoming forced retirement from Holman Gallery, Milton Storey did have influence.

Milton finished preening for the environmental hazard and started toward my office. "You'd better scoot," I said to Jane, "or he'll have a chance to ask you why you still haven't gone out with his son."

Jane grimaced and darted past Milton just as he entered the room. The sudden movement confused him for a moment, and his gaze jerked from her exiting form and to me several times before he settled on my face.

"What can I do for you, Milton?"

"I was just telling Sarah about the deal with Shamus Montgomery. She'd be willing to take your place as a model." Milton tucked his hands into his pants pockets and inclined his head. "She's young and thin."

Young, thin, and plastic. I glanced toward Sarah and knew exactly what was on her mind. It would be a cold day in hell before I'd let her parade around in all of her manmade glory for Shamus Montgomery. I wasn't exactly convinced I could pose for him, but I knew I couldn't allow her to do it either. "Mr. Montgomery made his choice. I did promise the man the gallery would secure the model he wanted." I leaned back in my chair, and watched Milton fidget.

Finally he looked out at Sarah and shrugged.

Miss Perky Tits glared at me and went back to her work.

My phone rang. Milton strolled out of my office, leaving the door open, which I hated. As I picked up the phone, Jane was at the door, gently pulling it closed. I was going to miss her when I went to prison for killing Milton.

"Hello."

"Ms. Rothell."

Shamus Montgomery. His voice was smooth and cultured, yet it woke something wild and nearly unspeakable in me. I wanted to be angry with him for his presumption. The truth was that I enjoyed his arrogance so much that I couldn't wait to tangle with him again. The fact that he'd called me so soon led me to believe that maybe he felt the same way.

"Mr. Montgomery. I'm glad you called. You didn't give me much time to consider your offer." My opening volley was met with a brief silence.

"It wasn't an offer."

Looking down at my desk, I sighed and then glanced out at Jane in the bull pen. She held up a piece of paper with SHAMUS MONTGOMERY IS A GOD written on it in big red letters. I glared at her and turned in my chair so I didn't have to see her or her stupid sign.

"I can assure you there are scores of women who would

happily strip naked and pose for you. I just don't happen to be one of them." That was a damn lie. Well, it was a half-lie. I could easily see myself getting naked with Shamus Montgomery; it was the posing part that put me off. I focused on one of my fingernails and frowned at the cuticle. It was a prime example of how I felt inside: ragged.

"I have a feeling that it's time you did something different," he said.

"I'm not stagnating," I snapped and then frowned, realizing that he hadn't said anything like that.

His silence wasn't comforting. I could almost hear the wheels turning in his head as he considered what my response had revealed. Closing my eyes, I waited for him to say something. Anything.

"Don't be late, Mercy."